FALSE FACE

Also by Veronica Heley from Severn House

The Ellie Quicke mysteries

MURDER AT THE ALTAR
MURDER BY SUICIDE
MURDER OF INNOCENCE
MURDER BY ACCIDENT
MURDER IN THE GARDEN
MURDER BY COMMITTEE
MURDER BY BICYCLE
MURDER OF IDENTITY
MURDER IN THE PARK
MURDER IN HOUSE
MURDER BY MISTAKE
MURDER MY NEIGHBOUR
MURDER IN MIND
MURDER WITH MERCY
MURDER IN TIME
MURDER BY SUSPICION
MURDER IN STYLE
MURDER FOR NOTHING
MURDER BY SUGGESTION
MURDER FOR GOOD
MURDER-IN-LAW

The Bea Abbot Agency mysteries

FALSE CHARITY
FALSE PICTURE
FALSE STEP
FALSE PRETENCES
FALSE MONEY
FALSE REPORT
FALSE ALARM
FALSE DIAMOND
FALSE IMPRESSION
FALSE WALL
FALSE FIRE
FALSE PRIDE
FALSE ACCOUNT
FALSE CONCLUSION

FALSE FACE

Veronica Heley

SEVERN
HOUSE

First world edition published in Great Britain and the USA in 2021
by Severn House, an imprint of Canongate Books Ltd,
14 High Street, Edinburgh EH1 1TE.

Trade paperback edition first published in Great Britain and the USA in 2022
by Severn House, an imprint of Canongate Books Ltd.

severnhouse.com

British Library Cataloguing-in-Publication Data
A CIP catalogue record for this title is available from the British Library.

ISBN-13: 978-0-7278-5057-7 (cased)
ISBN-13: 978-1-4483-0590-2 (trade paper)
ISBN-13: 978-1-4483-0589-6 (e-book)

All Severn House titles are printed on acid-free paper.

Typeset by Palimpsest Book Production Ltd.,
Falkirk, Stirlingshire, Scotland.
Printed and bound in Great Britain by
TJ Books, Padstow, Cornwall.

Bea Abbot ran a domestic agency whose watchword was discretion. She'd recently remarried her ex-husband, Piers – an internationally renowned portrait painter – and the agency was doing well . . . until . . .

ONE

B ea knew something was wrong as soon as Piers let himself in to the house. Normally he'd dump his kit in the hall, drape his leather jacket over the newel post at the bottom of the stairs and yell, 'Anyone at home?'

Today he dumped his kit on the floor in silence. Next, he aimed his jacket at the newel post. It missed, slipped to the ground, and he ignored it.

Bea was in the kitchen, taking a break from the agency to prepare something for supper. She suspended operations at the stove, feeling a wave of . . . what – tension? Bloody-mindedness? – accompanying him as he joined her.

She said, 'What's wrong?'

He ignored that to kiss the back of her neck, saying, 'What a picture we make of domestic bliss! You, slaving over a hot stove and me, the weary wanderer home from the chase, but alas, without anything to show for it. Is the Brat staying at school or coming home this weekend?'

The 'Brat' was Bea's ward, a clever, lanky teenager with a mind of her own. Despite calling her a brat, Piers was actually very fond of her.

'No,' said Bea, 'she isn't. What's wrong?'

He was taller than her even when she was hearing high heels. His body against hers didn't feel as comfortable as it usually did. It felt bony. His voice cracked. He cleared it. 'Shall we take a credit card in one hand, some sunscreen in the other and light off for parts unknown? We deserve a holiday, don't we?'

This was serious.

Piers might be tall, dark and sexy. He might handle life with a light touch, but there was an undercurrent of strong feeling here that warned her to take him seriously. So what had he been doing to cause this desire for a holiday?

At intervals over a period of some weeks he'd been painting the portrait of Karina, a 'national treasure', star of stage and screen. He'd said he found her amusing at first and thought he'd caught her pretty well on canvas, but last night he'd said he'd be glad once he'd finished the job.

Karina had refused to go to Piers' studio for her sittings but had arranged for him to set up his easel in the conservatory at her Belgravia mansion instead. Today was to have been her last sitting.

Bea tasted the chicken dish she'd been cooking and put the spoon down. 'What's brought this on?'

Piers didn't reply, but opened the back door and stepped out on to the balcony. He was breathing hard. He said, 'I need air.'

As their early Victorian house was built on a rise in the ground, at street level there were three steps up from the pavement to the portico sheltering the front door, while across the back of the house there was a cast-iron balcony and a curving staircase which led down to the garden one storey below.

Piers grasped the balcony rail as if he were a shipwrecked sailor clinging to a lifebelt. He said, 'I've always thought of myself as a pacifist but maybe I'm not. At the moment I'm having fantasies of murder and mayhem and that includes Karina herself. Can you see me as a robot, crying "Exterminate!"?'

He was making a joke of whatever it was that had happened. It was his custom to defuse a difficult situation with humour, but this was different. There was an undercurrent here of distress, even of violence. It was most unlike him.

Piers painted notables of all sorts: captains of industry whom he sometimes likened to robber barons; politicians whom he said should be in the dock and not in the House of Commons; women whose beauty relied on surgery. He made a very good living at what he did. The critics were unanimous in commending him for capturing the intrinsic nature of his sitters. He also painted unsung heroes and heroines without a fee if their faces appealed to him.

He had a reputation for being good-natured and easy-going.

Bea waited for an explanation and didn't get it. Eventually she said, 'You've finished? You said you'd only need one more session with Karina.'

No reply. She didn't think he'd even heard her. She raised her voice slightly. 'I'm cooking chicken a la something-or-other with new potatoes and greens for supper.'

He didn't move. Their large black cat, Winston, appeared from nowhere. Adept at weighing up a situation, Winston considered attracting Piers' attention by winding round his legs but, sensing this would not be acceptable at that moment, he slunk off down the stairs to chase a bird which had strayed on to his territory.

Piers said, 'I had to leave the painting and my easel behind. I haven't signed the portrait and it doesn't look as if I'm going to be paid for it. On balance, I think it's best for me to emigrate.'

His tone was deliberately light, but he frequently used humour to cover what he was feeling.

She said, 'Want to tell me about it? And what do you fancy for lunch?'

'I'm not hungry. I'll go for a walk or something.'

She'd never known him refuse food before. She put her arms around him from behind. He was trembling with tension. She held him close but didn't speak.

He made a coughing sound. 'Let me go. I'm not fit to . . .! I'm so wound up . . .'

She didn't let go. If anything, she held him even closer.

She waited. Gradually the tension eased. He sighed, deeply.

She said softly, 'You've had a bad day, right? We'll have a light meal to build up our strength. Cheese and fruit. Then we'll have a coffee, and you can tell me all about it.'

It was a toss-up whether he'd stay or stalk out of the house to walk off his distress. He said, 'You have to know. Yes.'

Bea put some cheese and salad stuffs out on the central island in the kitchen. She found some crunchy bread rolls and heated them up.

He took one small mouthful, rather as if it were medicine. And then another. He made himself eat. He took some green grapes, got those down, and finally cleared his plate.

When in doubt, feed the brute.

Finally, Bea encouraged him to have a cup of coffee and to move to the big living room next door.

He sank into 'his' armchair and closed his eyes. Then said, 'Look, this is real trouble. If we run away . . . No, that won't do. There's too much at stake. On balance, I think you'd do best to divorce me all over again.'

She ignored that, to say, 'I wouldn't mind a holiday. Where shall we go? I've never been to Australia. Come to think of it, I have distant relations in New Zealand and we could look them up. First you'd better tell me why we have to run away.'

'It's absurd. I still can't believe it. But we – you and I – have been accused of conspiracy to rob Karina of some valuable jewellery, not to mention stealing the hard copy of the book she's been writing. The portrait I was painting was to have gone on the cover, so they've kept that, too.'

Bea half laughed. 'How . . .? But that's ridiculous!' She waited. His expression didn't change. This was serious. 'Start from the beginning.'

He spread his hands wide. 'I don't know where the beginning is.'

'Well,' said Bea. 'You've told me a couple of stories about Karina which make her sound a bit of a drama queen. I've seen pictures of her in the papers. She was stunningly beautiful in her heyday. She must be in her fifties now? Or early sixties? Is she still beautiful?'

'She's beginning to show her age. She's had a little cosmetic surgery but not much. She does wear a selection of wigs because her hair has become thin over the years. She has a powerful presence. Her voice is honey, or the shriek of a witch in a storm. She's a falcon, a bird of prey with a wicked, shining look in her black eyes. She's an actress with many different faces. Mind you, I have wondered once or twice . . . is she burned out and ready to retire? I've heard she had a voracious appetite for sex once, but . . .' He shook his head. 'I would say she's still active, but not voracious. Am I seeing the last flicker of the life force that she once had?'

He stopped abruptly. 'I didn't know I was going to say that. No, she's nowhere near finished. I know because I've painted her hands like claws, with a selection of heavy rings on them, and I've given her hair a hint of serpents twisting through it. The portrait's as good as anything I've ever done. Probably good enough for the National Portrait Gallery. And yet . . . and yet I'm not satisfied with it. Have I only seen what she wanted me to see? What is the real Karina like?

'Five times I've turned up, painted when Karina made herself available, ignored the goings-on, chatted to whoever turned up wanting a sympathetic ear about the latest crisis in their life, and come away. Today, I arrived in good time, but there was a long delay before Molly – not the housekeeper – came to the door to let me in. Molly is Karina's ghostwriter. I told you about her, didn't I? Came through your agency. A bit flaky, but good company on the whole.'

'I don't have a ghostwriter on my books. What's her name again?'

'Malone. Molly Malone.'

Bea grinned. 'As in the folk song?' She made a stab at singing a couple of lines. 'Molly Malone, who "Wheeled her wheelbarrow, through streets broad and narrow? Singing cockles and mussels alive, alive-oh." Poor girl, to be lumbered with a name like that.'

'She makes a joke of it. Her parents had christened her Mary and that was all right, but at school there was another girl called Mary in her class so they called her Molly instead. She likes it.'

'Clever.' Bea switched on the computer in her brain and shook her head. 'Doesn't ring a bell. I'm pretty sure no one using the name of Molly Malone has been through our books, though if she registered under the name of Mary Malone, I might not remember.'

'Maybe she called herself a personal assistant? Karina's command of grammar is uncertain, and her attention span that of a gnat, so she needed a professional to knock out a book which wouldn't scare the horses. The fact is that Karina got the contract for her memoirs on the understanding that she'd need a ghostwriter, and Molly got the job through your agency. I understand there's been a bidding war over the rights to the book, and it's destined to be the next big bestseller for the Christmas market. The manuscript is overdue for delivery and unless Karina delivers next week, she'll miss the publication date.

'Molly has been there working on the book, on and off, for four or five months. I'm not sure how experienced she is at the

work, but on the whole I think she's probably making a reasonable job of it. I hear what's going on because Karina kills two
birds with one stone. While she's posing for me, she has Molly
sitting in to talk over various points she'd queried. Molly has
recorded what Karina has chosen to remember – or perhaps to
make up – and then had the thankless task of trying to tone down
those parts which would land the lady in court for libel.

'I tell you; Karina's brought a blush to my cheek on occasion,
and I thought I'd heard everything. I suspect that despite Molly's
best efforts, the publisher will have to have lawyers go through
the manuscript to remove any actionable material before it's sent
to the printers. Even with those bits removed, Karina probably
has spilt enough beans to upset a lot of people, and yes, even to
make the Christmas bestseller list. She's dropped all sorts of
hints to me about this important person and that while I've been
painting her. Some of which I believe – well, not the bit about
the bishop – but quite enough to make a stir.'

Bea was wide-eyed. 'Which bishop?'

'That's something which will only be revealed on publication.
The last time I was there, Molly queried what Karina swears
she said to the Queen at some function or other, and what the
Queen said to her. And no, I can't believe the Queen said *that*
and neither could Molly, so they were having a bit of a ding-
dong about it. I don't know who won.

'So that's who let me into the house this morning. Molly. I
could hear someone ranting and raving in the upper floors, but
that's not unusual in that household. Molly put a finger to her
lips to warn me not to speak. She took me through to the conservatory at the back and warned me to expect ructions. Apparently,
Karina had decided to wear a different necklace for her last
sitting with me, even though I'd made it clear I didn't want to
change what I'd already painted. She'd gone to the safe or wherever she keeps the stuff, and found that an antique diamond and
sapphire necklace and a diamond ring had gone missing. She'd
accused the housekeeper of having stolen them, and the poor
woman was creating blue murder.

'Molly said' – and here Piers couldn't resist a shadow of his
usual grin – 'she said the thief was more likely to have been one
of Karina's sons who are still at the juvenile stage of playing

practical jokes. I thought she was probably right. Molly said she'd been glad of the work but had found it more difficult than she'd expected. She said she'd had enough of trying to sort out an approximation to the truth from the fantasies which Karina had been chucking at her. She asked if I'd heard any talk about the death of one of Karina's husbands, ages ago. I said no, and was that in the memoirs? She said, "No," and started fiddling around with her laptop and memory stick, so I went over to the painting, worrying about what I still had to do to finish the picture. There was a shadow I'd put under Karina's chin. Should I take it out, or leave it? I decided to leave it but perhaps tone down the orchids in the background and then that would be that.'

'Orchids?'

'She has a "thing" about orchids. The conservatory was filled with them. That's how she thinks of herself, as an exotic. A Venus flytrap is more like it. She'd wanted me to paint her with orchids in her hair and I'd done so, but I wasn't happy about that, either. Usually we decide   the client and I   what she should wear and that's what I paint and I don't make any changes. But Karina was always changing her mind. First, she wanted the orchids, then she didn't and then she did. She tried putting on a different necklace each time till I had to say, "Enough!" I was going to be as pleased as Molly to finish with the job.

'I remember looking at my watch and hoping Karina would turn up soon. It's not unusual for her to be anything up to half an hour late for her sittings, but woe betide me if I'm not ready to start the moment she appears. Molly started chattering away about ghostwriters not always getting credited for their work on a book, and was I covered for extra when my painting appeared on the cover of Karina's book. I said, "Teach your grandmother!" because of course I had.

'I thought that if Karina was having a row with the housekeeper, she might be some time yet. And yes, I could hear people screaming and pounding up and down the stairs. I heard the housekeeper shouting that she'd never been accused of theft in all her born days, and she wouldn't ever, not ever, and she was collecting her clock and her knives from the kitchen and leaving the house that minute and she'd be obliged if they would give her, there and then, the money they owed her.

'Molly and I looked at one another. She rolled her eyes, and I must admit I had to wipe a grin off my face. We could hear the current husband – he's the only one in that household, it seems to me, who does have periods of sanity – bleating that Karina didn't mean it, that she would soon calm down and that the family relied on the housekeeper to keep the household running. Which, from my own observations, was quite true. But the woman was set on leaving and I don't blame her.'

'How many husbands and sons are in attendance on Karina?'

'Two of each. One divorced but still living there. And the current one. How they put up with her tantrums, I do not know. According to Molly, this housekeeper has lasted longer than most. I was wondering if I could persuade Karina to let me take the painting away to finish it when she burst in, wearing her usual bright red-and-gold caftan with wig to match.

'She was followed by the rest of the family, all shouting at one another and at her, some urging she should give the house-keeper another chance, others saying that maybe it wasn't her because they'd searched her belongings and not found anything, and one of the husbands saying they should call the police and have the woman arrested. I really believe they'd forgotten that Molly and I'd be there for they stopped short when they saw us. And then . . . oh then, I saw Karina's brain click over.

'I could see her decide that if it wasn't the housekeeper who'd stolen her jewels then it must be someone else who had access to the house. Molly was at the end of her work on the book. So yes, Karina turned on Molly. "Of course, it was you all along! You knew where the safe was! Traitress! After all I've done for you!"

'I stood there with my mouth open while Karina actually *howled* at the girl. The others joined in. Wide open mouths, red-faced, spitting out their malice. It was unnerving. One of them – a son? – shouted that Molly was a treacherous rat. Can a rat be treacherous? Another tried to stand up for her, saying they'd no proof that she'd taken anything, but he got drowned out by the others, demanding she handed over the jewels or they'd call the cops. Molly backed up against the wall, saying she hadn't, and wouldn't. She was as white as paper and shaking, and I don't blame her.

'Karina picked up Molly's handbag and emptied it out on the floor. No jewellery. She grabbed the girl's jacket, tore it off her and upended that, too. Molly cried out. I expostulated, in vain. One of the lads held Molly fast while another patted her down, making her cry. Someone grabbed her laptop which, in his haste, slid out of his hands and crashed to the tiled floor with a loud crunch! He then slipped and stepped on it. The screen disintegrated. We looked at the wreckage, and realized that nothing was going to be able to put Humpty Dumpty together again.

'All I could hear was people's heavy breathing. The current husband accessed what passes for his brain. "Hrrm. We need what's on the laptop, don't we? We have to deliver the manuscript of the book next week, right? No book, no money. Right?"

'That brought them all up short. It occurred to me to wonder if Karina was quite as wealthy as she had been. It must cost a fortune to keep that big house going and support all those men. The money from the book wouldn't be hers till the manuscript was delivered and accepted, would it? I could see them working out that it might not be a good idea to offend Molly, but before they could act, the girl crammed her belongings back into her handbag, picked up her jacket and the remains of the laptop and ran off, down the hall and out of the house. One of them started to laugh! Then another! I couldn't see what they were laughing at. They hadn't located the jewellery; they'd assaulted their ghostwriter and destroyed her laptop.

'If I'd had any sense, I'd have abandoned the painting and gone after her, but instead I tried to act as the voice of reason. I said I didn't think Molly would have been stupid enough to steal from a client. Karina didn't like that. She seated herself in her big chair and swung her head round at me. She said it had suddenly become clear to her that Molly and I must have been sent from the same agency under false pretences and that we'd gained access to her house in order to steal her jewellery.'

Bea shot upright in her chair. 'What! You can't be serious?'

His shoulders twitched. 'If you say something loudly enough, suspicion becomes a certainty. It was crazy! One lad said he'd never liked me, and that I was always to be found in a corner with the girl, plotting how to rob Karina. Another said that Molly must have stolen the goods and passed them to me to take home.

The current husband produced a file he had on Molly, and said he'd been suspicious all along of the coincidence of our both coming from the same agency. And – the clincher! – when he looked at Molly's details, they found that she'd given her home address as my studio in the mews here!'

Bea frowned. She did, in fact, own a mews cottage at the end of the street, which Piers used as his studio and office.

She said, 'What! But that can't be. You haven't let it out to anyone recently, have you? You're round there almost every day for this and that. So how did she get that address?'

A nasty thought wormed into the back of Bea's mind and started to incubate. 'I wonder, though . . . No, I'd remember if we'd ever been asked to supply staff for Karina, wouldn't I? This just doesn't make sense.'

Or did it? Her mind started to gnaw on the problem. Now, suppose . . .

Piers lifted his hands in despair. 'I don't understand anything. By this time the pack were all baying for Molly's blood. One of the sons got his mobile out, trying to ring her. She didn't pick up, for which I don't blame her. The current husband said that he'd seen Molly transfer everything from her laptop to a memory stick every evening before she went home. He wanted to know which of them had checked her handbag for it. No one admitted to that.'

Piers rubbed his eyes. 'I think I laughed out loud. It was a farce. I said, half in jest, that they'd have to pay a ransom to Molly or they wouldn't be able to deliver the manuscript of the book in time. The realization that they might not be able to set the tills ringing at Christmas time got them upset again.

'And so they turned on me. One of the boys suggested Molly had passed the memory stick on to me to keep for her and the two of them jumped me. I objected. Loudly. They laughed. They searched me, viciously. I tried to keep still, not to let them see how . . . I was appalled. Shaking. Humiliated. They didn't find the memory stick, of course. I said I was going straight to the police to charge them with assault and illegal detention. I reached for my jacket but one of the boys was quicker. He searched my pockets and came up with a solitaire diamond ring. Not mine. Not my style at all. Very much in Karina's style.'

Bea said, 'Ah. Had the same lad put the ring in there earlier, or did he have it on his person and was clever enough to "find" it in your pocket?'

'I don't know. At that point I felt as if I'd been concussed. I protested I had no need to steal. She, that horrible woman, sat there, licking her lips, enjoying the scene. She's like those women who took their knitting to watch the aristocrats being guillotined in the days of the French Revolution. I think she likes to watch people being hurt.

'One of the lads said Molly had corrupted me to help her steal the jewels, and where was the necklace? Another said Molly must have stolen it a couple of days ago and passed it to me to get it out of the house without throwing suspicion on her. As if I would ever!'

'No,' said Bea. 'You've never been interested in jewellery. Never even bought me any.'

'Do you want some?' Piers was trying for a light tone.

'No. I'm beginning to get an idea about what's happening here. Go on. Back to the crime.'

'They started arguing among themselves about sending for the cops and charging me with theft, but by that time I'd got my phone out. I said, "I have the police on speed dial to report that you've assaulted me. Do you want to speak to them, or shall I?"

'That brought the current husband up sharp. He said, "If we do that, we lose all hope of getting the memory stick back. No, no police. The man's right: we'll have to pay the woman something to turn the goods back over to us if he doesn't have them."

'They didn't like it. They all looked at Karina. She was nibbling a forefinger, eyes half closed, turning over various permutations in her mind. I didn't wait for her to decide. I put on my jacket. I collected my cards, wallet and so on. Only, when I packed away my paints and lifted the painting off the easel to bring it away, one of the sons intervened.

'I was to leave the painting on the easel. They said they'd give me twenty-four hours to return the memory stick to them and when I'd done that, I could have my easel back and they wouldn't press charges. Naturally, I was not to expect any payment for the portrait and if I failed to retrieve the memory stick, they would go to the press to brand me as a thief and I'd never work again. Karina nodded, and smiled. She reminded me of a poisonous snake which has just ingested a tasty meal.'

Bea said, 'Surely no one would believe that of you!'

'I'm afraid they would. Do you remember Tony . . .? No, you probably don't. Another portrait painter. Pretty good, too. A spiteful young girl alleged he'd tried to have sex with her when he was painting her father. The police were called in, and eventually it became clear she'd lied but the story got around and he lost work. The last I heard of him he'd taken up chicken farming in Wales.

'No one wants a rapist or a thief in the house. If Karina spreads a rumour that I stole from her, then I'm finished. I don't know what to do, apart from emigrating, changing my name and starting all over again. I have no idea where to find Molly. She's certainly not living in my studio. No one is. Which reminds me, can you find me a cleaner to give it a regular going over? I assume Molly lied when she said she'd got the job through the agency here, but how did she know about the mews? I can't see her as a thief, but how do I prove my innocence? I'm so angry, I could . . . Bea, what on earth am I going to do?'

She leaned over to stroke his cheek. 'Piers, you're too close to the action to see the pattern, but I can see one and together you and I will sort it out.'

He was not convinced. 'The moment that woman tells one of her friends that I stole from her, everyone in the world will know. I'm finished!'

'She may think she holds all the cards, but she doesn't. For one thing, she's reckoned without your ability to recall exactly what people look like and what they said. She's also involved me, which I think I may say is a big mistake.'

Piers couldn't see it. 'It's no use. Molly is obviously a professional jewel thief. She took me in completely and disappeared. I'm due to paint a couple of senators over in Washington some time. I'll bring that forward and disappear to America till this has all died down.' He was only half joking.

'That's exactly what they'd like you to do. Look, if I can trace Molly Malone by the end of the working day, will you hold off booking your flight to America till then?'

TWO

Piers said, 'What can you do? What can anyone do?'
'More to the point,' said Bea, 'is what you can do. Have you still got your sketchpad?'
He nodded.

She fetched his kitbag and dumped it on his lap. 'I don't care if you use pastels, pencil or a red biro, but you have five minutes to give me a sketch of Molly.'

He found his sketchpad and a pen. He looked at them as if he didn't know what they were for. 'My mind's gone blank.'

Bea folded her arms at him. 'Does she dye her hair? Does she wear four-inch heels? How old is she?'

'Ridiculous!' Then, as if hypnotized, he started to sketch.

Bea watched.

Piers drew a young woman – perhaps twenty-five? Maybe a little older? – with thick, coarse, dark hair which probably curled naturally. It had been cut in a longish bob. Her face was slightly on the plump side, her eyebrows plucked to a thin line, her mouth slightly open as if she were talking. Her nose had a bit of a blob on the end. Her eyes were sharp, looking off to the left. Nothing extraordinary about her except perhaps the thinness of the eyebrows. Piers sketched in the lapels of a good quality shirt, with a thin chain around her neck. Molly was, according to Piers, middle class, reasonably intelligent, unmemorable.

Bea studied the sketch. She was pretty sure that she'd never met the woman and if she had, she had a feeling she wouldn't have liked her. Now, why was that?

Bea shrugged. The main thing was that she knew how to find this Molly Malone. Ever since Piers had reported that the agency had been involved in the woman's appointment to Karina's household, Bea had been working on an idea which caused her no pleasure at all.

There was a leaky mouth downstairs in the agency, wasn't there? And Bea was going to have to ferret it out and deal with it. Yes, sir!

She looked at the clock, narrowing her eyes in thought. The office downstairs would be busy at this time of day, but she hadn't been needed or Lisa, her relatively new office manageress, would have phoned up with a query. At least, Bea hoped so. Lisa had come with good references. Bea had judged the woman to be a safe pair of hands while privately wishing she had a little more sugar and spice in her makeup. Now Bea had to face the possibility that Lisa had allowed a traitor into the camp.

Bea looked at her watch. She had an appointment with a client in half an hour. Could she locate Molly before then?

No, because this mess was going to take time to sort out.

Piers let his hands fall away from his sketchpad.

Bea said, 'Sign and date it.' He did so and she took it from him. 'Don't do anything about anything till I get back.'

'I can't just sit here and—'

'Start making sketches of everyone concerned, from Karina down to the housekeeper.' She paused. 'No, change that. Do the housekeeper next and bring it down to me in my office. What's her name, by the way?'

'No idea.'

'Of course you have. You've heard it. You may not have taken note of it, but it's somewhere in your head. So, do her next.'

She checked the time by her watch as she made her way to the hall. She had twenty-five minutes before her appointment. She took the stairs which led down to the agency.

She was spitting mad. She knew, she just knew that some member of her staff had colluded with this Molly to get a job with Karina. They had used access to the agency to learn how Piers worked and that he had a studio in the mews nearby. Lisa must have known what was happening. Had corruption crept into the office and worked its oily way up to her office manageress?

It didn't bear thinking about.

Bea glanced at her watch again. Twenty minutes to her appointment. Could she get someone else to interview this particular client so that she could bring out the thumbscrews and get to work on whoever it was who had embroiled the agency in Karina's affairs?

No, better not. Long-term clients who came back year after year sometimes became good friends and what's more, they merited a pot of tea and good china teacups.

Bea paused on the threshold of the big office and told herself to calm down.

The staff were busy in a muted sort of way. Lisa looked up from her computer and signalled with her slightly anxious smile that all was well. One of the girls was laying out the teacups ahead of their client's visit.

Bea held up her hand to attract attention. Two of the girls were in the middle of telephone conversations and couldn't stop, but the others did.

Bea held up Piers' sketch. 'I have something here for Molly. A good likeness, isn't it? Which of you knows how to contact her?'

Nobody looked worried. Amused smiles were on the faces turned to Bea. They knew Molly all right, and the knowledge didn't stir them to anxiety. They knew and liked the girl? How come? Well, that was what Bea was going to find out.

Three of them, including Lisa, looked towards the girl who was making the tea. She – the latest recruit to the office – looked up and waved her hand. 'Is that one of Piers' sketches? He's good, isn't he? She'll be thrilled.'

Lisa said, 'How's Molly doing? She was so happy to get that job. There's no problem, is there?'

Bea relaxed a notch. She'd gambled that someone in the office must know Molly and she'd been right. How else could the girl have been able to produce paperwork from the agency, know about Piers' work, and have details of the mews cottage?

How much had Lisa known about it? Bea's mind whirled around and round and stopped right there. Lisa hadn't been with Bea long, but she had proved herself a reasonable second-in-command during that time. She had no dress sense, but that wasn't a crime in itself. She would wear a cardigan – *a cardigan!* – to work. Bea had always dressed well and considered it a matter of self-respect to do so. But if that were the only fault she could find in the woman, then so be it. And if Lisa had made a mistake, well, that wasn't the end of the world, was it?

Bea said, 'I have a client coming at three . . .' Prompt on cue, the doorbell rang, and the girl nearest the door went to answer it. Bea said, 'So I'll be quick. I'm told Molly ran into a spot of difficulty at her job this morning. My husband would like us to help her, if we can. So, could I see Lisa and anyone else who knows Molly in my office at four o'clock and we'll have a chat about it? If Molly herself rings here before then, could you pass the call on to me?'

Their client had arrived. Bea went to meet her, all smiles. The smiles were deserved because this woman employed only the very best of staff for an exclusive hotel, and was about to open a second. She wanted to discuss taking on extra staff and Bea was delighted to help her choose the best.

Bea told herself to relax. First things first. 'How are you doing? Do come through to my office. Tea is on its way.'

Because of the slope, Bea's office was reached by a short flight of stairs down from street level at the front, but at the back French windows let on to the garden. Bea threw open the windows and turned her mind from mayhem to maids.

Although the door to her office had been shut, Bea was conscious of an argument going on in the big office next door. A couple of voices were raised, and quickly hushed.

The client looked interested. She'd heard the ruckus, too.

Bea sighed. She confided, 'A girl who was sent out by the agency appears to have run into a spot of bother this morning. I don't know exactly why but my manageress is dealing with it.'

The client rolled her eyes. 'Was she chased around the furniture by her employer? Or did she misspell his name?'

They both laughed, as the client had intended. Bea relaxed. This client was taking the agency's problem the right way. 'I'm not sure,' said Bea, 'but I'll look into it later. Actually, I've just thought that it might have happened while I was on holiday—'

'Ah, I remember. You got married again, didn't you? Congratulations. A delightful man. What insight he brings to his pictures! He made a really good job of capturing the likeness of my brother's wayward daughter. Fortunately, she's calmed down in recent months, but . . .'

Indulgent smiles all round.

Nearly an hour later, Bea saw her client out and was able to turn her attention to Molly's misdoings. 'Lisa?'

Lisa didn't look happy. But she got to her feet, picked up a folder from her desk and followed Bea back into her office, closely followed by the new girl, Jolene.

Jolene was a wisp of a girl with her hair in cornrows. Jolene had a flair for figures which was a valuable asset, but she didn't always understand the difference between being funny and being rude. Jolene was sulking. Had Lisa been having a go at her?

Bea waved them to seats.

Jolene said, 'You're not going to sack me, are you? I didn't do nothing wrong.'

Lisa was not amused. 'Oh, don't whine, Jolene. I'm sorry, Mrs Abbot. I suppose we did bend the rules when we took Molly on and she applied for the job. If it's led to trouble then I'll take responsibility. What's happened to her?'

Bea made calming motions with her hands. 'Let's start at the beginning. You employed Molly while I was away on honeymoon?'

Jolene flounced in her chair. 'There wasn't no harm in it. She was looking for a job and we was short-staffed with you away and two of us on holiday. She came in with me to look after the filing and stuff. She was a load of laughs. Lisa didn't mind, did you, Lisa? My mum said we should always help our friends.'

Lisa looked anxious. 'That's true. We were short-handed and she did help out. Is something wrong?'

Jolene said, 'Molly's mum was a friend of my mum's from way back when they was kids, see? Molly come up to London to find a more interesting job than she could get back home. She wanted to go into publishing but couldn't get anyone to take her on, so was keen to register with an agency for some temp work in the meantime. Mum said as we could put her up for a while, and she came in to work with me to help out while you were away. She made the tea, ran errands, did a spot of filing. Then this job with Karina came in – a ghostwriter, of all things! – and Molly said she'd like to try for it. It'd look good on her CV and might help her get a foot in the door at a prestigious publishing company. It was perfect for her.'

Lisa explained, 'Molly had an English degree and she'd done

all these courses in creative writing and that. We hadn't anyone
else on our books who'd got her background, so I said she could
apply but to be clear about her lack of experience to date.'

Bea said, 'I didn't see her name on the wages sheet when I
returned.'

Lisa flushed slightly. 'I know it was a bit irregular, but she
signed on to work for us as a temp under her own name, which
is Mary Ann Pocock. She liked to be called Molly and there was
nothing wrong with that. We paid her for the work she did for
us under that name, and she paid us the usual registration fee
when she went for the job.'

Bea sat back in her chair. 'I begin to see. She was born with
the name of Pocock but wanted to change it – for which one
cannot blame her – and so invented another for herself when
she signed on and went for the job with Karina.'

Jolene bubbled up. 'A new name for a fresh start in life. She
wanted to keep her first name, Molly, because it was easy to
remember. We all talked about what she might like to call herself,
and we had a bit of a laugh about it and . . . well, Molly Malone
sounded all right, and she could make a joke out of calling herself
a girl who sold fishes . . .' Her voice trailed away.

Bea sighed. 'By law you can call yourself whatever name you
like. Was she going to change her name by deed poll?'

Lisa said, 'She said she was, because of getting new National
Insurance numbers and all that, but I don't know if she's got
round to it or not yet.'

'Didn't her family object?'

Jolene was fast recovering her usual sprightliness. 'There's
only her mum back in the Midlands and she said she didn't mind,
and my mum said she didn't see no harm in it, and Molly said
she'd got no friends down here yet. She said she'd spin some
yarn about losing her papers in a fire at home and ask to be paid
in cash till she could get herself sorted.'

Lisa said, 'It all seemed like a bit of laugh, but now . . . You
say she's in trouble? Has she been found out? It's no big deal,
is it?'

Bea had to think about that. 'If it had only been a question of
using a false name . . . Well, I don't think her employers would
have liked it. They might have regarded it as deceit. I personally

have not liked to hear that the agency registered someone under a false name.'

Lisa reddened. She said, 'No, I see that now. I ought to have told you. I'm sorry.'

Bea accepted this. Yes, Lisa had been, well, imprudent. But there had been no intent on her part to deceive. Or had there? She said, 'I'd like to see the records of Molly's employment with us and of the job we recommended her for.'

Lisa handed over the file of papers.

Bea read them through, and then turned back to the name of the client. 'The job came in from a firm of solicitors in Knightsbridge. They were looking for a PA with an English degree, not a ghostwriter.'

Lisa said, 'I sent through her details, and they asked her to go for an interview to this house in Belgravia, to see a Mr Fletcher. He said he had a client who wanted to dictate her memoirs to someone who could correct her grammar and so on. Molly said he was ever so stiff and really old. Then she found out she'd be working for a celebrity. She had to sign a contract promising secrecy and we only found out that Karina was the celebrity when she told Jolene, but that wasn't till some weeks after she started.'

Bea slapped the folder down on the desk. 'How come she said her home address was in the mews at the end of this street?'

Lisa shot out of her chair. 'What! But . . . No, that's not possible! Jolene?'

Jolene wriggled. 'Well, it was just . . . Look, I know it was a bit cheeky, but the thing is that she didn't want to say she was living with me and me mum in a tower block in Acton. I mean, it don't give the right impression, do it? And she was planning to move somewhere nice as soon as she'd earned enough, so . . . There was no harm in it, was there?' Her voice died away. 'It sounded all right, the way she said it.'

Lisa was hopping mad. 'Jolene! How dare you!' She turned to Bea. 'I didn't know! I left it to her and Molly to fill in the details.'

Lisa was speaking the truth? Probably.

Bea was resigned. 'Molly tried to pretend she was living in a better part of London than she really did, so gave her address as my husband's studio flat in the mews nearby?'

Jolene was defiant. 'It was just like using a postal box. She filled out a form for the post office so that if any mail went there, it would be forwarded to us. Honest, it all went like clockwork, and the tales she told us about Karina, well! You wouldn't believe if it hadn't been Molly.'

Bea and Lisa stared at Jolene. Bea thought that the sooner she got rid of the girl, the better. Apart from her sloppy grammar, Jolene didn't seem to know the importance of telling the truth when a lie might be more convenient.

Lisa looked as if she'd either like to throttle Jolene or commit suicide, she wasn't sure which. Or burst into tears. Mm. Lisa needed to toughen up, didn't she?

Jolene shuffled around on her seat. 'You said Molly was in a spot of trouble?'

Bea said, 'Molly was accused of stealing some jewellery from her employer.'

Shock! Horror! From both women. 'What? Molly? Never!'

Bea said, 'No, I don't think she did it. I don't even know if her employer had worked out that Molly was using an alias. Nevertheless, it's a nasty situation and, because she's involved the agency, we've been dragged into it. Jolene, has Molly tried to contact you on her phone today?'

No one was supposed to receive or make private phone calls at the agency, unless in dire emergency. That way, no one missed incoming calls.

Jolene got out her mobile phone. She shook her head and was about to put it back in her pocket when Lisa leaned over to take it off the girl. 'Let me see that!'

'Watch it!' said Jolene as she tried to snatch it back and missed.

Lisa exclaimed, 'Why, what's this? She's called you twice in the last fifteen minutes!'

Jolene said, 'I *told* her we're not allowed to take calls in office hours.'

Lisa appealed to Bea. 'Mrs Abbot, are we in trouble? Are the police involved?'

'Not yet, but they will be unless we sort something out pretty quickly. Jolene; you're very young and I'm prepared to believe that you acted in good faith but you did help Molly to bend the rules and I can see that the police might take a dim view of that.'

Jolene burst into noisy tears. 'It's not my fault!'

'Crocodile tears, Jolene. It's about time you grew up and took responsibility for your actions. Molly is still living at home with you? Yes? Good. Now, I need to talk to her.'

She glanced at her watch. Nearly five. How time flies when you're having fun. 'Lisa, give Jolene back her phone. Now, Jolene; I want you to ask Molly to come to see me this evening and we'll see what can be done. Meanwhile . . .'

A tap on the door, and a girl brought in a piece of paper which she put on Bea's desk. She removed herself after a lingering look at Lisa and Jolene. Bea realized they'd been gossiping next door, wondering what had gone wrong that Lisa and Jolene were still in with Bea.

Bea reached for the paper. 'Ah, this is a sketch of someone who is part of Karina's household. Do either of you recognize her?'

She held out the sketch, which was of a middle-aged woman with a heavy jowl. Bea's private thought was that the woman would have a light hand with pastry and smell of warm currants.

Lisa leaned over to see. 'N-no. I don't think so. What's he written at the bottom? Sherry? Brandy? Has she got something to do with alcohol?'

Bea said, 'This is a sketch of the housekeeper at the place Molly has been working. Piers has been trying to remember what the woman was called. Jolene, do you recognize her? No? Have either of you had a phone call from a woman urgently wanting a post as housekeeper today? No? It's a long shot, but I'll just try next door.'

She put her head round into the main office. 'Has anyone here had a phone call today to make an appointment for a cook or housekeeper who needs another job urgently?'

One of the older women put up her hand. 'Mrs Hennessey, you mean? She rang about an hour ago saying she'd walked out on her job for good and sufficient reasons and wanted to know if we might find her another straight away. Is that who you mean?'

Bea said, 'Tell me about her.'

The woman consulted her computer. 'She's a cook and housekeeper, been on our books for some years now. We placed her with a retired couple four years ago. Six months back her employers went into a retirement home at short notice and we found her another placement with . . .' She frowned. 'Ah, yes. A Mr Fletcher. I think he's a solicitor and he was enquiring for a reliable woman to look after someone who has a house in Belgravia. Mrs Hennessey's only been there about six months. I don't know why she's left.'

'I do,' said Bea, 'and it's not her fault.' She held up the sketch Piers had made. 'Does anyone recognize her? Good. Now, I'd like to see her here tomorrow morning. Would you ask her to come in and yes, see what else we can find for her straight away?'

There was a commotion back in Bea's office. Lisa's voice was raised sharply. Jolene was shouting.

Bea turned back into her office, thinking she'd made a mistake giving Jolene an opportunity to phone Molly back. Because that was what the girl had been doing, wasn't it? Yes, Lisa was standing over Jolene in a nose-to-nose confrontation. Jolene was laughing. Lisa wasn't!

Bea was annoyed with herself and with Jolene. 'You were talking to Molly on your phone?'

'If I was? So? She's back home, packing to leave, going to a friend's place till things calm down. And you needn't think you can ring her on this phone now because she doesn't want to talk to you.'

Lisa appealed to Bea. 'I did remind Jolene you wanted to speak to Molly!'

Bea cut her off. 'I know. And Jolene knows she shouldn't make private phone calls at work. Jolene, Molly's in trouble. Maybe I can help her, but to do that I need to speak to her.'

Jolene was defiant. 'You can try all you want to ring her but she's not going to pick up. She's got something that everyone wants and she's going to make sure she gets the best price for it.'

Bea said, 'Will she answer if the police ring her? Yes, the police. Jolene, this isn't some silly prank. This is serious. Her employer accused Molly of the theft of some jewellery. Now, I'm pretty sure she didn't do it—'

'Don't be daft. She wouldn't!'

Bea exercised patience. 'I agree. And yes, I think she's been very badly treated and yes, I'd have run off, too, if I'd been in her position. She's due an apology—'

'And her wages!'

'Now that's another matter. Was she paid weekly or monthly? As a PA, or as a ghostwriter? Do we know what sort of contract she signed, if any? Lisa, do we have a copy of her contract with this Mr Fletcher? No? Well, now; if she accepted the job as a PA then she's owed her wages and that's all. If she signed a contract as a ghostwriter, then she's obligated to deliver the goods within a certain time frame for a set sum of money.'

Jolene shrugged. 'After what they've done to her? She can flog the manuscript to the highest bidder.'

'It depends on the terms of her contract as a ghostwriter. She's been working for Karina, presumably for a fixed sum. So the copyright belongs to Karina, and not to Molly. Agreed, Molly has to be paid for it, but she can't hawk it around, hoping for a better offer. Actually, she doesn't need to because she's in a strong position. She has the manuscript and Karina needs to deliver it to the publisher next week or the book won't come out in time for Christmas. The family has to pay Molly off *now*.'

'Well, they haven't paid her for it yet! What's more, they've broken her laptop and assaulted her, so she can claim damages for that as well.'

'I'm inclined to agree with you,' said Bea. 'Her best bet would be to go to a good solicitor and get them to sort it out for her.'

'She hasn't the money for that. She's been living with us rent free, because they only give her a coupla hundred on account when she started work and nothing since. She owes our mum for rent, and what's more, she's borrowed for her tube fare to work every day and all.'

'All the more reason for her to get this sorted. I know a good solicitor—'

'You're not listening! Molly's no money for that! You people are all the same. You've no heart! I thought you'd be willing to help someone who's been so badly treated, but you're all alike, you lot! Think only for yourself. Well, I've had it up to here! It's way past six, and I'm off home! And don't expect me to come back in the morning. You can keep your poxy job, so there!' She stormed out to the main office, snatching up her jacket and handbag on the way out.

Lisa bleated, 'Oh, Jolene! No!'

Jolene made a noisy exit, slamming the outer door.

Bea took one deep breath. And then another.

Lisa twisted her fingers. She was trembling. 'Oh dear, I don't think . . . the young people nowadays, no respect for . . . but going off like that . . . but maybe you wouldn't have wanted her to stay after . . .? I do understand I ought to have reined her in . . . Do you want me to tender my resignation?'

Bea thought that sometime soon Lisa would probably decide the job was too stressful for her and find an excuse to resign. At that point Bea would accept the resignation, but not now when Jolene's departure meant they were already one short in the office.

She stifled a sigh for her previous office manager, who'd been a cheerful and efficient second-in-command. Ah well, Betty had gone on to pastures new and was enjoying herself there.

She said, 'No, Lisa; mistakes have been made and the agency has been put in an uncomfortable position, but we'll just have to see what we can do to put it right. As for Jolene, it's clear she hasn't fitted in here and it's best she goes. Let me have her address and telephone number before you leave this evening and I'll send on whatever money is due to her.'

Lisa trembled her way to her desk and set about shutting down for the night.

Bea hesitated. Somebody had mentioned a name that she'd heard before.

Bea concentrated. Ah. Bingo! Mr Fletcher. That was it. She'd heard the name not once but twice. She had a mental picture of a puppeteer pulling strings for Karina. Now, how to contact him?

THREE

Thursday, early evening

B ea turned off her computer, locked the French windows that let on to the garden, checked that all was well in the main office, tested the outer door to the street to make sure Lisa had secured it properly, and went up the inner stairs to the first floor.

She found her husband on the phone, sitting with his laptop at the big table in the front window. A quick glance informed her that he'd recovered his balance. He'd showered and changed. He was now wearing a white silk shirt and black jeans.

She took a moment to appreciate what a pleasant picture he made. He'd always been lithe and lean, though he took little exercise. His charm hadn't diminished with age, though his dark hair was now turning grey at the temples and there were crows' feet forming around his eyes.

He heard her come in but held up his hand to prevent her from speaking while he finished his phone call. And then he said, still without looking at her, 'I believe I owe you an apology. I haven't had the black dog sitting on my shoulder like that for years.'

'Idiot!' said Bea, giving him a quick hug. 'I loved it. For once I felt you needed me as much as I need you.'

'Ha!' He swung round to look at her. 'You're looking pleased with yourself. You found Molly, did you?'

'I did. Apparently, she enjoyed herself working in the office while we were away on honeymoon. Everyone liked her. When the job with Karina came up, she and my staff conspired to invent a new name for her since the one she'd been given at birth did not amuse.'

'So, she isn't Mary Malone?'

'That wasn't her birth name, no. Her real name wasn't one you'd want to carry through life and I understand why she wanted to change it. Legally, you can call yourself any name you like, and she has. I don't know if she's changed her name by deed poll or not. Anyway, I found out where she was living and almost got her on the phone before things went wrong and I lost contact. So, how about you?' She looked at the laptop. 'What's that? A contract?'

'For Karina's portrait.'

'I'm right in thinking it was a Mr Fletcher who approached you to paint her portrait? It wasn't a member of her family?'

'That's right. He got in touch with me through my agent. Clients do tend to pass my name along to their friends if they like what I've done for them, but this was . . . I think he said he'd seen something of mine at the Royal Academy? No, it was in the Mall Galleries. He said that an anonymous admirer of

Karina's had asked him to find someone to paint her portrait as a birthday present. As an added inducement to me to accept the commission, the publisher of her forthcoming memoirs would use the portrait on the cover of the book. That's not unusual. I met Mr Fletcher at my agent's to discuss the matter. Next day he took me to meet Karina in Belgravia, when we talked about how many sittings I'd need, where I'd paint her, what she would wear, and so on.'

Bea asked, 'Was this Mr Fletcher a member of her family?'

'I don't think so. He didn't live there, and I never saw him again after those two meetings. He looked and acted like a solicitor.' Piers seized his sketchbook and started to draw the portrait of a man in his late fifties or early sixties with all the hallmarks of a professional. A grey man. Intelligent, guarded in manner.

Piers said, 'I was trying to find his telephone number when you came in, but it's not on the contract and my agent's phone is busy. If anyone knows what's going on at Karina's, Mr Fletcher does.'

'I agree,' said Bea, 'and I happen to have the telephone number here. You see, you are missing several links in the chain. This Mr Fletcher of yours has had dealings with the agency before. It was he who asked us to find Karina a cook-housekeeper. That's the woman whose face you drew for me. Her name's Hennessey.'

A flicker of a smile. 'I knew her name reminded me of drink.'

'It was also Mr Fletcher who asked us to find a PA slash ghostwriter to turn Karina's memoirs into a publishable book. On both occasions the agency sent him someone to interview and only when they'd passed muster with him, did it transpire that the jobs were for Karina and her household.'

'So when a portrait painter was needed, they asked him to come up with someone?'

'I think,' said Bea, 'that this Mr Fletcher acts as man of business for Karina and her family. Whenever they need someone, they ask him to oblige. I suspect he may be their family solicitor.'

Piers was looking at the contract on his laptop. 'I was supposed to bill Karina when the portrait was completed. Want to see what our diva looks like?' He attached his smartphone to his laptop and transferred the image of the portrait.

In silence they contemplated what Piers had done. He'd often said that he didn't know exactly what effect he was going to get when he started to paint.

Karina had wanted to be painted as an exotic – as an orchid – and that's precisely what Piers had done. The woman loomed out of the darkness with a beauty which had more than a hint of cruelty about it. The red brocade of her gown matched the red tints in her hair. Orchids were hinted at in the design of her robe, and she had another in her hair. And yes, Bea thought they were a trifle obtrusive and Piers had been right to think of toning them down.

Piers said, 'She must be in her late fifties, possibly early sixties, but sometimes . . . the way she looked me up and down . . . and all the time she would be stroking . . .! No, it's not my imagination. She still wants sex.' He was amused, a little, that he could still stir the senses of an older woman without any effort on his part.

Bea hid a smile. Piers had always been a magnet for sex. Put him in a room full of people and the women would be instantly aware of him.

The doorbell rang.

Piers said, 'Are we expecting someone?'

Bea shook her head and went to answer the summons, hoping it might be the elusive Molly Malone on the doorstep.

But no. It was a grey man with grey hair in a grey suit. There was a slight flush on his cheekbones and his jaw was rigid as he enquired, 'Mrs Abbot?'

Bea opened the door wide. 'Come in, Mr Fletcher. We were just talking about you.'

He stepped in as if testing the temperature of the sea with his toe. The set of his shoulders indicated that he was not a happy bunny. He was carrying a canvas bag, which Bea recognized as being the one in which Piers stowed the collapsible easel he used when visiting sitters in their own homes. She took it off him and laid it on the hall chest.

Piers appeared in the doorway to the living room, recognized the bundle and said, 'Thanks for returning my easel. I'd be lost without it.'

Mr Fletcher compressed his lips. 'I was asked to do so. It is

your property. If you would be so good as to sign this receipt
for it?' He extracted a sheet of paper from his pocket and held
it out to Piers, who scanned it, picked up his jacket and went
back into the living room, saying, 'I've got a pen here,
somewhere.'

Mr Fletcher followed Piers into the living room. He moved
stiffly, giving the impression of a man suffering from a bout of
acute indigestion.

Piers took his jacket to the table in the window while Bea
gestured Mr Fletcher to a seat.

She said, 'Would you like a cup of coffee or tea, perhaps?
No? I wonder, were you expecting something in exchange for
the easel?'

Hard grey eyes fastened on hers. 'I was led to believe that
yes, you might possibly have come across something which
belongs to my client. As you can imagine, she is in considerable
distress at the loss of so much valuable property. She was going
to call in the police but had second thoughts. She felt that doing
so would advertise the fact that she keeps valuable jewellery on
the premises, and amount to an invitation to all and sundry to
burgle the house.

'She acknowledges that it was, in retrospect, a mistake for a
member of her household to accuse your husband of theft. It was
perhaps understandable that he took offence and decided to
retaliate. It would have taken only a second or two for him
to pocket something which did not belong to him.'

Bea glanced across at Piers, who was frowning down at the
receipt, reading it through. He had his 'wooden' face on. Bea
expected him to join in the conversation, but he didn't seem
inclined to do so.

She turned back to Mr Fletcher. 'Do sit down, Mr Fletcher.'

She indicated a high-backed armchair and sank into her own
seat beside the fireplace. Piers signed the receipt and handed it
to Mr Fletcher. Instead of joining in the conversation, he then
returned to look out of the front window.

She said, 'My husband was outraged at being manhandled and
accused of theft.'

'Naturally. Naturally. But let us suppose that he had, in a
moment of quite understandable annoyance, pocketed something

which did not belong to him? Once he had calmed down, he would regret his action and then he would start to wonder how to return the object without any fuss or the intervention of the police. Hence my offer to return the easel and see if this matter can be brought to a satisfactory conclusion with the least possible aggravation to all concerned.'

He spoke to Piers' back, which remained resolutely turned to the room.

Bea couldn't understand why Piers failed to speak up. She said, 'My husband did not steal anything, so your journey was in vain.'

Mr Fletcher was not giving up. He gave a little cough. 'My client would not wish to be the instrument of ending your husband's career, which would undoubtedly happen if she were forced to call in the police. His momentary aberration would be fodder for the media and his career would be over. When you have thought over my offer, I am sure you will find it has considerable merit.'

Frowning, Bea looked across at Piers. His back was still turned to the room. Why was he acting like this? She said, 'As a matter of interest, what is it that Karina wants most? The memory stick, or the jewellery? We haven't got either, but it would be interesting to know which she values most highly.'

Mr Fletcher steepled his fingers. 'I really cannot say.'

Bea said, 'Personally, I think she'd want the memory stick more than the jewellery. A wise person wouldn't keep valuable pieces of jewellery at the house, whether she has a safe or not. She'd keep them at the bank and take them out for display on important occasions. I'd guess that she's had replicas made for everyday use. Oh, she screamed blue murder when she discovered – or said she'd discovered – a missing necklace and ring this morning, but I believe she did that for another reason. Am I right, Mr Fletcher?'

Mr Fletcher said, 'No comment.' He turned in his chair to look at Piers, who was still looking out of the window.

Bea said, 'I'm curious about your position in this affair, Mr Fletcher. You appear to be acting on behalf of Karina. In what capacity, may I ask? Solicitor?'

'There is a family connection,' he said, still with his eyes on

Piers. 'When he died, Karina's second husband appointed me the executor of his will, and guardian of their son. Her fame has laid her open to approaches from many people who would like to separate her from her wealth. I have become a sort of . . . a barrier, shall we say? . . . between her and those who do not have her best interests at heart.'

'Hence your unusual arrangements to vet members of her household before they actually know who they will be working for? Hence your use of our agency to locate suitable applicants?'

'It is a system which has worked well in the past. Perhaps not so well now.'

'You are referring to Molly Malone?' Bea tried to hide a smile. 'She's done it on you good and proper, hasn't she? Piers says she'd picked up quite a few items of gossip while working for Karina. I'm beginning to wonder how stable Karina's finances may be. To run that big house and all those hangers-on—'

'Members of the family only.' Mr Fletcher was in a cleft stick. He couldn't actually bring himself to say so, but his manner indicated that he did indeed deplore the extravagance of the household.

'Of course. Husbands, ex-husbands, and sons. Expensive, very. I wonder if she makes a habit of accusing members of staff of theft so that she can sack them without paying their wages?'

'No, no.' But he shifted uncomfortably in his seat.

'Who thought up that little ploy? Was it Karina herself – or one of her entourage?'

'Not Karina. No, of course not.'

'She did stage that playlet in order to get Mrs Hennessey to leave in a huff, didn't she? Perhaps she's pulled this stunt off before in order to save wages? I must ask around at other employment agencies and enquire if they know of her. If her name is mud elsewhere, then it is not perhaps surprising that she asked you – whose name is not connected to hers – to find some staff by working through an agency which she hadn't used before?'

A tinge of red blossomed on his cheekbones. 'I cannot possibly comment.'

Bea grinned. 'I bet you were furious when you discovered what she'd been up to. To sack her cook-cum-housekeeper is one thing, but to get rid of her personal assistant and her portrait painter on the very same morning is overdoing it. I'd have liked to have been a fly on the wall when she explained to you that she'd sacked not one, not two, but three people in order to avoid paying what is owed them.'

He said, 'It is true that she does find herself temporarily embarrassed, yes. Her position in society, her fame . . . it is only natural that she lives up to that . . . Shopping at Fortnum & Mason and Harrods, hosting parties at the Dorchester, patronizing a French couturier . . . it is the sort of thing expected of her. But there is a considerable sum of money due to her on delivery of the manuscript of the book. It is expected to do well. There was a bidding war for the rights, several foreign language rights have already been sold. Lucrative television interviews are being arranged, and after-dinner speeches booked. There may even be cameo spots in television series. There will be a great deal of media interest.'

'So, she believes the book will put her back on the map and you have been sent out to rescue the manuscript and soothe over the hurt feelings of the wrongly accused so that they don't jeopardize her chances of fame and fortune by suing her for wrongful dismissal. I doubt if madam will go so far as to apologize to any of those she accused of theft, will she? No, I don't suppose she will. And yes, you will have cheques in your pocket to compensate and neutralize Mrs Hennessey, Molly Malone, and Piers. Am I correct?'

'The first two, yes. Partially. If I can get them to sign a release. As for Piers' cheque, that depends on his returning the memory stick. They still believe he might have it.' Fletcher hoicked some papers out of an inner pocket and smoothed them out on his knee.

Bea said, 'Well, I'm pretty sure I can put things right for Mrs Hennessey. She has taken jobs through our books before and always given satisfaction. I imagine you have been generous and added a bonus for the aggravation she suffered this morning? Yes? If you will send me a good reference for her, signed by Karina, then I will do my best to find her another post straight away.'

His lips thinned, but he nodded. 'She has to sign a release, forbidding her from talking to the press or anyone else about Karina. You understand?'

'I shall be seeing Mrs Hennessey tomorrow morning. I will give her your cheque and advise her to sign the release once the money is in her bank account. Now, as for Molly Malone . . .' Bea shrugged. 'Have you a cheque for her, too?'

He steepled his fingers. 'I am only authorized to pay for a replacement laptop. And we need the memory stick before we can talk about anything else.'

'Ah. Yes. There I cannot help you.'

'She came highly recommended through your agency. Your reputation is at stake.'

Bea winced. 'To a certain extent, that's true. I can leave messages with her family, asking her to contact you, but that's as far as I can go. Piers doesn't have your memory stick, so what happens about payment for him?'

His fingers twitched. 'Perhaps he'll change his mind about holding on to someone else's property, and then I'm sure something can be arranged. Meanwhile, Karina is sending her portrait to the publishers so that it can be featured on the cover of her book.'

Piers interjected, 'The portrait is worthless until I sign it.'

The grey man said, 'Karina is not particularly pleased with the poor likeness that you have produced. She has authorized me to offer you half the amount on which we agreed originally, subject to your returning the memory stick, of course.'

Piers puffed out a laugh. 'That's par for the course, isn't it? Employ someone to do a job, then renege on the deal. Have you yourself seen the portrait?' He swivelled his laptop round to show Mr Fletcher what he'd done.

The grey man stood up, put on a pair of rimless glasses and bent over to look at the screen. 'Ah,' he said. 'This reminds me of the extravaganzas produced by Gustav Klimt. Predatory women wearing clothes made of luxury fabrics. I quite like it, myself, but I am not the buyer.'

Piers held out his right hand, with a memory stick on his palm. He said, 'Oh, I rather think you are.'

The grey man held out his hand for the tiny object. 'So, you had it all along?'

Piers closed his hand on it. 'No. I found it a moment ago. It was in the pocket of my jacket when I looked for a pen to sign your receipt. I've been trying ever since to work out who put it there, and when. And why.'

Mr Fletcher's eyes were on Piers' hand. 'It doesn't belong to you. I'll return it for you, shall I?'

Piers threw the tiny black memory stick in the air and caught it again. Then he tossed it over to Bea, who fumbled the catch but managed to hold on to the stick.

Piers said, 'That memory stick is not yours. I'm not exactly sure who owns it. Is it the one Molly was using? And if so, why did someone put it in my pocket?'

'It's not your property and you have no right to hold on to it.'

'Then whose is it? Not yours, surely.'

Mr Fletcher was finding this conversation difficult. 'I am acting on Karina's behalf, to retrieve property which is rightfully hers.'

'At what point does the memory stick become hers? When was Molly due to deliver the book, anyway? When she got paid for it? I wouldn't mind a sight of the contract you signed with Molly, which might tell us when the memory stick ceases to belong to her and becomes Karina's property.'

Mr Fletcher took out a folded handkerchief and dabbed at his forehead. 'The girl was paid to produce the manuscript by last weekend. There was a slight delay, an argument over the text, nothing to worry about. I'm sure that that is Molly's memory stick. Let's see what's on it, and then you'll know it's hers and you can hand it over to me.'

Bea took a hand in the game. 'I can understand why Karina wants to keep her reminiscences secret till she's satisfied she's employing someone trustworthy. It is only sensible for her to get you to negotiate her contracts. But her history of terminating people's employment is not brilliant. Look at what's happened today!'

Mr Fletcher dabbed at his forehead again. His unease grew.

Bea guessed he was an honest man, finding himself in a difficult situation.

Bea went on, 'I presume you drew up the contract with Molly, yes? Did it cover Molly as a PA or as a ghostwriter? When was she supposed to be paid? Weekly, monthly, or in one lump sum on delivery?'

'I really don't . . . can't . . .' His voice sounded strangled.

Bea said, 'I'm told that Molly was living with friends, and that she was so short of the readies that she had to borrow money from them to get to and from work. It doesn't sound to me as if she were paid weekly or even monthly. How many months has she been working on this project? Four or five?'

Dab, dab, dab. 'She was paid a small advance. The rest will be due when she delivers the manuscript. That is standard procedure for ghostwriters.'

Bea said, 'Is it? I've never had to deal with this sort of thing before. I must look it up. Have you a cheque for her completion of the book?'

He hesitated. 'I . . . No. Not yet. You've shown me a memory stick. How do I know it was hers, and that it contains the manuscript of the book? It could belong to, well, anyone.'

'True.' Bea put the memory stick in her pocket. 'Perhaps it belongs to some member of Karina's family? They could have pinched the original when they searched Molly, and put it into Piers' pocket to confuse the issue. Or perhaps they substituted one of theirs and retained Molly's? Have you any suggestions?'

Mr Fletcher turned to Piers. 'Which member of the household put the memory stick in your pocket?'

Piers narrowed his eyes. 'I think it was one of the two lads who manhandled me. They turned me round and round and patted me down. One felt in the pockets of my jeans. Another picked up my jacket and investigated the contents. That was the one who "found" the solitaire diamond there. I've been trying to replay in my mind who was standing where and what they did. Was the one who searched my jacket, the same one who put the memory stick in it? And why did they do it? To confuse the issue, or to incriminate me as a thief? I'm not sure who did it or why. Does it matter?'

The grey man did his little cough again. 'It might make a difference. It was definitely one of the sons? The blond or the redhead?'

Bea's mind leaped to the truth. 'Mr Fletcher, exactly how involved are you in this matter? You said there was a family connection . . . to whom?'

He threw up his hands in a gesture of surrender.

She'd guessed right.

He tapped his fingertips together for a count of ten, and then decided to play ball. 'Did I hear you offer a coffee, earlier? Or tea, preferably Earl Grey. Or, possibly, a small sherry? Dry rather than sweet?'

He was going to talk. Hurray.

Once they were all comfortably seated and Mr Fletcher had been provided with a dry sherry, he relaxed. 'My family were mill owners who worked their way up from nothing, sold out at the right moment and joined the landed gentry. My mother was a deb, my elder brother and I were privately educated. My brother – Lance – inherited the money and the country estate. He stepped into our father's shoes as to the manor born. He was a "golden boy", a great sportsman, racing cars all around the world, jet set type, always in the tabloids.'

'Got it,' said Bea. 'He married Karina?'

Mr Fletcher nodded. 'At the time they met, she was still married to her first husband, whom she divorced in a blaze of publicity. They had had one child, Alexander, whom she adored in public but . . .' A shrug. 'She was set on a career in films so, with many tears, she handed him over to his father's parents to rear.

'As soon as the divorce was through, she married Lance in a fantasy of a romance, in a private plane flying high over the Med. They duly produced another son – my nephew Teddy – who was looked after by a series of nannies. Karina was getting bigger and bigger parts in films which caused problems in her marriage to Lance. The long hours of filming, the pressure of being constantly in the limelight, all took their toll of their relationship. They were both alpha males, if you see what I mean. Their life together was . . . tumultuous. They separated and reunited, only for my brother to die in an accident.'

Bea remembered that Molly Malone had dropped hints of a suspicious death to Piers. Had she been referring to the second husband's death? How suspicious had it been?

Mr Fletcher continued. 'Unlike Lance, I had never been attracted to the bright lights and as the second son I had to earn my living. I trained as a solicitor, married a lovely girl I met at the local tennis club and settled down in suburbia.

'When Lance died . . . Well, you can imagine. His affairs were in a mess. Debts everywhere. Lance had named me as his executor. So that's how I became involved in Karina's affairs. I found a tenant to take the country house on a long lease and installed a manager to run the estate. I met with creditors and arranged plans to pay off the debts. My aim was that by the time Teddy reached twenty-five and inherited, he could reclaim his birthright and have a decent income.

'Karina was devastated by Lance's death. To complicate matters, at long last she had an offer of a part in a Hollywood film. So she put aside her grief and made herself look to the future. She needed a fresh start, away from everything that reminded her of Lance, so she upped sticks and left.

'Alexander was settled with his grandparents, but Teddy was weakly and still clinging to his nanny. Karina thought it would be all wrong for him to be brought up with all the razzmatazz that was attached to Hollywood children, and proposed that my wife and I look after him while she was away. And that is how Teddy and his nanny moved in with us.

'The lad takes after my brother in so many ways: brave, handsome and with considerable charm. We would have adopted him, but Karina kept saying that one day when things calmed down, she'd be able to have him back to live with her. We wanted him to grow up with a balanced view of the world, to recognize his privileged position, and to be ready to run the country house and estate in due course. Unfortunately Teddy doesn't want to know about any of those things.

'His nanny was partly to blame. She was star-struck. She cut out all references to his mother's triumphs in Hollywood from the magazines and talked constantly to Teddy about the important people Karina was meeting. Poor boy! He was so proud of her. Karina did send him extravagant presents at intervals but then . . . she'd promise to ring him on a certain day and he'd get so excited, looking forward to hearing from her and . . . she often forgot and he'd be devastated. She insisted he had the best of private educations and of course that was only right and proper—'

Bea said, 'Who paid the bills for that?'

He pinched the bridge of his nose. 'We did, of course. She was so beautiful, she stunned the eye. But she's never been very practical, can't remember dates and times, that sort of thing.

Needs someone to look after her. Her life in the limelight must have seemed like a fairy story to a boy brought up by a solicitor and his wife living in suburbia. We sent him to Harrow where he traded on his mother's name to gather a coterie of boys who were also impressed by her stardom. We understood. We must have seemed very dull by contrast with the way his mother lived.

'I sound bitter, I know, but looking back I can see that it was inevitable Teddy would leave us to go back to her. When she eventually came back from the States and moved into the house in Belgravia, he dropped out of university and declared he was going to go into a partnership with Alexander to "manage Karina's career". It pretty well killed my wife. There wasn't anything in particular wrong with her, you know. Grief, mainly. I took early retirement to look after her. We tried everything but she just faded away.'

He contemplated his empty glass and set it aside without asking for another. He was not the type to drown his sorrows in drink, was he?

Piers said, 'I understand. You don't want it to be your nephew who put the ring or the memory stick in my pocket. There are two sons, one redhead and one blond. Am I right in thinking that Teddy is the blond boy?'

'He is. Was it he who put the memory stick in your pocket? Was it he who palmed the ring off on you?'

Piers shook his head. 'I honestly can't say. Those two boys grabbed me and whirled me round. Then one of them – and no, I can't be sure which one it was – put his arms round me from the back while the other searched me. I can't even be sure whether it was the same one who put the memory stick in my pocket that also "found" the ring there.'

Mr Fletcher lowered his eyelids. 'I understand. I can make excuses for him, but . . . he is only twenty years of age, twenty-one next month. As far as the courts go, he is an adult and must be treated as one. But it's an uphill struggle.'

'Debts?' said Piers.

Mr Fletcher sighed. 'He's unlucky. No, that's not quite true. He lacks judgement. He bought a share in a racehorse which broke its leg on its next race and had to be put down. Three months ago he signed a contract to buy a World War Two biplane, dreaming of becoming some sort of daredevil pilot. He crashed it on landing after his first solo outing. Wrote it off! I've had to sell one of the farms on the estate to pay the bills, which reduces his income in the long run.

'Once upon a time, he depended upon my judgement but recently . . . he told me the other day that . . .'

He reddened, then decided to come clean. 'He said that the sooner I kicked the bucket the better so he wouldn't have to listen to my lectures any longer. He said that he didn't need to worry about the future because he'd inherit my estate when I died. I was angry and let him see it. I said I was going to change my will and leave everything to the Cats' Protection League. I meant it at the time, but of course I soon calmed down. He said I wouldn't disinherit my brother's son and of course he's right.'

His eyes shot around the room. He swallowed. 'Actually, I have been wondering if it would be the only thing that might bring him to his senses . . . me changing my will. I even got as far as . . . no matter. Every time I think I can go through with it . . . I step back from the brink. But . . . his latest idea is . . . incredible! He has some crazy idea of setting up a film company with Alexander, which is ridiculous. I can't get through to him.' He extracted his handkerchief again and blew his nose.

Bea was silent.

So was Piers.

Mr Fletcher was not in an easy place, was he?

For some minutes now, Bea had been conscious of her mobile phone vibrating. She took it out. An unknown caller. It was routine at the agency for the phone there to be switched through to an agency at weekends and in the evening. Had Lisa forgotten to do that?

Bea hesitated about answering the call, but finally did so.

'Mrs Abbot? Is that Mrs Abbot?'

A woman, youngish. Warm. A hint of an Irish brogue? No. Midlands. Not a voice Bea recognized. She said, 'Speaking.'

'I'm Molly, Molly Malone. You don't know me, but I worked for the agency for a time. I'm sorry, it's rather late, I know, but . . . I'm just wondering, is Jolene still with you? I was supposed to meet her but she hasn't turned up and I've tried her place but she hasn't been there, either. So I just wondered if by any chance she was still at work for some reason.' The voice tried to laugh but didn't quite make it. 'I mean, it's all getting rather heavy.'

'No,' said Bea, sitting upright. 'Jolene left early, just after six. As a matter of fact, we've been wanting to speak to you because—'

'Later, perhaps. I'm so worried about Jolene. I'm afraid . . .!' Buzz. Molly had ended the call.

Bea looked at the clock. 'That was Molly. She'd arranged to meet Jolene – that's a girl who works . . . who used to work . . . in the agency here – and she hasn't turned up. She hasn't been home, either. I'm beginning to get a bad feeling about this.'

FOUR

Thursday evening, supper time

The timer rang in the kitchen and Bea got to her feet. 'Supper's ready.'

Mr Fletcher struggled to his feet, grimacing slightly. Had he a bad back?

'Of course. I must be on my way.' Once on his feet, he made no move to hand over the cheques he had brought with him, or to leave. Perhaps he was going home to a ready meal in an empty house?

Piers said, 'Would you care to take potluck with us?'

'Of course,' said Bea, departing for the kitchen. 'I've just to put some frozen veg on. You won't mind eating in the kitchen, will you? We only use the big dining table in the front on high days and holidays.'

The landline phone rang, and Piers answered it. He listened for a moment, said, 'No, I'm sorry. She left early.' He cradled the phone and joined Mr Fletcher on his way out to the kitchen, saying, 'That was Jolene's mother. The girl rang her mother earlier saying she'd be a little late for supper, but she's long overdue.'

Mr Fletcher eased himself on to a kitchen stool. 'This is the girl Molly was supposed to be meeting? Ah, well. Youngsters these days have no sense of time.'

Piers said, 'Jolene is the girl who got Molly the job with Karina; the girl whose family took Molly in as she had nowhere else to live in London; the girl who gave Molly the details about the mews house which I use as a studio and which Molly gave as her address when applying for the job with you.'

Bea picked it up. 'This is the girl who thinks Molly has been hard done by and who is prepared to help her get her revenge on Karina, who has treated her so badly. This is a girl who threw her job back in my face this afternoon because she didn't think I was doing enough to help Molly. This is a girl who has a temper and is not, I'm sorry to say, very good at handling people.'

'Dear me,' said Mr Fletcher in the voice of one who didn't want to be bothered hearing about other people's problems.

Bea insisted. 'Jolene made arrangements to meet Molly after work, telling her mother she'd be late home for supper. But she failed to turn up. Now her mother is alarmed because the girl hasn't appeared, as she doesn't think the girl's behaviour is typical. Personally, I think it would be absolutely typical of a teenager's behaviour except that her mother says Jolene isn't like that. So, how worried ought we to be for Jolene, on a scale of one to ten?'

'Five,' said Piers, getting some beer out of the fridge.

Bea said, 'Eight. If I were her mother and Jolene hasn't turned up by ten o'clock tonight, I think I'd be justified in contacting the police. Otherwise, not.'

Mr Fletcher produced a faint smile. 'In my experience young people are always late for everything. They are quite unable to comprehend the fact that their behaviour may inconvenience other people.'

Was he speaking of his nephew, Teddy? Yes, probably.

Mr Fletcher said, 'I'd like to wash my hands, if I may.'

Piers said, 'I'll show you.' He indicated the ground floor loo.

Bea threw some frozen veg into a pan of boiling water and took the casserole out of the oven. She dropped her voice to a murmur. 'What do you think, Piers? Is Mr Fletcher the genuine article?'

Piers set the table. 'I'd say so, yes. What you see is what you get. Self-discipline and service to others. He's a lonely widower who appreciates home cooking.'

Still speaking in a low voice, she took hot plates out of the top oven. 'You switched memory sticks? The one you threw me was one of yours, wasn't it?'

'It was. Misdemeanour on their part has led to misdirection on mine. They mess me around. I retaliate. What memory stick do you think the grey man uses?'

'One with a football logo on? White and blue?'

'The one they printed for England at the World Cup?'

Mr Fletcher reappeared, looking slightly more substantial. 'Ah, home cooking.'

Piers waved him to a seat. 'You're lucky. We often have takeaways. Depends how busy we are.'

Mr Fletcher said, 'Sometimes I dream of my wife's apple and blackberry crumble with clotted cream. You have children, don't you?'

Bea ladled food on to the plate in front of him. 'Please excuse no serving dishes. Yes, we have a son, grown up and flown the nest. Also, my ward Bernice is around most weekends but, as it happens, not this one. Boarding school. Making friends. Will probably take her A levels early. She's growing up fast.'

'Ah, I think I saw her portrait in the Mall Gallery. Quite a beauty.'

'Quite a handful,' said Bea. 'But worth it.'

Keep the conversation on this level and we may discover why he wanted to stay for supper. Or is he – as Piers says – just a lonely widower seduced by the scent of my cooking?

A slight colour came into Mr Fletcher's cheeks. He managed a second helping of the chicken dish once he'd cleared the first and did justice to the fruit and cheese that followed.

'Coffee?' Bea bundled the used tableware into the dishwasher.

'I won't say no. Excellent meal. Excellent.'

The doorbell rang. Hard.

Bea looked at the clock. Five minutes to eight. Jolene or Molly? Jolene's mother? Or . . .? She said, 'I'll go,' and went to open the front door.

Standing in the porch were two handsome young men, one

blond and one redhead. Casual clothes which had cost a mint, haircuts by masters. Mightily pleased with themselves and with life.

'Hello-o-o,' said the redhead. 'Mrs Abbot, isn't it? Or may I call you "Bea"?'

Even as Bea assembled a frown, he assumed forgiveness for his breach of good manners. He said, 'Forgive the intrusion. We were looking for the portrait painter, who seems to have gone missing from his house in the mews. We had to get on to his agent to get this address.' He grinned. 'He didn't take much persuading, I'm happy to say.'

What persuasion had the lad used? Physical force? Surely not! And yet that is the message he seemed to be conveying.

The redhead pressed Bea back into the hall, followed closely by the blond, who closed the door behind him. They were both smiling, relaxed, sure of themselves.

Bea stiffened her back. 'We're not in a position to welcome visitors this evening. I must ask you to leave. Ring for an appointment in the morning.'

'No, no. No need for that. No need at all. A quick word. He has something of ours, you see. He took it by mistake, of course. We're not talking larceny, petty or otherwise. A little something that's gone astray and needs to be returned to its owner.'

Bea's temper rose, not unmixed with fear. 'I'm asking you to leave my house, now!'

She was ignored.

The blond looked past Bea and whistled. 'Hello, hello! If it isn't the Nunkie-Dunkie! What are you doing here, old boy?'

Bea winced. The language was careless, the lack of respect jarred.

The redhead laughed. 'Let me guess! He's trying to curry favour with the matriarch. He's her very own, good little errand boy, isn't he?'

Bea drew in a quick breath, telling herself to be calm. These two golden lads had a strong sense of entitlement, they respected neither age nor sex and probably gave their allegiance solely to the few whom they considered their equals.

If she remembered correctly, they had both dropped out of university and were sponging off their mother for board and lodging. They needed a lesson in how to behave to others with at least a veneer of politeness.

Piers was standing in the doorway to the living room, with his mobile phone in his hand. He spoke to Bea. 'You want them to leave? Shall I call the police?'

The redhead surged past Bea. 'There's the painter fellow! Tally-ho! You set us a fine trail to follow!'

'No!' Mr Fletcher stumbled his way out to the hall to confront the boys. 'Teddy! Alexander! This is not the way to behave. You can't force your way into a private house and—'

'No force required,' said the redhead, holding up his hands. 'Look, no hands!'

'None!' Teddy followed him, grinning. 'We called to collect a piece of property which by some mischance – some accident, shall we say? – ended up in the painter fellow's pocket. It was meant to provide a diversion, but somehow it slipped through the net. We return it to its owner, least said, soonest mended. Eh, Nunkie? You haven't managed to lay hands on it yourself, have you? No. Thought not. You hardly know how to tie your shoelaces nowadays, do you?'

Mr Fletcher's features sharpened and he looked as if he were going to rebuke the youngster for his rudeness, but all he managed to say was, 'Boys, boys! This is not right, indeed it is not. Yes, I came here to settle various matters for your mother. I am in the process of negotiating for the memory stick to be handed over, but—'

'There's no need to pay for services badly rendered,' said the redhead, who seemed to be enjoying himself hugely. 'We'll see to getting the memory stick back.'

'Absolutely,' Teddy chimed in. 'A few minutes alone with the painter person will surely do the trick, without any expenditure of the readies!'

Piers said, 'Bea, I'm phoning the police.'

The redheaded Alexander lowered his head and charged at Piers . . .

Who side-stepped and . . .

Mr Fletcher cried out, 'No!' He managed to deflect Teddy's rugby charge but, in doing so, he was thrown off balance and crashed into the lintel of the door behind him. His head met the wood with a thud . . .

Piers caught one of Alexander's flailing arms and impelled him into the kitchen where he stumbled head-first into the island.

Winston the cat had been sitting there, sampling the butter which had been overlooked when Bea cleared the table. The cat objected to being interrupted, fluffed out to twice his size and hissed at Alexander, while . . .

Teddy laughed . . .

And Mr Fletcher rebounded on to the floor and lay there like a disjointed doll, his eyes closed.

Teddy stopped laughing. He took a step forward. 'Nunkie?'

The doorbell rang.

Piers knelt down by Mr Fletcher, feeling for a pulse.

Bea said, 'Get out! Both of you!'

Teddy lost his smile, considering the odds and not liking them.

The doorbell rang again.

Bea drew a deep breath and opened the door, thinking that any caller would be welcome in this situation.

Someone in an all-enveloping, dark-blue, caped macintosh stood on the doorstep, hesitating, unsure whether to advance or retreat.

Teddy saw her at the same moment and exclaimed, 'There she is! Alexander, she's here!'

The woman looked beyond Bea, spotted the two young men, gave an inarticulate cry and disappeared back down the steps into the night.

Alexander wobbled to his feet. 'What? Who? That something cat scratched me!'

Teddy dragged his mate to the front door and out. 'That was Molly! After her! Which way did she go?' The two disappeared.

Piers said, 'He's got a decent pulse.'

Indeed, Mr Fletcher was showing signs of regaining consciousness.

Bea slammed the front door closed and leaned against it, breathing hard. This was altogether too much!

Piers helped Mr Fletcher to his feet and helped him to hop to the nearest chair.

Bea thanked the Lord for their deliverance and promised herself that Winston should have a special treat for playing his part in routing the intruders. Which reminded her to put the much-licked butter out of sight to be dealt with later.

Now, what was the damage for Mr Fletcher?

His colour was poor but he was the stiff-upper-lip type, wasn't he? Only his eyes looked strange and he was holding on to his head with both hands. Concussion? He said, 'Sorry! So sorry to be such a nuisance! The boys are just playing, you know, don't realize their strength.'

To which Piers and Bea responded with raised eyebrows.

He said, 'I'm all right.' Which he clearly was not. He tried to rise, turned a nasty shade of yellowish-green and collapsed back into the chair. 'I may have sprained my ankle. I'll call a cab to take me home. Just . . . if I could rest a minute?'

Bea took off his shoe and black sock, revealing an ankle which was indeed swelling nicely. She wiggled his foot, and it did wiggle. Not broken, probably, but badly sprained. 'Is your bedroom upstairs? Do you live in a flat?'

He gasped with pain. Then tried to control his voice. 'I sold our house after my wife died and bought a flat in Knightsbridge. Second floor, no problem. The stairs keep me fit. I'm fine. A little rest . . .'

'Is there no one to look after you at home?'

He shook his head, and repeated, 'If you can call a cab for me? I'll be all right.'

'Cold compress,' said Piers, and went to organize it.

Bea followed Piers into the kitchen. Speaking softly, she said, 'Concussion. And he's no one at home to look after him. He must go to hospital for an X-ray.'

Her landline phone rang.

This would be Jolene's mother, right?

It was. The woman's voice was high and tight with anxiety. 'Have you seen her, have you got her there? It's not like her, not at all. She is back with you, isn't she?'

'No, I'm afraid not. She left hours ago.'

'Yes, I know. She rang me, said she'd had a row with you, all about nothing. I told her, you'd better go back and say you're sorry and, if she hasn't done so yet I'm sure she will when she's calmed down. She really enjoys working for you, every day different, which suits her down to the ground. Are you sure she's not with you?'

'Definitely not.' *And I don't think I want her back, anyway.*

'She always lets me know if she's going to be late, but she said it would be an hour, no more. She said she was meeting Molly. You know about Molly moving out of here and looking for a new place to live, don't you? Such a good job. So interesting, just what she was looking for, but I understand that some people can be a little difficult to work for, and Molly was glad this project was coming to an end and she could take her money and move into a place in Kensington, rather than traipsing out here every day.'

'Yes, yes,' said Bea. 'I know there was an unpleasant incident this morning at work and Molly left in a hurry. The family friend who hired Molly came round this evening to talk about payment. Perhaps you can pass the message on to Molly when she surfaces?'

'I would if I could. Molly did say she'd pay me rent for putting her up all this time, and between you and me, I could do with a little something at the moment. She said she'd let me have her new address but she hasn't done so yet. These youngsters, they'd forget their head if they weren't screwed on. She took her tote bag with her for tonight, and said she'd be back tomorrow for the rest. The thing is she said she was meeting with someone who promised to get her her money, and she asked Jolene to go with her because she said this man – at least, I think it was a man, I assumed it was a man – could be difficult. Jolene said it wouldn't take long, perhaps they might have a drink in a pub or something to celebrate and then she'd be on her way home. Only, she hasn't.'

Bea shivered. 'Who were the girls meeting, and where?'

'She didn't say.'

'They seem to have missed one another. We had a phone call from Molly earlier, asking where Jolene was. Molly turned up at the door here a while back . . . only she ran away before we could get any sense out of her.'

The woman at the other end of the phone was silent. A long, indrawn breath. No words came.

Bea said, 'I think you'd better ring the police and report Jolene missing.'

The phone clicked off.

Piers had been listening as he soaked a clean tea towel in cold water. 'Both missing? I don't like the sound of that. I'm going to ring for an ambulance to take Mr Fletcher to the hospital. He's the sort that will walk around on a broken leg, swearing he'll be all right in a minute. One of us should go with him or he'll get a taxi to take him home, swearing he'll be perfectly all right. Which he won't be. What do you think?'

'I don't think either of us should stay here on our own. I'm not sure those two boys will catch Molly, but if they don't, they'll be back here looking for that memory stick. Plus, I've a feeling Molly will also return. She's tried to contact us twice. Third time lucky. I'll stay if I can organize backup.'

Piers knew what she meant. 'You get Hari,' said Piers, 'and I'll ring for an ambulance.' He took his cold cloth next door, getting out his mobile as he went.

Bea pulled the phone towards her and pressed a well-known number.

Hari was Maltese by birth and British by education, married to one of Bea's oldest friends. He'd been a professional bodyguard at one time but was now an independent security consultant. He was a man who could slide through locked doors faster than other people could sort out which key to use.

He answered the phone straight away. 'Well, Bea. What fine mess have you got into this time?'

'We have a man here who needs to go to hospital for an X-ray. Piers will go with him, but only if you can come and babysit me. On the danger list, we have a young girl from the agency who's gone missing, together with a ghostwriter and a memory stick. Oh, and some cheques. There are also two young thugs who haven't heard of the Marquess of Queensbury rules and wouldn't bother to abide by them even if they had. Interested?'

'Mm. You brighten up my day. I've been on a job today which has been driving me nuts. The client is a faded pop star who believes he needs round-the-clock protection for his forthcoming tour of Hungary. He's suffering under the delusion that he's still shaggable, but the evidence is all to the contrary. His manager says he's hardly sold a ticket in weeks and the tour's going to be cancelled anyway. When do you need me?'

'In half an hour? And possibly stay the night?'

'Are the two young thugs that dangerous?'

'Yes,' said Bea. She said no more, as her throat had
closed up.

'Twenty-five minutes,' said Hari and clicked off.

The paramedics arrived, ignored Mr Fletcher's protestations,
loaded him into a wheelchair and took him out to the ambulance.
Piers went with them. As they drove off, Hari slid out of the
dusk and followed Bea into the hall. Chunky of build, he was
light on his feet. And hungry.

He kissed Bea on the cheek, said, 'My darling wife sends her
love. Have you any food? I missed lunch today, watching the
pop star drink his way into oblivion. Fill me in on your problem
while I'm eating.'

Bea gave him the remains of the casserole, while reporting on
what had been happening. She said, 'It's a mess. Piers hasn't
finished or signed the portrait and hasn't been paid for it. I think
he'd quite like to cut his losses and move on, but our agency is
involved because we supplied Karina with the ghostwriter and
the cook. And, to make matters worse, with Piers. Also, one of
our staff – a young girl called Jolene – took umbrage this afternoon and stormed out. She's supposed to have been meeting the
ghostwriter, but didn't. I think young Jolene thought she was
going to have a splendid adventure, accompanying her hard-done-
by friend into battle, but I'm very much afraid she's found that
the fairy at the bottom of the garden is a pitbull with sharp teeth.'

'And the two young men?'

'Karina's sons by different fathers. Some brains, no respect
for the law of the land. They took part in accusing and then
manhandling the cook, the missing ghostwriter and Piers. They
pretended to find stolen jewellery so that Karina could dismiss
all three without payment of monies due. One of them put the
memory stick holding Karina's memoirs into Piers' jacket pocket,
but he doesn't know which one it was.'

'Why did he do that? To incriminate him?'

'I suspect muddled thinking. They were already accusing him
of stealing jewellery so probably thought it would help their
accusations of theft. Mr Fletcher came here to soothe hurt feelings and retrieve the memory stick, but he doesn't know if the
one Piers found in his pocket is the right one or not. Mr Fletcher
then got trampled on in the rush and Piers is nursemaiding him

to the hospital. Mr Fletcher says it's just a sprain but I think he's concussed to high heaven and I don't think he can manage the stairs back at his flat.'

She looked at the hall. Stairs led up to the first floor and down to the agency. A man with a badly sprained ankle wouldn't be able to manage those stairs, would he?

If Mr Fletcher were sent home from hospital, he wouldn't be able to manage the stairs to his flat. He'd be welcome to stay here, but . . . No, the stairs were going to rule that out.

Bea dished out cheese, shooed Winston the cat off the table yet again, and said, 'It looks like being a long night. Piers thinks that the two boys will be back at some point in search of the memory stick, and I think Molly might also try to make contact. I'll put some coffee on. I've just thought . . . I may be wrong, but I want to check something in the living room.'

She returned to the living room. Closed her eyes. Waited five seconds and opened them again. Yes, something was not right. Something was out of place. Mantelpiece? No. Table in the window with Piers' laptop and sketchpad on it? She drew the curtains against the night. Nothing seemed amiss there.

Side table with lamp on it. No.

She checked that the French windows leading on to the wrought-iron balcony across the back of the house were locked, which they were. She drew the blind down and pulled the curtains across.

She turned round and looked at the room from that angle.

Ah. Two cushions on the settee had been changed over. They almost, but not quite, matched though only Bea, who had bought them from the same shop but at different times, knew that. The one which had been put behind Mr Fletcher's back was now on the wrong end of the settee.

A tiny thing. Not noticeable at all, really.

She picked both cushions up and shook them about. Underneath one was the paperwork Mr Fletcher had brought with him. Two cheques, two releases. He must have put them down on the settee when called in for supper . . . or hidden them?

'Yes?' said Hari at her elbow. He was sipping coffee, his eyes bright.

She held up the two cheques drawn on Mr Fletcher's private

account. One was for Mrs Hennessey with a form saying that in consideration of this payment, she would be keeping quiet about the way she'd been sacked. The other cheque was for Molly to cover the loss of her laptop. The covering note acknowledged receipt of the cheque and indemnified young Teddy for the destruction of the laptop.

'Mr Fletcher wasn't taking any chances. He couldn't make excuses for Karina's behaviour but he did try to make up for what his nephew Teddy had done. He was prepared to stump up from his own funds to replace the damaged laptop. I hope he can recover the money he's advanced to silence Mrs Hennessey. He's gone all cloak and dagger, imagining . . . what? That the boys might get hold of the cheques and destroy them? He knows someone has got to use some diplomacy to get those releases signed. Faced with being removed to hospital he's left them for me to find.'

Someone pressed the doorbell in tentative fashion. Not sure they wanted to be heard?

'That will be Molly,' said Bea. 'She's got a lot of questions to answer and I'm not sure I want to give her Mr Fletcher's cheque yet.' She thrust the papers back under the cushion and pulled the curtain in the front window aside so that she could see who was standing in the porch.

A hooded figure stood there. Blue mac, rather too large for whoever was wearing it. No way was Bea going to open the door to a stranger. She set the mental picture of her earlier sighting of Molly against what she saw now and nodded to Hari. 'Let her in.'

The figure in the all-enveloping mac stepped into the hall, half prepared to turn and flee. 'Mrs Abbot? Sorry to call so late, but I really, really need to speak to Piers.'

'Come in, Molly,' said Bea. 'I'm delighted to see you. Jolene's mother has been on the phone. Her daughter said she was meeting you for some reason but hasn't returned home yet. Have you any idea what may have happened to her?'

'Yes, but . . . No, not really.'

The girl looked as if she'd like to back away into the night, so Bea said, 'Look, you're safe here. Let me introduce you to Hari, who's a black belt and has various other skills as well.

Take off your mac, and ring Jolene's mother. Piers had to accompany someone to the hospital but will be back soon. Are you hungry?'

Molly shed her mac, revealing herself to be a buxom lass with short, dark hair and a complexion which ought to be roses and cream but which was now sallow with fatigue and anxiety. 'I don't know what's happened to Jolene. I can't stay because the boys are looking for me.' She sniffed the air.

Bea was a good cook and the chicken casserole had been particularly tasty. And fragrant. Bea saw hunger momentarily overcome prudence only to be beaten back.

Molly said, 'If you'll give me the key to the mews house, I can go there and wait for Piers.'

What on earth did she mean by that? She couldn't mean that Piers had said she might stay there, could she? Definitely not. He wouldn't. So why does she think I'd let her have the keys? This requires investigation.

Bea swept Molly into the kitchen, pushed the box of tissues at her, and opened the fridge door. 'He won't be long, with luck. Meanwhile, I'm sure you could do with a cuppa and something to eat.'

Now, what have I got? Hari had finished up the casserole, hadn't he? Ah, eggs. Scrambled egg in a bap. That should do. And a nice hot cup of tea. Put the kettle on.

Hari put his head into the kitchen. 'I'm going to check the house is locked up for the night. Is young Bernice coming back for the weekend?'

'Not this weekend, no.'

'The door to her quarters up top is kept locked while she's away, right? I'll check it, though. Back in a tic.' He vanished.

Bea set about making Molly something to eat.

Molly looked around her. She flinched away from the kitchen window, which showed a darkening sky outside. She said, 'I'm all of a jitter. How long will Piers be? Can you ring him and tell him I'm here?'

'I don't think he can use his mobile where he is, but I'll try him in a minute if you like. Now, a cup of tea won't take long. I understand you were meeting Jolene, and she's gone missing. Is that true?'

The girl was running her tongue over her lips, frowning, looking at her watch. Uneasy. Unsettled. 'We arranged to meet opposite the pub. I admit I was a few minutes late. As I arrived, I thought I saw her getting into a car. But that couldn't have been her, could it? I waited and waited but she didn't come and I tried to ring her but she's not picking up.

'I don't know what to do. I thought of going to the police. Then I thought that was silly, because she couldn't go missing from outside a pub in a busy street, and surely she wouldn't have been so stupid as to get into a stranger's car. Would she?'

'I suppose it depends whose car it was. You told her who it was you were supposed to meet, didn't you? I'm wondering . . . Why did you ask her to join you? Weren't you happy about meeting this someone by yourself, and asked her to come along for backup? So, who was it you were supposed to meet?'

'No one you know.'

'Someone Jolene might know? Would she know any members of Karina's family by sight?'

A tinge of colour. 'I didn't say it was one of them.'

'I'm guessing here. Someone rang you, or perhaps you rang them, suggesting you meet up to hand over the memory stick of Karina's memoirs. You agreed because they offered to give you a cheque covering the work you'd done on them. So, who was it?'

'No, no. You've got it all wrong.' Tears sprang to her eyes.

Temporarily, Bea gave up. 'Oh, well. I expect you'd like to freshen up before you eat. The loo is first on the left in the hall. Food will be ready in a minute.'

'You don't understand. I don't want anything to eat and I can't wait. I didn't want you to hear about it like this, but you'll have to know sometime because I've got nowhere else to go and will have to move into the mews house. Piers and I, you see . . . I didn't want to have to tell you but . . .' She cast down her eyelids and looked away.

'Tell me what?' Bea's smile faded. Was the girl really trying to say that Piers had been taking an interest in her? Surely not!

FIVE

Thursday, late evening

Molly produced a cat-like smile. Her eyebrows rose. She plucked at the neck of her T-shirt. And then . . . oh, yes . . . here it came . . . the upward glance, as quick as a lightning strike, checking that her meaning had got across to Bea.

And then, a little wriggle, beautifully timed. 'Oh, well. You know how it is. Even you must admit he's fit. He's older than I'm used to, but sexier than anybody else I've ever met. I didn't take him seriously at first, but then . . . seeing him so often . . . and I know he never meant to hurt you, you being rather past all that sort of thing, but . . . one day he looked at me and the next we were rolling around on the floor together.'

Bea felt as if someone had punched her in her midriff. The eggs she had been scrambling were congealing in the pan. Moving like an automaton, she picked up the spatula and deposited the eggs into a buttered bap.

I'm going to grab that little minx by the hair and ram the bap down her throat and then I'm going to . . .

I'm not going to do anything. I'm not going to beat her up because it wasn't true! Never, nada, nothing. It did not happen. No way.

Piers is undoubtedly the sexiest man I know and occasionally in the old days he had spread himself around when invited to do so, but he'd promised me when we finally got together again that he'd put all that behind him, and I believed him.

At least, I think I believe him.

I did believe him. I was content to believe him . . . to fool myself into believing him.

But suppose he's still playing around?

Devastation!

I can't bear it!

I have to bear it.

Oh, he'd still got plenty of time left for me, but . . .

How dare that little chit imply that I'm past it!

The kettle whistled.

What a noisy kettle! Why don't they make noiseless kettles nowadays?

Moving with care, Bea transferred the egg-filled bap to a plate, pushed it over the tabletop to Molly, and turned back to make a pot of tea.

Molly was preening herself, checking her reflection in the back window that had turned into a mirror as the light faded outside. She said, 'Of course Piers doesn't want to hurt you. Naturally. He said you'd be civilized about our little affair, that you'd take the news well. And I can see he's right. He did say that he didn't want a divorce, though when he hears my lovely news, he might change his mind about that. I gather you own this house and have your own career so you won't be any the worse off when he leaves you.'

Bea poured a mug of tea out for Molly and one for herself. As she stood there, opposite to the girl, she saw a shadow change shape in the hall. Hari stood there, just outside the door to the kitchen, listening. And grinning.

Yes, grinning. Bea couldn't understand why he was grinning. Her brain had gone blank.

Too much was happening, too fast. The girl said she'd been having an affair with Piers. *No, that could not be true! Could it?*

The girl had hinted she was pregnant with his child. *Impossible! I don't believe her. I don't want to believe her.*

And she was talking of divorce?

Molly picked up the bap. 'Thanks. This looks good. Dunno when I last ate. You're pretty good, aren't you? Taking it so well. Piers and me, I mean.'

Bea looked at the mug of tea in her hand and considered bringing it down on the head of the girl in front of her. With intent to kill.

Or she could make an excuse that she hadn't put any sugar in the girl's cup of tea, and lace it with arsenic. Except that she didn't have any arsenic. Where did one get arsenic from nowadays, anyway? Wasn't drain cleaner supposed to be toxic enough to kill? She had drain cleaner.

She set down her own mug and thought back to what Piers had told her about this girl. He'd been alone with her now and then, while they were waiting for Karina to appear for her sittings. He'd said that on those occasions Molly would chatter about this and that, and he would get on with the portrait. When he'd spoken to Bea about her, his tone had been slightly indulgent but also irritated because he said that Molly would chatter on while he wanted to concentrate on the painting.

He'd called her 'flaky' and said something about not being sure she was really up to the job of ghostwriter.

Flaky. Ah. As in *imaginative*?

What else had he said about her?

He'd said that Molly had gossiped about members of the household; she'd complained about the extravagant tales which Karina had come up with; and the fact that she wouldn't be paid till the project was finished.

If Piers had been speaking of a girl he'd been having an affair with, there would surely have been a consciousness in his voice, a caress here or there, and there hadn't. Could he have been pretending? No.

Hari had grinned because he'd worked it out that the girl was lying.

Bea made herself look at Molly. The girl put on an innocent, wide-eyed smile.

Bea got it!

In spades, she got it. Back in her teens she'd come across a girl with just such a wide-eyed, innocent look, who'd fooled everyone into believing she was the daughter of a pop star until someone discovered the girl had been adopted at birth and didn't know who her parents might have been. Bea remembered that there had been a division in the class between those who believed the girl and those who didn't, and how this had led to dissension and a lot of unhappiness as friendships split.

Bea had been one of those who had condemned the girl as a heartless, congenital liar, and it was only as she grew up she realized that the unhappy, adopted child had invented a background for herself which had – at least for a while – made life tolerable for her.

Had Molly done the same thing? Bea thought about what the

girl had had to put up with that day, being accused of theft and manhandled . . . No, no! It had been altogether wrong of her to claim someone else's husband for herself. But perhaps, at a stretch, it was understandable.

Understandable, yes. In a way. But Molly had carried it too far. It was almost as if she had been trying out a new persona for herself, to see if she could get away with it.

Bea simmered down. She thought she could understand how Molly operated, but she couldn't forgive it. Anger fought with pity. Pity lost.

She thought back to the sketch Piers had made of Molly. The girl had been looking out of the picture, up and to the left and talking. So that was how he envisaged her. Looking elsewhere for a different life.

Bea seated herself and tried to make her voice conversational. 'How many times have you tried this on with other men?'

Molly's face flooded with colour. 'I don't know what you mean.'

Bea said, 'It's quite an art, being able to blush to order. At least you have the grace to be ashamed of yourself. I nearly put you over my knee and gave you a good spanking. I might have done, too, if I hadn't recalled that it might be regarded as an assault. What you said just now is actionable. Slander. The courts are hard on people who slander others, and once the media get hold of a case like that, I understand that the perpetrator gets a rough ride. Rough enough to scarper any idea you might have of earning your living as a ghostwriter or working in publishing.'

Molly hid her face in her mug and said something inarticulate. Was that an apology? No, probably not.

Do fantasists ever face up to their inventions? If found out, do they invent another background for themselves instead of owning up to what they've done?

Bea noticed that the girl's plate was empty. 'Would you like some bread and cheese to follow? Or fruit?'

'He did try to kiss me!' Defiant.

'Nonsense!' Bea was on sure ground here. 'You're not his type.'

'How would you know?' Silkily.

Bea laughed. She couldn't have done anything to disconcert the girl more.

Molly bridled. 'I don't know why you laugh. He's not the first to sniff around me.'

Hari sank into a chair next to Bea and helped himself to a banana. He said, in a conversational tone, 'I'm Hari, and you're Molly, right? You stink of sex.'

'What!' This time the girl lost colour. 'How dare you!'

Bea sighed. 'That's a bit rich, Molly. You can't come the innocent after accusing my husband of fathering a child on you.'

'Oh, oh! How could you!' Molly spurted tears.

Bea lifted her mug in a salute to her. 'Tears to order! That's another thing I've always wished I could do.'

Was she being a little rough on the girl? No, not after she'd slandered Piers.

Bea pushed the tissue box in Molly's direction. 'Mop yourself up and tell us how you got into this mess.'

Molly snuffled. 'I'm only here to see Piers. He'll see me right. He's always been so kind to me.'

Bea was amused. 'Piers is kind to everyone. He finds it eases his path through life. It doesn't mean much. He paints. That is what he does. What he is.'

With a spurt of spite, Molly said, 'He doesn't like Karina much. He as good as told me so. If I told her that, he could whistle for his payment.'

'Another porky,' said Bea. 'Yet another lie. You really are a tiresome brat, Molly. Whether Piers likes Karina as a person or not, his portrait will add to her fame and that's all that she cares about.'

Molly cast around for another dart to throw at Bea. 'He promised me I could move into the mews cottage and live there, free, till I'm paid for the book.'

'Chance would be a fine thing. The mews cottage is not his. It's mine. He uses it as his studio and office. He can't offer it to anyone to live in.'

'Are you going to turn me out, with those two horrible boys tracking me down and threatening all sorts? And you know there's a stalker with a knife loose on the streets.'

'Is there? I hadn't heard anything about—'

'It's all over social media, but you probably don't even know what that is. I could be found dead in the gutter by the morning, and much you'd care! You're a hard-hearted, wicked woman, and I'm not surprised that Piers looks elsewhere for comfort.'

Bea felt rather than saw that Hari had paused his ingestion of the banana and was looking at her. If Bea gave the signal, he'd throw the girl out of the house, here and now.

Bea steadied her hand around her mug and thought about it. 'You're afraid that the stalker has come across Jolene?'

'Much you'd care, even if she does work for you.'

'She doesn't work for me now. She walked out of the agency this afternoon. There was a disagreement about how your application for the job was handled and she left. I believe she contacted you straight away and you arranged to meet her . . . in order to confront someone? That's correct, isn't it? You were afraid of whoever it was, and that's why you asked Jolene to join you. You saw Jolene step into the car and drive off. Knowing Jolene, I imagine she thought she could deal with whatever the man dished out. Foolish of her. So who was it?'

'I was too far away to be sure it was her. It could have been anyone.'

'Come off it. Of course you know who it was you'd arranged to meet. You may not have been sure that it was Jolene who stepped into the car at that distance, which is why you waited for her to appear. But she didn't materialize, did she? And since then . . . nothing. Aren't you concerned for her?'

Molly looked away. She shrugged.

Bea would very much like to have tied Molly up somewhere – to the banisters, perhaps? – and give her a good whipping. 'You led that girl into a trap and left her there.'

'No! That's ridiculous! How was I to know that . . .? Oh, nothing's happened to her, I'm sure. She'll turn up tomorrow with some tale of meeting a friend and forgetting to tell her mother that she was staying the night with her. So if you'll just give me the keys to the mews house, I'll be on my way.'

Bea held on to her temper. Tightly. She felt it might escape and attack the girl if she let go of it even for a second.

Hari, beside her, was on his phone. 'Piers? You're somewhere you can take the call? Yes, it's me. Safe and sound. How are you getting on? . . . Ah, yes, the usual waiting time in Accident and Emergency. They've done some X-rays and are now waiting to see a doctor? Will they keep him in overnight? . . . Yes? Because of the concussion? Yes, that's sensible . . . He did what? Gave your name as his next of kin?'

Hari's eyebrows signalled his surprise, and Bea's rose, too.

Mr Fletcher had given Piers' name as his next of kin and not that of his nephew? Uh-oh. Does this mean that Mr Fletcher considers his nephew to be an untrustworthy lout? Mm. He's probably right about that.

Hari passed the phone over to Bea. Piers was talking. '. . . We're waiting to see a doctor now. Mr Fletcher thinks they'll strap him up and he'll be all right to go home. I doubt it somehow. He's the colour of a wax candle. What a tangle!'

Piers wasn't best pleased about all this, was he?

'Fine,' said Bea. 'Problems proliferate. Molly is here, insisting you have agreed to let her stay in your studio.'

The phone barked, 'No way! What the . . .! She did ask me, but I told her I wouldn't dream of . . .! Why on earth does she think . . .? I don't let anyone but you into the studio, you know that! Tell her to get lost!'

'Oh, I will, I will,' said Bea. 'When do you think you'll be able to get home?'

'Heaven knows.' A groan. 'You know what hospitals are like. If Mr Fletcher's allowed home . . . no, I don't think he'll be allowed to leave. I think they'll keep him in overnight. I'll hang around till I know what's happening and let you know when I'm on my way. Hari is with you, and you've put the alarm on, haven't you?'

'Sure.'

Bea ended the call and produced a smile for Molly. 'Well, my dear? You've been fed and watered, your fantastic tales have been listened to and rejected, so I think you'd better be on your way.'

Molly's eyes widened. 'You can't turn me out without anywhere to go. Anything might happen. I might be found dead in a ditch tomorrow morning.'

'You said that nothing had happened to Jolene, so what have you to be afraid of?'

Molly winced. She shuffled on her seat. 'I'm sure she's perfectly all right, really.'

'Who were you meeting? Who was going to pick you up in a car?'

'No one. I arranged to meet Jolene and she didn't turn up.'

Bea pulled the landline phone towards her, switched the sound up and rang the number from which Jolene's mother had contacted her. 'Bea Abbot here. I'm concerned for Jolene. Has she turned up yet?'

'No, she hasn't! I'm worried sick! I've been on to the police and they said she has to be missing more than a couple of hours before they can take any notice. Her dad's off to work on the night shift and ringing me every half hour to find out if she's turned up yet and I'm biting my fingernails. I've got a neighbour sitting with me, and we're ringing everyone we can think of to see if she's landed up there. You haven't any news?'

Bea looked across at Molly, who was trying to pretend this conversation had nothing to do with her.

Bea said, 'Molly has turned up here wanting somewhere to stay. At first she said she thought she saw Jolene get into a car and be driven off, and then she said she was too far away and must have been mistaken.'

Jolene's mother almost snarled. 'That girl! She's nothing but trouble! I rang the place she's working at thinking Jolene might have gone there but they haven't seen her, they didn't know who I was, they didn't know Molly was lodging with me, or anything. They seemed to think Molly was living in some posh place in Kensington. As if! Whatever lies has she been telling them? I wish I'd never set eyes on the girl but there, her mother and I go back a long way and when she turned up on the doorstep begging me to let her sleep on the couch, well . . . which reminds me that I rang her mother, too, and Molly hasn't been in touch with her, either. What's got into the girl? She isn't half going to get the rough side of our tongues when she condescends to turn up.'

'I'll remind Molly to ring her mother,' said Bea, disliking the girl more and more.

'What's the girl done with our Jolene to make her behave like this? If Molly's led my Jolene into danger . . . I don't know what I'll do to her, but all I can say is, she'd better keep out of my way, or I'll . . .' She gulped. Tears came. And then the phone crashed down.

Molly fiddled with her hair and hummed a little song. And no, the tune was not that of 'Molly Malone'. She said, 'Don't look at me like that. My mother knows I'm all right. I get my ups and downs, but I'm never down and out. I'll ring her in a little while. I haven't done anything wrong, you know. I've worked my socks off writing a book for that dreadful old woman, I've had to fend off the advances of those two horrible young men who've both got arms like tentacles, and just when she ought to be on her knees thanking me for having gone the extra mile, Karina accuses me . . .! Me! Of stealing some of her manky jewellery that's probably all fake, anyway, and in dreadful taste! Oh, oh, OH!'

Tears welled up in her eyes and spilled over her cheeks.

'Bravo!' said Hari, and clapped his hands twice.

Bea ignored the tears. She thought of Mr Fletcher's cheque. She could give that to Molly now, couldn't she? No, she couldn't. She wasn't going to give the girl the sniffings off a used tissue.

Bea put on a creamy tone of voice. 'How bad is the damage to your computer? Can you get someone to take out the hard drive, and will you be able to get the book off it?'

Molly's tears stopped. She took a tissue from the box, and carefully wiped away all signs of distress. She said, 'I dropped it into a computer repair shop this afternoon. They said they'll have a go but can't promise anything, and in any case they're so busy they won't be getting round even to have a look at it for a few days.'

Bea worked out what that meant. 'The book has to be delivered on Monday or the publisher will miss his deadline. Piers said you backed up everything every day. To the Cloud? Or only on a memory stick?'

'A memory stick. And before you ask, I haven't got it. I thought I'd put it back in the laptop case, but it isn't there. It must have dropped out when that lout trod on it. My only hope is that Piers had picked it up.'

'No, he didn't,' said Bea, picking her words with care. 'He has his own memory stick, of course, but the design is different. His is black with some sort of logo on it. What's yours like?'

'White, with a blue trim.'

The memory stick Piers 'found' in his pocket might well belong to Molly. And if so, presumably it has the book on it?

Now why am I not telling her that he's still got it? Why am I not giving her Mr Fletcher's cheque straight away?

Is it because I don't like her and she's caused so much trouble she deserves to suffer for a while? That's not very nice of me, but . . . darn it! I don't care!

Besides which, we haven't checked that the one Piers found in his pocket really is hers, and that it does contain the book. It might be the infantile ravings of someone who has nothing to do with the book.

Molly put her head in her hands.

Oh, these theatrical gestures!

Molly sobbed, 'If he hasn't got it . . . oh, what am I going to do? You've got to help me! Those boys are coming after me, I know they are! They like to knock people around, you know, just because they can! They like hurting people!'

Now was that true? Can anything Molly says be taken as gospel?

Molly tried a different tack. She lifted her head and looked around her. 'I'll have to get a move on. If they've discovered I lied to them about where I've been living, they'll come back and I'd as soon as not be here when they do. You've got to let me move into the mews cottage.'

'I don't have to do anything of the kind,' said Bea. 'Piers doesn't want you there, and that's that.'

And that should have been that, except that someone leant on the doorbell, and someone else thumped the door. 'Come on! Open up!'

Molly shot to her feet, wide-eyed. 'It's them. I've got to get away! I can get out through the office and up to the street that way, can't I? There's no other way out of the house, is there? What can I do! If they find me, they'll kill me!'

'No, they won't,' said Bea, though she wasn't overly confident about that.

Hari said, 'We've no need to let them in.'

The doorbell was ringing continuously, the door was being pounded . . . would it stand up to the attack? Yes, of course. It was a well-built, stout, early Georgian door that would withstand everything except a battering ram.

Molly seized her mac. 'I'll take the stairs down to the agency and you let them in. Once they're inside, I can escape up the front stairs out on to the street!'

The noise at the front door was thunderous.

Bea hesitated. The girl's fear seemed real, and what Bea had seen of the boys confirmed that yes, they wouldn't stop at physical force to get what they wanted. If Bea rang the police, then Molly would be trapped inside the house and the boys would realize that and return as soon as the police had gone. Bea doubted they'd be arrested and taken to the police station. And what might they say to the police about Piers? On balance it was perhaps best to go with Molly's plan.

Bea said, 'You'll need the code to the agency front door.'

'No need. I know how Lisa does it. The same numbers but advance one each week.' She was on her way out to the hall, disappearing down the inner stairs. 'Tell Piers to ring me. I'm sure he'll say I can take refuge in his . . .' The door halfway down the stairs banged shut behind her.

Hari said, 'Where's the key to that door on the stairs? It wasn't there when I looked earlier.'

Bea took the spare from the cupboard. 'We don't usually bother to lock it mid-week. Here, lock it after her and hide the key.'

Hari disappeared down the stairs. 'Don't let them in till I get back.'

'No.' Bea looked around for evidence of Molly's visit. One mug of tea, one dirty plate, a couple of used tissues. She swept them away into the dishwasher and the bin.

The thundering on the door continued. The landline phone rang.

Bea picked up the phone and could hardly hear what was being said at the other end. 'Who is it? Sorry, let me . . .!'

There was a crack of breaking glass and she shot out into the hall.

The fanlight over the front door contained some old glass held in place by a tracery of ironwork. The glass had been smashed in and the delicate pattern of ironwork, made brittle with age, had been shattered and hung by a thread here and there.

Hari charged down the hall, bellowing, 'Stop that!' The crunch of broken glass underfoot made Bea feel sick.

Her phone had gone dead.

She followed Hari down the hall. 'Do we phone the police? Or let them in so that Molly can escape?'

Hari looked at her. 'It's up to you.'

She dithered.

He said, 'Signal if you want me to get rid of them.'

She killed the alarm and opened the front door, narrowly missing a fist in her face.

'What,' she said in her iciest tones, 'on earth do you think you are doing? Look what you've done!' She stepped back, again treading on broken glass, giving them room enough to follow her inside. She didn't risk a sideways glance at the stairs going down to the agency front door, but allowed herself to be pushed back and back . . .

Hari had his phone out, but he wasn't talking on it.

The redhead was laughing. 'And who's this old man, and what's he doing here? Acting as guard dog?' 'Old man' was probably the most insulting phrase they knew.

Bea said, 'He's a family friend. Just look what you've done to the fanlight!'

'That wasn't us! That was . . . that was the wind!'

The blond was also laughing. 'You want to be sure of your facts . . . Granny!'

Hari held up the phone. 'Shall I ring the police, Mrs Abbot?'

The redhead said, 'Don't bother. Mrs Abbot – or rather Bea, my dear! – we only want what's ours. Give it to us and we'll be out of your hair.'

The blond was prowling around. 'Where's the painter, eh? And where, oh where, is our dinky little ghostwriter bird?' He held up a tote bag. 'We found this in the area down below. She must have dropped it when we spotted her earlier. She'll be back for this, won't she?'

Molly's? Of course, she must have chucked it down the stairs when they caught sight of her. Which means that, oh dear, she will be back for it.

The redhead, Alexander, pushed Bea's shoulder, forcing her back down the hallway and into the living room . . .

Away from the front door. Pray God this gives Molly time to escape!

Alexander was smiling. He had prominent incisors which should have been dealt with in childhood. He advanced on Bea. 'There you go' – *push* – 'back into your burrow, little rabbit' – *push* – 'we aren't here to make trouble, unless' – *push* – 'you force us to.'

Bea stepped backwards into the living room.

Hari stepped back into the kitchen . . . and back . . . and back.

The blond – Teddy – said, 'The painter can't have left. He must be here. Where's he hiding, eh?'

He slammed the front door to and more glass tinkled down into the hall.

Piers will be furious. He loved that fanlight, which is original to the house. But at least Molly has a chance to get away.

Alexander gave a cursory look around the kitchen. 'No one here.'

Teddy followed Bea into the living room and looked around. 'No one here, either. Where's your old man, Bea? Out shagging the local talent?'

'At the hospital,' said Bea. 'Thanks to you.'

'What? I don't believe you.' An uneasy laugh. 'Alex, are you going to search upstairs or shall I?'

Hari said again, 'Mrs Abbot, shall I ring the police?'

Alexander said, 'Don't come the old Cock Robin with me! She won't want you to ring the police, because you know that if we did, we'd accuse your painter friend of theft.'

A good point. Should I let Hari ring them? Has Molly had enough time to leave? If so, I could ask Hari to deal with those two louts. Only, it is true that they could destroy Piers' reputation . . .

Alexander said, 'Bluff all you like, you can't fool us. Tell us what you've done with the goods and we'll leave you in peace, rather than in pieces.' A hoarse laugh.

These two think they're invincible, don't they?

A key turned in the lock.

SIX

Thursday, late evening, continued

S omeone exclaimed, 'What the . . .!'
Piers! That must have been him on the phone just now,
saying he was on his way back.
The two boys swung round. 'Who's that?
'Is it the police?'
Bea said, 'That will be Piers back from taking Mr Fletcher to
the hospital. When you knocked him over, Teddy, he didn't only
sprain his ankle but got concussion as well.'
Two heads swung back to her. 'What? Really?'
Bea almost smiled. 'I assume Teddy will wish to take
responsibility for looking after him.'
Teddy's mouth hung open in shock.
The front door was pushed open, and Piers stepped in. He
looked at the glass on the floor and up at the fanlight and exploded.
As Bea said, he really cared about beautiful objects. 'What the
. . .! Who? You two! That fanlight was put in when George
the Second was on the throne and it's lasted all these years,
through the Blitz, through everything, and you . . . you vandals!'
The blond said, 'It's nothing. She wouldn't open the door, so
we had to get in somehow, didn't we?'
The redhead said, 'Don't get your dander up, old man. It's
just a broken window. It's easily mended.'
Piers was incandescent. 'This terrace, my lad, has heritage
standing. Any alterations, any improvements have to go through
committees that don't like change, and by definition to replace
anything broken costs an arm and a leg. I assume you have a
private income and can afford to go around smashing things, which
is fortunate for you because you're going to have to pay for this.'
'Where's Uncle?' said the blond, trying to change the subject.
'What have you done with him? Is it true he's sprained his ankle?'
Dear me! Does Teddy actually feel some responsibility?

Alexander wasn't having any. 'Tripped over his big feet, eh? Such carelessness!' And brayed out a laugh.

Teddy stopped looking concerned and started looking relieved. 'Yeah, that would be it. Old people do fall over their feet. They don't look where they're going.'

Piers shut the front door, with infinite care. His jaw was tight. Bea thought he was having some difficulty preventing himself from hitting young Teddy.

Bea hovered, not knowing what to do. She could feel Hari looking at her for instructions.

Piers tossed his jacket on to the hall chest, and said, 'They're keeping him in overnight. Concussion. If he looks better tomorrow, he'll be allowed to go home. That is, if suitable caring arrangements can be made for him. You'd better start thinking how that can be organized and paid for.

'I'll get on to the heritage people tomorrow to make a temporary replacement and to find out which specialist firm reproduces such things. The ironwork will have to be specially commissioned to match the original and as for the glass, you can't put modern glass in. The original handmade glass has a greenish tinge and that's what will be needed for this job. I'll be contacting you when I get a couple of estimates for repair. Meanwhile, you'd better make yourselves scarce or I'll change my mind and call the police to have you arrested for wilful destruction of property.'

Teddy said, 'Get it on your insurance.' Half defiant, half miserable. 'Anyway, it wasn't me.'

Alexander laughed aloud. 'So, sue me!' Alexander was the leader of the two, wasn't he? He thought he was invincible, untouchable. He liked to smash things. He said, 'We came for our property and we're not leaving without it.'

Bea said, 'What property? You're holding Piers' portrait but you don't own it till he's signed it and been paid for it. As for the memory stick, that's not your property either, not until Molly has been paid for it. Why don't you ask Karina who picked it up and what they did with it? Someone in your family was very busy staging thefts and arranging to pull diamond rings out of bystanders' pockets. Why don't you ask who has the most to gain by accusing outsiders of crime?'

Piers snarled at the couple. 'You'd better get out of my way. I want to take pictures of the damage. Then you're going to take a dustpan and brush – no, we'd better use the hoover – and clear up the mess you've made. We don't want people cutting their feet on broken glass, do we? And Teddy, I'm sure your uncle would be pleased if you ring him on his mobile to ask how he's doing.'

Piers took his smartphone out of his jacket pocket and started to take photographs.

Smiling, Hari put his phone away.

Alexander brayed out another laugh.

Teddy arranged a smile on his face. 'Oh, Nunkie will be all right. And I . . . well, I've got plans for the evening.'

Hari extracted the hoover from the cupboard in the kitchen and dumped it in front of the two. 'Which of you are going to hoover the mess up?'

Alexander said, 'Get lost! Old man. Come on, Teddy. We're out of here.'

The two boys, laughing wildly, crunched down the hall, and out of the front door.

Hari grunted. 'Small boys will do anything to avoid clearing up their own messes.'

Bea leaned against the wall. She was feeling more shaken than stirred. Her voice cracked as she said, 'I'm sure Mr Fletcher would say that Teddy was such a lovely boy and has been led astray by that nasty half-brother of his.'

Piers put the alarm on. 'I can't remember ever being so angry. Twice in a day.' He stumbled over something. Molly's tote bag, which had been left behind by the boys.

Bea took it off him. 'I suppose Molly dropped it into the area when the boys surprised her on their earlier visit, and they picked it up when they arrived just now. They'll have rifled through it, I suppose, but just to make sure . . .'

She took the bag into the kitchen and turned the contents out on to the table. Toiletries, a pepper spray – useful if you wanted to walk the streets at night – underwear, jeans and a top, a pair of flat shoes, a filmy white dress and high heels, makeup. All the odd bits and pieces you pick up when you intend to be away for a couple of nights.

Bea commented, 'She doesn't wear a nightdress or pyjamas, and it looks as though she expected an evening out with someone else paying the bill.'

Piers put the kettle on. 'No memory stick? Have you still got mine?'

'I've got the one you threw to me earlier, yes. I assume you've still got hers.' She put everything back into the bag and zipped it up. 'I fear Molly will be back for her bag any time and before she does, we'd better see what's on the blue-and-white stick you found in your pocket.'

Piers filled the kettle. 'I'm bushed. I couldn't care less. I suppose the one I've got is Molly's, but I wouldn't put money on it. Anyone else for a cuppa before bedtime? Hari? How about you? Or do you want to get back home?'

Hari fingered his chin. He said, 'This is all too easy. No, I don't mean that . . . or do I? I'm missing something.'

'Not like you,' said Piers, who liked to drink a glass of hot water before going to bed. 'I must admit, I'm incapable of thought for the moment.' He took his favourite mug from the cupboard and filled it to the brim.

Bea thought she was too tired to think, too. So much had happened and yet . . . and yet . . . Hari was right. Something was not as it should be. They'd missed something, somewhere. Every nerve insisted the day was not yet over.

Hari went to the back door and tested it. 'I went the rounds when I arrived. Everything's locked that should be locked.'

Piers closed his eyes and sipped hot water. 'This is the best treatment for indigestion there is. No one's coming back tonight. I'll deal with the broken fanlight tomorrow.'

Bea had caught the fidgets from Hari. 'I wish I could agree with you that we can go to bed in peace and quiet. Those boys think we've got something of theirs. They've tried to rescue it and failed. They don't consider the day is over at ten in the evening. They're the sort who party all night and go to bed with the dawn. They'll try again. And as for Molly . . . words fail me. But that little madam is not going to doss down on a park bench when she can talk her way into someone's bed. I only hope she doesn't come back here, but I wouldn't count on it.'

Piers waved his mug around. 'Tell her to get lost.'

Bea ran her fingers back through her hair. 'What's really bugging me is Jolene going missing. I don't understand why she's disappeared. We keep overlooking that because she wasn't part of the scenery at Karina's and she's nothing to do with memory sticks.

'What do we know? She set out to meet Molly by arrangement. Molly thought she saw the girl getting into a car, but couldn't be sure because she was some way away. Molly then waited for Jolene but the girl didn't turn up at the meeting place and she didn't go home. Jolene isn't like Molly. She isn't the sort to sleep away from home without telling her parents what she was doing.

'I can understand why Molly set up the meeting. She thought she'd get compensation for her laptop and payment for work done in return for handing over the memory stick. Only by that time she'd lost it, so in fact she hadn't anything to bargain with when she met . . . whoever it was.'

Piers was trying to follow Bea's reasoning. 'I get that. Someone at Karina's picked it up, recognized it for what it was and instead of screaming "Eureka!" he or she planted it in my pocket. And why they did that, I can't imagine, unless they thought they could implicate me in the theft and thereby save themselves from paying for the portrait. Does that make sense?' He drained his mug. 'It's beyond me.'

Hari shook his head from side to side. 'In the heat of the moment someone thought it was a good idea and only later realized it was a dumb thing to do?'

Piers put his mug in the dishwasher. 'Let's call it a day. Everything will look better in the morning. Hari, are you staying for the night? It's getting late and the spare room bed is always made up and ready for visitors.'

Hari said, 'What Bea says is true. There's a dark undertone to what's been happening. I'll tack something over the fanlight but I'm not leaving. And I won't sleep till I remember what it is that's bothering me. There's something scratching at the back of my mind . . . what have I seen or heard? I did see something on Facebook or Twitter . . . somewhere . . . but where? About a man holding up girls – prostitutes, I think – with a knife, but

. . . Well, I'll go round the house once again. You don't like to think those boys will come back, but I'm with Bea on this.

'I've come across the type of man that redhead is before. They've been brought up to believe they're something special. They like noise, loud music, loud cars. They like to *make* noise, to crash into things, to make people jump. Some people say it's a kind of defence, that they're trying to make their mark in a world which is ignoring them. It'll have been the redhead who climbed up to look through the fanlight and smashed it in with his boot.'

Bea said, 'Before we go to bed, Piers, can I use your computer for a moment? I'd really like to know what's on the memory stick you found in your pocket.'

Piers shrugged but followed her back into the big room. His laptop was still there. He delved into his jacket pocket and retrieved a blue-and-white memory stick. He plugged it in, and a menu appeared on screen.

She drew in her breath. Yes, this memory stick did belong to Molly. There were short stories and articles galore. Molly had been trying to break into publishing, hadn't she?

A large file was marked 'Star Gazer'.

Piers clicked on that, and up it came. And yes, the first page answered her question. This was the story of Karina's chequered life.

They crowded around to look. Piers switched to the end. And yes, there was the story of what had happened when Karina met the Queen.

Bea said, 'How do you two feel about this? I'm going to suggest we delete it from Piers' laptop, but take another copy on another memory stick, just in case this one goes missing.'

Piers produced one of his black sticks. 'Use one of mine? I have several.'

Bea and Hari shook their heads. 'Too easy to get confused with your other ones.'

Hari delved into a breast pocket and came up with a bright red stick which he handed to Piers, who copied the book on to it. Piers then deleted the copy he'd put on his laptop.

Hari said, 'No, that's not enough. We need to delete it thoroughly . . . Here, let me.' He seated himself, drew the laptop towards him, and began to do various complicated things to confuse anyone who might try to find the copy of the book.

Bea weighed the red memory stick in one hand and Molly's blue-and-white one in the other. 'What do we do with these?'

Piers said, 'The blue-and-white belongs to Molly till she's paid for her work and we'll give it to her when she surfaces again. I know the boys are after it, too, but they've no legal right to it yet. We'd better hide it somewhere.'

Bea said, 'Can you remember now which of them might have put it in your pocket? For instance, was it one of the boys, or one of the husbands?'

He shrugged. 'I'm too tired to think straight. Perhaps it will come to me in the morning. I'm off to bed.' He drifted out to the hall.

Bea pocketed the red stick. 'Well, if the boys come and make themselves unpleasant, I suppose we could give them any old memory stick with any old stuff on it, and keep the original till Molly comes back for it. I'll keep the red one somewhere safe for the time being, just in case the deal turns sour.'

She looked around. Where should she hide the blue-and-white memory stick? It would be best to put it in a drawer full of them, which meant going down to the agency rooms . . . from which she could hear . . .

And then she yelped, 'Downstairs! Didn't you hear it?' She set off for the door. 'Where's the key? Hari, give me the key to the door on the stairs. There's someone in the agency rooms below. You can only hear water running in the toilet downstairs if you stand at the front of the house overlooking the street. That's what I just heard. Molly was supposed to have left by the door to the street when we got the boys to step inside the hall, but suppose she forgot the code and couldn't get out? Hari, you didn't check the agency rooms after Molly had gone down there, did you?'

Hai said, 'Let me go.' He closed the laptop, fished the key to the door on the stairs out of his pocket and disappeared down the stairs . . . to reappear with a bedraggled-looking Molly in tow.

Molly was crying again. This time the tears did seem real. 'I couldn't get out. Lisa's changed the code! Oh, oh! Have the boys gone? Oh, and is that my tote bag? Yes, it is.' She pounced on it. 'I had to drop it at the bottom of the outside stairs when the boys appeared and I thought for sure they'd take it. And oh!' She'd spotted the blue-and-white memory stick which Bea was still holding. 'Oh, you've managed to find it? However, did you do that? It wasn't in the laptop case, and I'd swear I'd left it there! I thought one of the boys must have taken it out of spite!'

She grabbed the stick from Bea and spotted Piers, who'd got as far as the stairs and had stayed there, leaning on the newel post. 'Oh, I'm so glad you've come back. Everything will be all right now, won't it? You'll let me have the key to the studio, won't you? I'll be safe there.'

Piers was too tired to be angry. He said, 'I told you before, Molly. I don't let anyone but Bea into the studio.'

'You can't be so cruel as to turn me out at this time of night! I haven't anywhere to go. I was going to sleep on the floor at another friend's house but it's way out past Cockfosters and I don't fancy the journey at this time of night. And I doubt if they'd let me in if I did manage to traipse out there. And I'd have to take a taxi from the station and I haven't enough money for that.'

Bea said, 'What about Jolene's mother? Won't she take you back?'

Molly fiddled with her hair. 'I owe them so much money for rent, you see, and besides, if Jolene isn't there . . . You haven't heard from her, have you? I mean, she's sure to turn up sometime. Isn't she?'

Jolene was still missing. Why did they keep forgetting about the girl? Surely Molly was right and she'd turn up safe and sound?

Molly appealed to Bea. 'You've got such a big house. There must be umpteen bedrooms not used. Can't you find me a teeny-weeny little bed somewhere? I could even manage on the sofa?'

Hari shook his head, Piers shrugged and Bea gave in. 'All right, Molly. The top floor is out of bounds. That's my ward's territory. She's not here this weekend, but you go near that on pain of death. You can use the guest room on the first floor. It's en suite, on the right at the top of the stairs. But remember to ring your mother and your aunt! And, if I find you harassing Piers, you'll be out on your ear, middle of the night or not.'

Molly dimpled and picked up her tote bag. Passing Piers with a high five – which he didn't return – she went up the stairs and into the spare room.

Hari's fingers rasped on his chin. 'That one needs watching. See how she switches from one mood to another? She reminds me of a professional con man I once knew. Changed the story of his life according to who he was with. Got caught out because he couldn't remember which date of birth he'd given to which of his victims. Want me to lock her into her room in case she starts straying in the middle of the night?'

Bea managed a smile. 'It *is* the middle of the night. You want to stay? Surely nothing else will happen tonight?'

'Want to bet?'

No, Bea didn't want to bet.

Hari said, 'I'm worried about the broken fanlight. I'll see to that and doss down on the settee. You get some sleep. Off you go.'

They had three hours of sleep before Hari drifted into Bea and Piers' bedroom and woke them up. 'There's been another attempt to get into the house. Want to look? Remember to put your shoes on. I've swept up all I could find of the glass from the fanlight, but there may be some shards still on the floor in the hall.'

They forced themselves to wake up. Blinking and yawning, Bea reached for her kimono. Piers collected his short towelling robe from the back of the door.

Down in the hall, the fanlight gaped open again. A black anorak, rather the worse for wear, lay on the floor beneath it.

Hari said, 'I haven't phoned the police.'

Bea and Piers looked from one to the other and failed to make sense of what they saw.

Bea tied her kimono around herself and ran her hands back through her hair to settle it. 'Is this night never going to end?'

Piers rubbed his eyes and yawned. 'An opportunist burglar? Someone who spotted the broken fanlight and thought he'd try his luck?'

Hari explained, 'The man was halfway through the fanlight when I heard him. I invited him to come right in and explain himself, he tried to back out, and stuck. He was fluent in the language of the gutter, but not helpful. I tried to help him further into the house, but he wriggled himself backwards and eventually dropped back into the porch and ran away, leaving his jacket behind. Oh, and I managed to get his picture before I left.'

Hari held up his phone, which showed a white-faced clown in a hooded jacket. He looked wizened. Not young. Startled, as well he might be, having come nose to nose with Hari when he'd thought the inhabitants of the house would have been asleep.

Hari said, 'Spoils of war. Let's see who we've got.' He picked up the black jacket and investigated its pockets. He held up a wallet. 'Name: Bernard Sanders. Probably known as Bernie. Address: a house in Belgravia. That doesn't fit the image. Two fifty-pound notes and an out-of-date leisure pass . . . in fact, two leisure passes, made out to different names. One smartphone, probably nicked. One four-year-old mobile, probably his. A light hammer and a glasscutter. He's an amateur. A professional doesn't go equipped to burgle, carrying his ID on him.'

Piers rubbed his eyes and took the phone from Hari to inspect the picture he'd taken. And concentrated. 'The flash distorts his face. Have I seen this man before? Maybe. But where? And when?' He thought about it, shook his head.

Then nodded. 'He looks like a man I spotted working in the kitchen at Karina's, something to do with a door that was sticking? I saw him as I passed by . . . five days ago? Six? Odd-job man? Occasionally acts as chauffeur for Her Highness?'

Bea pressed her fingers to her forehead. 'He knew the fanlight had been broken, so he must have some connection to the two boys. They failed to find Molly or the memory stick here earlier, so they asked someone else to investigate for them? He wanted payment in advance and they gave him the two fifties?'

A door banged open, and Molly appeared at the top of the stairs. 'What's happened? It's not the boys back again, is it?'

She looked at the jacket and it seemed to mean something to her. She came down the stairs, slowly. She was wearing a singlet and pants. Nothing else. Her figure was ripe. Bea took one look and knew the girl was pregnant. And, if not by Piers, then by who? Or should it be 'whom'?

Piers said, 'For heavens' sake, Molly, don't you have a dressing gown or something? Here, look at this.' He showed her the picture on Hari's phone. 'Do you know this man?'

'Heavens! Isn't that Bernie? He has a jacket like that. He's the gardener or odd-job man at Karina's. He fixed a chair with a wobbly leg for me to sit on.'

'Bernard Sanders,' said Hari, 'trying a new trade. Not very good at it. There's no question now, we have to call the police.'

'No!' said Molly, explosively. 'I mean, they wouldn't like it if Bernie was arrested for doing something they asked him to do.'

'Who,' asked Bea, 'do you mean by saying "they" wouldn't want us to call the police?'

Molly backtracked. 'Well, I don't know, do I? Someone in that household. They're all hiding something, so . . . Any one of them could have asked Bernie to get the memory stick back for them. It's a prank, that's all.' Even she must have realized how lame that sounded.

'Nonsense!' Piers looked at Molly with the eyes of a weary father whose teenaged daughter had kept him waiting for her safe return from a party which had gone on long after curfew.

Bea noted his annoyance and was heartened by it. No way had he been Molly's lover.

Bea said, 'Come off it, Molly. This has gone too far. That fanlight is going to cost the devil and all to repair. The boys came for the memory stick and failed to find it. They got Bernie to come looking for it. They need teaching a sharp lesson. If they stump up for the damage, well and good, but we can't rely on that. If we make it an insurance job, we have to have proof that there was a break-in, which means we have to report the matter to the police and get a crime number.'

'Yes, well . . .' Molly seemed to be thinking hard. 'I'm sure this can be settled quietly, without going to the police. The boys do go off the track occasionally, I admit, but the thing is that they really do care about the book and yes, they did the wrong thing, asking Bernie to find the stick . . . That is, if it was them, which we can't know for sure, can we? But if it was them, I agree that was very naughty of them, but it doesn't justify them getting a criminal record. I mean, it's just bricks and mortar, and I'm sure if you explain to Karina that you have enough proof to send Bernie to prison, she'll be only too willing to cover the cost of the repair.'

Molly was smiling. 'You see, everything is going to work out perfectly well. No need to call the police. It wouldn't look good for Karina, just as the book is coming out. It might well damage sales. We can ring her in the morning, and I'm sure she'll sort it out.'

Well, well! Here's a change of tactic. One minute she's running away from the boys and begging for sanctuary, and now she's taking their side? Has she been on the phone to her lover at Karina's, and been fed this line? If she isn't involved with one of the boys – and no, I don't think she is – then which of the men in that household is pulling her strings?

Molly clutched her upper arms and shivered. 'Oh, goodness me, Piers is right, and I should have brought something to wear at night. Jolene's place is nice and cosy and I didn't think I'd need to cover up. Look at the time! Let's all go back to bed, and in the morning we'll have a confab and sort it all out.' And up the stairs she went at a lickety lick, signalling no more talk tonight.

Hari looked at Bea and Piers.

All three raised their eyebrows.

Piers said, 'I take it all back. I'm not going to run away to America. We have to get this sorted.'

Bea felt her way through various possibilities. 'Molly is unreliable, but sometimes comes up with the right idea. My first thought was to hand the jacket and its contents over to the police, but that does risk the wrong sort of publicity for Piers. On the other hand, if we let Karina know that we are holding evidence that one of their household tried to break in here, it puts us in a strong position to get this sorted without anyone else knowing about it. It's blackmail, of course, and I don't like it, but it might be the easiest way out of the situation.'

Piers yawned. 'Molly's pregnant, isn't she? I was slow to pick that up. The currents flowing between different people in that household were so confusing that at the time I let them flow over me, but I rather think it's relevant now to find out who she's been sleeping with. I must think about that.'

Hari said, 'I don't like it. There's a nasty feeling I get when

I hear a professional liar spreading tales. They don't have any compunction about lying. Amoral. And therefore never to be relied on.'

Bea said, 'Even though she's a good liar, we ought to be able to beat the truth out of her. What's been going on so far is irritating, annoying – even more than annoying – but it's getting desperately important that we get at the truth. We keep forgetting that Jolene went to meet someone at a time and place where someone was expecting to find Molly, and Jolene hasn't been seen since. You say there's a man running around with a knife. Suppose Jolene has fallen foul of him? If she hasn't turned up by tomorrow morning then we have to give Molly such a hard time that she comes up with at least part of the truth.'

'Agreed.'

Finally, Bea and Piers left Hari and went up to bed. Slowly. It had been a tiring day and they had much to think about.

Bea had left the red memory stick on her dressing table. 'What are we going to do with that? What if Molly doesn't hand hers over as per contract? Are we obligated to let Karina have the one we've copied? And what are we to do about the portrait? I can't think straight.'

They climbed back into bed and moved close to one another.

Piers switched off the light. 'I've a feeling we're going to regret not having gone straight to the police when the boys broke the fanlight.'

Bea stared into the dark. She thought he was right, but that, given the circumstances, she didn't know what else they could have done. The threat to Piers' reputation was too powerful to resist. Wasn't it?

'On the other hand,' said Piers, snuggling closer to her. 'If Karina's going to play games, there's no reason why we shouldn't respond in the same way.'

Bea wriggled into a more comfortable position. 'How?'

'Dunno, yet. I'll give it some thought.'

And, thought Bea, a prayer for Jolene might be in order . . .

SEVEN

Friday morning

Bea, Piers and Winston the cat breakfasted together. Hari appeared, said he was popping back home for half an hour to tidy up the case he'd been working on, and would be back by ten at the latest.

Neither Piers nor Bea felt like talking. Bea turned the radio on low, so that it murmured a companionable background noise. Both of them listened to the news on the hour in case there'd been a report of Jolene's body having been found somewhere. No such report was broadcast.

Winston made more noise scuffing his food down than his carers did.

There was no sign of Molly. Bea took her first cup of good coffee and unlocked the back door. She went to stand on the balcony overlooking the garden below. Winston brushed past her legs and slunk down the cast-iron staircase to investigate a movement in the bushes under the nearby wall.

Bea relaxed, closing her eyes, feeling the warmth of the early morning sun on her face.

Piers came out to join her. He put his arm about her, and she moved more closely towards him, feeling his warmth, his strength, along the length of her body.

He said, 'Molly did come on to me once. My second visit. I hadn't really noticed her before. I was concerned with how to light Karina, how much background, exactly which shade to paint her hair . . . you know how it is. Polite conversation was all on the surface and I was concentrating on my craft. On my second visit Karina was late and Molly started telling me about herself and her ambitions in life. Slightly irritating.

'She came to stand close beside me and I moved aside, instinctively. She was in my space. She said something about liking what she saw. She could have been commenting on what I'd done for the portrait, but we both knew she wasn't. I shook my head and went to my kitbag for something – anything – to let her see I wasn't interested. She got the message. She didn't try it again.'

Bea said, 'Mm,' acknowledging what he said. She considered saying that she'd never doubted him but didn't. The truth was that she had doubted him and he'd probably known it. It was best to let the subject die.

She looked at her watch. 'I'm due downstairs in the agency in fifteen minutes. Shall we ring Jolene's mother to see if she's turned up all right?'

He drained his mug. 'I'll do it. Her phone number's on the pad, isn't it? I'll put the phone on speaker.'

He made the call while Bea cleared the breakfast things away.

The phone rang for a long time before it was answered. A man said, 'Yes?' Abruptly.

Jolene's father?

Piers said, 'I'm calling on behalf of Mrs Abbot. She's concerned about Jolene.'

A long pause. 'Well she may be.' The voice was thick with tears. 'The police found Jolene this morning. Dead. Under one of the railway arches. I have to go down to identify . . . But it's her all right. It's her bank cards and . . . They knew this man was going around, raping and killing at knifepoint. They knew, and what did they do about it? At least he didn't get round to interfering with our girl. They think that's a consolation, but . . . Why couldn't they have caught him before . . .?'

The phone went dead.

There was a stir in the doorway. Molly stood there, dressed in yesterday's clothes, every hair in place. No sign of a disturbed night. She said, 'Another knife crime? Not Jolene, is it?'

Piers stayed silent but nodded.

Wide eyes showed that she was shocked. Bea warmed to her. Only, she then thought, is the girl pretending to be shocked, or is her reaction genuine?

Molly spoiled the good impression she'd made. 'Oh, dear,' she said, in the tones of one commiserating with the death of an acquaintance. 'Poor Jolene. She was always in the wrong place at the wrong time.'

Piers and Bea stared at Molly, who didn't blush but who did shift from one foot to the other.

Molly shrugged. 'London's known for it. I suppose it was that man who's been on the news lately, attacking girls. I wonder if they'll ever find him? Knife crime is such a common thing in London, isn't it?'

Bea felt anger build up inside her. She said, 'This can't be the same attacker. Jolene got into a car which was meant to be picking you up. You have to tell the police who you were supposed to be meeting.'

Molly flashed her teeth at them. 'Oh, that! That wasn't anything to do with anything. I . . .' A quick flutter of the eyelids as she thought up another story. 'Well, if you must know, I'd arranged to meet someone through a dating site. Jolene was jealous of my success with men. I told her I was due to meet someone new and she decided to meet him instead. She ought to have known better.'

Bea started to say something hasty but managed to swallow the words.

Piers worked it out. 'You're protecting the man you were supposed to meet last night? The man who took Jolene away in a car? I mean, that's a lie about meeting someone from a dating site, isn't it? I grant you, that might work with some people but not with the police. They'll want to know which dating site, and when you had time to tell Jolene about it.'

'Oh, that's all right,' said Molly. 'I joined the dating site. It's all on my laptop, which has unfortunately been damaged and is now beyond repair.'

Bea unstuck her tongue. 'Molly, Jolene's dead and you're responsible for having led her into a dangerous situation.'

Molly shrugged. 'I'm sorry she's dead, obviously, and her parents must be very upset about it, but they do have another daughter who lives close by with her husband. I expect she'll be round to comfort them soon.'

Piers' hands closed around the back of a chair. He held on to it, tightly. He said, 'Molly, your life isn't going to be worth tuppence if you keep shielding a murderer. Don't you realize . . .?'

'It's nothing to do with you what I do and what I don't do. I hold all the cards, and I'm going to play them my way. I've got my memory stick back and I'm going to make Karina pay and pay before I hand it over. Jolene shouldn't have tried to meddle with things she didn't understand. Don't look so disapproving. Perhaps I can get enough money out of Karina to give some to Jolene's mother and to pay for your fanlight to be replaced. Those boys really do need teaching a lesson, don't they?'

Piers said, 'Are you saying you think it was the boys who enticed Jolene into a car and stabbed her to death?'

Molly was amused. 'I wouldn't have thought so, would you? All mouth and no trousers, those two. Think they're movers and shakers, but when they're up against real men, they can't cut the mustard.'

Bea clutched her head. 'Molly, you're not being sensible. Someone killed Jolene because she meddled in your affairs. They knifed her and dumped her. They may have made it look like the work of the man who's going around raping girls at knife-point, but you know and I know that it wasn't the same.'

'I know nothing of the kind.' Molly looked at her watch. 'Have you any good coffee made? I could do with some breakfast and you'll want to check out what's happening at the agency before the staff start work at ten.'

Piers scraped his chair back over the floor. 'Bea, I've had enough. We have to cover ourselves. I'm ringing the police to tell them we may have some relevant information about Jolene's death. I'm also going to contact the insurance people about the broken fanlight. And the Heritage people. They'll send someone round to assess the damage and tell us what to do next.'

Molly was ready for that, too. 'Of course you can contact the insurance people if you wish, but wouldn't it be better to hold off till I've sorted things out this morning? The boys are going to bring the portrait over at ten o'clock for you to sign. Remember, you don't get paid till you've done that? I've agreed to hand over the memory stick to Karina when my terms have been met. And then I'll be on my way and you can do whatever you like.'

So saying, she whisked herself out of the kitchen and down the stairs to the agency rooms, saying that she wanted to say hello to the girls and would get herself a coffee with them.

Bea said, 'The nerve of the girl!' She was torn between anger and amusement. Anger won. She said, 'What's the betting she'll have the girls entranced by her stories of Karina and her ménage, and in ten minutes' time she'll be looking through our Situations Vacant to see what might suit her next?'

Piers drew the phone towards him. 'All bets are off. I'm not dancing to her tune. I'm going to do what we should have done last night. I'm going to speak to the police and tell them what we know. I'm also reporting the damage the boys did, and the overnight attempted break-in. I hope you're with me on this. I know there's a risk they might try to smear my reputation but I'm prepared to take it.'

Bea hesitated. There was a danger in doing as he suggested. No, he was right. She said, 'Do it.'

His call to the police about Jolene was passed on to someone who took a note of it and said they'd ring him back. His mention of the broken fanlight was passed through to a local police station. Again, Piers was told someone would get back to him in due course. And that was that. Frustrating.

He said, 'I need the names of the insurance company and the Heritage builders. Where can I find them? Down in your office?'

Bea said, 'They're in the home address book on the table by my chair in the living room.' She'd been doing some thinking. 'Have you come to any conclusion about which member of Karina's court has been to bed with Molly?'

'No.' He frowned. 'Not really. At a guess it's any one of three. When I'm through phoning, I'll try sketching each one and see if anything stirs at the back of my mind.'

Bea looked at her watch. She had a few minutes to spare before she was due in her office, so she went down the stairs into the garden, to replenish the seed in the birdfeeder and to deadhead the rose bush by the pond.

It helped her to think. Yes, Piers was right; they had to report the break-in to the police. Yes, Molly was right; if they wanted payment for work done, they should play along with Karina's story. And no, it was all wrong to ignore Jolene's death, which was not, could never have been, a random knife crime.

Or was it?

It was a fine, bright autumn morning. The sky was blue with a trace of light cloud here and there. The birds were active.

There'd been no frost as yet, so the bedding plants in the big stone urns were still blooming. The trees, on the other hand, were feeling the stress of the colder weather and had assumed the dull green hue which occurred before they started to turn yellow and drift to the ground.

Winston appeared from nowhere, leaped on to the garden seat and proceeded to give himself a thorough wash.

The sun was warm on her face. Shadows thrown by the tree at the bottom of the garden split and wavered in a light breeze.

All was right with the world but it was a different matter with the people who lived in it.

Bea closed her eyes and concentrated. *Dear Lord, we are doing the right thing, aren't we? Yes, I'm sure we are. Self-interest tells me to do nothing till Piers has been paid. Yes, he deserves to be paid. Yes, Molly does, too. But . . .*

No, I hold no brief for Molly.

But poor little Jolene, who thought she knew what she was doing . . .

And now we're threatened with an invasion of the body-snatching boys, who will try to overwhelm us with their superiority.

Dear Lord, please show me what to do!

A cloud of sparrows descended on the garden, aiming for the pond but, being brought up short by the presence of Winston, retreated to the branches of the tree where they made a great fuss, swearing at him from a safe distance.

Winston gave them one long, considering look and hesitated. Wasn't presenting a perfectly groomed appearance to the world more important than chasing them away? On the other hand, they were making quite a racket and that was disturbing his peace.

He leaped from the bench and shot up the tree, causing the birds to flee.

Bea thought that there wasn't always safety in numbers and went up the stairs to find Piers still on the phone, trying to get through to someone. He saw Bea and said, 'I'm ringing to see how Mr Fletcher is.'

Bea remembered the cheque Mr Fletcher had left for Molly and winced. She knew she ought to have given the cheque to Molly last night. The lads had destroyed the girl's laptop and it was only right that she should be compensated for that. Yes, Bea knew she'd behaved badly, and would have to apologize and hand the cheque over as soon as possible.

Which reminded her. 'I'm overdue downstairs. Hold the fort?'

She dropped a kiss on the nape of Piers' neck, which made him laugh and reach for her. She slid away, removing herself from temptation.

Descending the stairs to the agency rooms, she heard a buzz of gossip and laughter. She stopped. Molly was entertaining them? Yes, she could hear the girl babbling on about something or someone . . . Wait a minute!

Molly was imitating Bea, trying to refuse Molly a bed for the night! Molly was making the girls laugh at Bea? How dare she!

As Bea reached the big office, she found that the girls were indeed laughing, turning in their seats to look at Molly who, with a mug of coffee in one hand, was clowning away in the middle of the room. Even Lisa was smiling. Well, authority is always a good target for a laugh. But not now, not when young Jolene was lying in the mortuary.

Jolene's desk was the one nearest to the stairs. It had a tiny teddy bear – her lucky charm – perched on top of it. Jolene wouldn't need her teddy any more.

Bea said, 'Morning, all.' Then, very quietly, 'Girls, perhaps Molly hasn't said, but we've just heard that Jolene was found this morning, dead from a knife wound.'

There was a murmur of shock and horror. Molly stopped clowning and flashed a look of malice at Bea.

Bea weathered that. She said, 'Yes, it's truly dreadful news. Our thoughts are with her family, who must be terribly distressed. Lisa, would you please organize delivery of some flowers to Jolene's parents and a card, too; one which we can all sign? I imagine the police will be around to ask questions at some point and we must do what we can to assist them. If any of you had contact with Jolene after she left here yesterday, the police will want to know about it. Molly told me she was supposed to meet up with Jolene last night but missed her. Isn't that right, Molly?'

Molly nodded. No smiles now.

The other girls were turning to one another, frowning, anxious, upset. And then turning to Molly . . . and then back to Bea. This time there were frowns in Molly's direction and no amusement at Bea's expense.

Bea said, 'We managed to find Molly a bed last night but she'll be going on her way in a minute. We wish her all the best in finding another job with a different agency.'

Bea let that sink in; there were to be no more easy introductions to Molly from the Abbot Agency, right?

Bea collected the eyes of her staff. 'We will have to look at replacing Jolene soon, but not just yet, I think. Lisa, can you check to see if Jolene's left any work unfinished, and give it to someone else to deal with? Our clients mustn't suffer because we're mourning Jolene.'

Lisa nodded.

Bea resumed her briskest tone. 'Is there anything else that needs my attention, Lisa? No? Good. We are expecting visitors upstairs this morning. Molly, a word?' Bea swept through into her office, expecting the girl to follow her, which she did.

Bea seated herself at her desk and booted up her computer.

Molly flounced down into the visitors' chair. She wasn't best pleased with the way Bea had interrupted her fun and games, was she? The girl said, 'It was only a joke. I was just going to tell them about Jolene when you came in.'

Bea opened the French windows on to the garden to let some air in and scanned the agency inbox on her computer. Yes, yes . . . and yes. Nothing which the girls next door couldn't deal with.

Molly stretched herself out in the chair, letting herself down till her head was resting on the back and her legs were straight out in front of her. Although Bea hadn't yet spoken to her, Molly took the initiative, saying, 'I slept well, thank you. And weren't the girls glad to see me! I hear there's a job going at this new hotel they're opening up. I quite fancy being a receptionist there. You'll give me a good reference, won't you?'

'No. I thought you wanted to break into publishing.'

'I did. I do. You know someone who can help me get in? Now that is good news. Who are they and when can I get an interview? With Karina's book behind me, they're bound to be impressed, right?'

Bea shook her head. 'I don't want you on the books of this

agency, either working here or going after any of the jobs that come in.'

'Is that sour grapes because your husband fancies me?'

Bea snatched at her temper and caught it just in time. She told herself she must be reasonable, that Molly might be this and that but she was a faulty human being who was only lying because she was out of a job and a place to live. Bea told herself that she was so much older and more experienced than Molly that she ought to regard the girl's lies as amusing rather than hurtful. How would she, Bea Abbot, feel if she were in the girl's shoes?

Answer: she wouldn't have found herself in such a position.

However, there was the small matter of the cheques and forms provided by Mr Fletcher, which she was honour-bound to hand over to the intended recipients. The sooner Bea was rid of them, the better.

Bea said, 'Mr Fletcher left you a cheque to cover the loss of your laptop, together with a release for you to sign that you will take no further action with regard to this matter. I left them upstairs in the living room.'

Molly returned to the vertical. 'What! That's nice of the old dear! Well, that's a start. And when I've collected what Karina owes me, I'll be well on my way.'

'I suggest you go back upstairs and pack so that you can leave as soon as you've handed over the memory stick and got your cheque. I don't want you hanging around in the agency and I don't want you bothering my husband—'

'Yes, that's what this is all about, isn't it? You can't trust him to be in the same room as me, can you? And quite right, too!'

Bea shot to her feet, and then told herself to calm down. 'I offered you a bed last night.'

Molly giggled. 'But not your husband's bed. You wouldn't risk that!'

Bea closed her eyes for a second or two. Then unclenched her fists and opened her eyes again. 'I'm amazed you've lived as long as you have. Out! Now! You may collect your cheque and sign the form upstairs, wait there till our visitors arrive, transact your business with them and then leave this house for good. Understand?'

'Oh, keep your hair on!' Molly wriggled herself out of the

chair and stood up. She was laughing. She said, 'Shoo! Boo! Silly old witch!' Then with a grin, she dropped her mug on the floor – where it bounced and spilled the remains of her coffee on the carpet – before she strolled out into the main office.

Bea put her forefingers to her forehead and counted ten, slowly.

She heard Molly saying her goodbyes to the staff. She was laughing, throwing kisses, saying she was being thrown out, oh dear, but old Mrs Abbot was such a cow, wasn't she!

Bea went to the door and watched as Molly waved goodbye and climbed the stairs to the first floor.

Heads swung, watching Molly leave, and then turning back to see how Mrs Abbot was taking her departure.

Bea said, 'I'm afraid Molly is sometimes economical with the truth. There have been . . . issues with her recent placement. We can't afford to let the agency acquire a reputation for lying. She will not be back. Now, do we have any carpet cleaner in the cloakroom? Molly upset her mug of coffee and you know how difficult it is to clean up.'

One of the older women said she'd deal with it. The others busied themselves with their phones. Order had been restored in the agency.

Bea realized that Molly was probably laying out her lures to Piers upstairs at that very moment. Bea stiffened her back. She must trust him. He'd said he'd contact the builders recommended by the Heritage people. They were specialists in repairs to listed houses and shared Piers' view of vandalism to such. They were going to make a meal out of repairing the fanlight. There would be forms to fill in, and arguments about who would pay what. She could do without all that.

Back to work.

An hour later Bea was free to turn her mind to Karina and her court. Up the stairs she went to find Piers alone in the living room. He'd lined up a series of pencil sketches on the big table, and was going from one to the other, occasionally adding a pencil stroke here and there.

He put his arm around her and explained. 'These aren't for publication. I tried doing accurate representations of the family at first, but that told me nothing about what they're really like.

Then I tried to recall everything I've seen and heard about them . . . which was quite a lot when I started to put it all together. So I tore up my first efforts and tried again, doing them as caricatures. I let my hand draw freely, tapped into my subconscious, that sort of thing. I'm not sure now whether what you see here are accurate portraits of the inner men or my imagination running riot.'

Bea said, 'Got it.' She picked up the one he'd drawn of Karina. 'You've drawn her this time as some sort of snake. No, not a snake. A bird of prey. Is she really that impressive?'

'She's an actress. She can portray herself as anything she likes. She can be charming, even mesmerizing. She can also be a Fury when opposed.'

Bea examined the caricatures of the two boys, Alexander and Teddy. They were superficially alike which was not surprising as they were half-brothers. They bore the imprint of an expensive education and of the air of privilege which this confers.

Piers said, 'Both went to university, both dropped out. Neither of them has ever been short of a penny, and don't intend they ever will be. Alexander is the redhead. He's the son of Karina's first husband. He looks good in front of the camera. I don't know what he studied at university but he's now trying to make some kind of a living as a social media influencer, specializing in clothes for young men. Some influencers can earn a very good living, promoting this product and that. Whether Alexander will or not, I don't know. He trades on his connection with his mother and her contacts, but to be fair, he's got a talent for communication. He did ask me to join him in a chat about my work and the portrait, but I didn't feel like helping him.'

Bea considered the sketch in silence. A handsome redhead, holding a mirror in his right hand. 'You're saying he's not just a pretty face, that there is a businessman behind the good looks?'

'He's ambitious and hard-working. He has a studio in the basement of Karina's house all set up for his daily podcasts. He has a diary filled with "go-to" events and A-list parties. He has delusions of himself as being above the law. Don't underestimate him. He has a sharp tongue and a media presence.'

'What about his father? He was Karina's first? What happened to him?'

'He was a businessman. Something to do with bathrooms? The marriage didn't last long, only a few years, if I remember correctly. There was just the one child, Alexander.'

Bea moved on to the drawing of Teddy, the blond. A handsome lad whose facial features were spoiled by a sneering mouth. Sharp eyes. Another suggestion of a bird of prey, but not as marked as in his mother.

Piers said, 'This is the second husband's son, Teddy, the one Mr Fletcher brought up. I can't say I took to him. He went to uni, started to make his name as a journalist of the scurrilous sort. Molly told me – though anything she told me you probably ought to take with a pinch of salt – that young Teddy wrote something which offended the wrong person and got him the sack.'

'Couldn't he have written his mother's memoirs?'

'Wrong sort of journalism. Too young to know what needs checking and what can be allowed through into print.'

'How come he and Alexander are such great friends nowadays?'

'Molly said Teddy had met up with his half-brother at a party and was persuaded into dropping out of university to join Alexander in his media career. He writes some of Alexander's material and sometimes acts as his cameraman. It's a good combination, writer and presenter. They talk a lot about working in the media and about helping to get Karina back into the lime-light. They want to set up a company to make a film featuring her career.'

Piers had made Teddy's mouth look as if he were about to say something nasty.

Bea said, 'To recap, Alexander is the older brother, the one more firmly established in the public eye, and Teddy is the follower? Was it Teddy's father who might have met with an untimely end?'

'I was told he was pushed and fell down the stairs. It's a three-storey house and the stairs are steep. I don't think there's anything in it, myself. The way they carry on in that household, any of them might have drunk too much and tumbled down the stairs. No one seems to have made a fuss about it at the time.'

Bea said, 'The first husband – the one who was in bathrooms

– would have paid alimony, but that wouldn't be enough for her to maintain such a big household, would it? As to the second, according to Mr Fletcher, his brother's finances were in a right old state when he died. So what is Karina living on? Royalties from repeats of her old films? Did the third husband have money? And what of the present one?'

'Good question. The third husband has a handsome face and not much personality. He's younger than her by, I'd say, ten years. He says he's attached to the film world but I couldn't make out how. Perhaps he's in marketing, or production? Was he in films himself? If so, his looks don't seem to have done the trick for long. She divorced him some time ago, but for some reason she still allows him to hang around.

'The current husband, number four, has no looks to recommend him but seems to keep the household running smoothly. Recently there have been reruns of her old films on various channels which should bring something in. I think, yes, that he might be a canny businessman. With age Karima may well prefer financial security to good looks in her bedfellow.'

Bea was about to move on to the next sketch when he put out his hand to stop her. 'You asked which of the men in the household was the father of the child Molly is carrying. The answer is that I don't know who the father of her child is, but I suspect . . . I don't *know*, I can't *know* . . . that she's had both the boys.'

Bea frowned. 'They're far too young for her.'

'Molly doesn't think that way. She would say that she has her *needs*. I wasn't aware of what she was like at first because I was concentrating so hard on the painting, but when she came on to me, I got it straight away. She likes sex. I don't think she much cares where she gets it. No, that's wrong. She uses it as a tool. She probably thought that giving it to the lads would help her because they are all over social media. I doubt if they thought anything of the kind. They're a formidable pair.'

Bea said, 'But they wouldn't let themselves be caught fathering a child on her, would they?'

'I don't know. Depends if she said she was on the pill or not. How far along would you say she was? Three months or four?'

Bea's eyes switched to the clock. Their visitors would be here in a minute, and wasn't that the builder's van drawing up outside?

'You think she has a go at every male she meets? She was talking about meeting people through a dating agency. I thought she'd made that up, but . . . No, surely anyone she met through an agency would be too wary to get her pregnant, wouldn't they?'

EIGHT

Friday morning, continued

P iers spread his hands. 'Your guess is as good as mine.'
Bea wondered, 'Does Karina know that Molly is promiscuous?'
He shook his head, gathering the sketches up and tapping them into a neat wad. 'At a guess, I'd say she does and she doesn't. She probably thinks – if she thinks at all about such an unimportant person as Molly – that the girl can keep the boys amused for a while but that she herself only has to twitch her little finger and they'd fall into line.'

'Do you think that's realistic? The times are changing. If her sons are doing well with their influencing work, they are, or soon will become, financially independent and can play about with whom they choose. Am I right in thinking they are living with her rent-free, coasting along, making use of her in order to set themselves up in their own careers? Do you think she's realized that they are using her?'

He looked troubled. 'Look, I go to a place, I paint whoever it is who's asked for me. That's what I do. Everything else passes me by. I don't usually have much to do with other members of the household. I never expect to have to do more than make small talk with anyone other than the person I'm painting.'

'What you observe about the household must affect your view of the sitter but, in spite of all the cross currents there, you have drawn Karina as the dominant character.'

He hesitated. 'Perhaps because I was there to concentrate on her? If I had to pick out the person who keeps that household going, I'd say that's the current husband . . . No, I'm not sure.'

There was a clatter on the pavement and the doorbell rang. At the same time, Hari bobbed up from the internal staircase and flashed them a smile to show he was back on board.

'The builders have arrived,' said Bea, and went to let them in. She'd met the man before when they'd needed to do a repair to the balcony at the back of the house, but not the woman who was accompanying him that day.

The man – Mr H, as he liked to be called – was the sort who talked a lot but did a good job when he got down to it. He treated her to a wide grin saying, 'Good to see you again, missus. How have you been?' He looked up at the fanlight. 'I can see from here what it is this time.'

'How did it happen?' The woman at his side was dressed in office black and carrying the latest of smartphones plus a laptop. Bea summed her up as a bean counter, happiest when working with technology. Her default expression seemed to be one of disgust at mankind who only lived to damage the environment, whereas his was one of patience, no matter what was thrown at him. They must be a good team.

Bea said, 'We were visited by two louts who thought it was fun to break their way into the house when the door hadn't been opened to them as promptly as they expected. Oh yes, we know who they are, all right. And yes, the police and the insurance people have been informed.'

Hari broke in. 'I took photographs of the damage. Do you want to take your own or shall I send them to your phone?'

'Keep them for the insurance people.' She sucked her teeth and took her own photos, then said, 'We can't start on ordering a replacement for the ironwork until the insurance people have agreed to cover the cost.'

Mr H said, 'You work out the cost and fill in the forms, while I put in a temporary replacement, right?' He crossed his arms, leaned against the wall and said how much it hurt him to see such wanton damage.

Bea smiled and prepared to listen to him, knowing that that was the quickest way to get something done.

Mr H launched into a rant about vandalism in the area. He did rather go on about it. He progressed to talking about how he *might* manage to recreate the original fanlight. He thought he knew where he could source some original glass that might be used to replace the smashed fanlight, but it would add to the cost, mind.

'Has to be appropriate,' said the woman. Turning on Bea, she demanded to know which pattern this particular fanlight had been – there were four different designs in this street.

Bea's mind went blank. She'd lived in this house for decades and couldn't for the life of her remember what the fanlight looked like. Fortunately Piers could recall the pattern, and duly sketched it out for madam. Then they all descended to street level to see if what Piers had drawn matched the ones in neighbouring houses.

The woman tapped away at her laptop, while Mr H opined that he doubted the police would be much good at finding the culprits when this was obviously vandalism by some of those yobs from off this patch, who never minded what they did so long as they caused maximum problems for everyone else . . . and so on. He checked that his stepladder was in order, counted over the tools he'd got in his truck, then shifted some dustsheets from one side of the hall to the other. He said he wouldn't mind a coffee if they had one going, as it was going to take him all morning to take out what was left of the fanlight and put in some plain glass as a temporary replacement.

He opened the front door and stood in the porch, looking up at the fanlight, measuring tape in hand.

The woman said she didn't drink coffee and got on with her calculations.

Patience was required, in spades. Bea and Piers retreated to the kitchen to brew up Mr H's coffee, but were interrupted before it could be made.

'Hey up!' Mr H yelled back down the hall to Bea. 'The circus has arrived in the street. You're not expecting visitors, are you? I need to get on with the job.'

Bea and Piers made haste into the living room to look out of the front window, with Hari on their heels.

A gleaming Rolls-Royce had driven up and double-parked in the street. Karina's two sons spurted out of the back of the car, one holding a camera, the other walking backwards, talking as he went. Filming the event?

A man in chauffeur's uniform opened the back door for Karina to step out into the road.

The woman certainly knew how to make an entrance. She was taller than Bea had expected, and yes, she drew the eye. She was dressed in a gold brocade sleeveless coat over a black silk shift, with a black velvet band around the mass of red hair which curled around her head.

The hair was a wig? Probably.

Emerald earrings swung from her ears, matching the flash and fire of large eyes, outlined with kohl. Her face was a triangle of pampered white skin.

With a flourish of invisible trumpets, Karina drew herself up to her full height, fully conscious of the camera recording every moment but seeming to ignore it. Despite the honking of cars drawn up behind her, she paused on the pavement to smile at anyone who might have the good fortune to pass by and admire her.

She was followed out of the Rolls-Royce by a distinguished-looking man in his late forties; a tall, handsome creature with silver frosting on well-barbered dark hair.

Bea muttered to Piers, 'Which one's that?'

'The handsome one? Third husband. Looks but no money. His profile is pretty near perfect, don't you think? He runs errands and makes himself useful to her. He cooks occasionally, I believe.'

Karina held out her right arm, without looking to see that her gesture was going to be obeyed, and the dark-haired man magicked a tall walking stick from somewhere – was it collapsible? – and put it in her hand. The cane had a skull's head carved on the ivory handle.

The chauffeur darted back into the car to extract Piers' portrait and handed it over to husband number three, who held it well away from himself since the paint was not yet dry.

Finally, an older man emerged from the car. He was balding, rather on the short side, with unmemorable features and a slight paunch. Pigeon-toed.

Piers said, in Bea's ear, 'That's the current husband, number four. Don't underestimate him.'

'What about the chauffeur? Is it the same man who'd tried to burgle us in the night? Hari, you saw him, didn't you?'

Hari shook his head. 'Might be. It was dark, so I can't be sure. He's the right size and build. Hard to tell now he's in uniform and wearing a peaked cap.'

The chauffeur closed the door reverently on the Rolls-Royce, slipped into the driving seat and smoothly took the monster away.

Meanwhile the two lads focused their camera on Karina, giving a running commentary on her visit to Down Town Wherever.

'Ta-ra!' said Piers, imitating a trumpet. 'Entry of the Queen of Sheba, with attendants. The scene is set for the descent of a national treasure on a member of her adoring public. She is accompanied by two of her swains and the event is being recorded by her two talented sons. Please note that members of the public are expected to be in awe of Her Graciousness. They will stand and stare and ask for her autograph and she will wave her hand and smile at them, and they will go away and tell their grandchildren that they once saw her in the street.'

In the street, Karina widened her smile but held up a hand. 'No,' she fluted, 'I'm not here to talk to the camera today.' Exuding modesty, she turned to mount the stairs to the house . . .

And came to a halt, as the front door was slammed shut in her face.

Karina's face became a tragic mask. What was this? Some peasants impeding Her Majesty's progress?

Bea was amused.

So was Piers, looking over her shoulder. He said, 'You know, I did expect some reaction from her when she learned the boys had broken the fanlight, but I thought she'd send husband number four over with soft words and something on account. This is a full-scale visitation. Of course, she does need that memory stick rather badly.'

'She expected a walkover,' said Bea. 'She's certainly not expecting the peasantry to revolt. Mr H is a master craftsman and he won't take kindly to being treated like a serf. He's not going to step aside for her, is he?'

One of the boys lifted his hand to ring the bell. Promptly on cue the door opened and a stepladder was thrust out into the porch, followed by Mr H with a dustsheet over his shoulder and the woman in black, who was gesticulating and talking on her smartphone. They looked at the visitors and clearly decided they could be ignored.

Faced with the unexpected Karina recoiled, causing husbands numbers three and four to step back sharply in order to avoid being knocked over. The handsome one – who must be a good ten years younger than his replacement – nearly dropped the painting, which was fielded by the older, paunchier one just before it hit the pavement.

'Watch it! The paint's not yet dry!'

'Sorry.' Handsome husband number three resumed possession, juggling the portrait this way and that. It was, unfortunately for him, just the wrong size to carry with ease.

Mr H turned his back on the would-be visitors and spread the dustsheet out in the porch. His attitude was that he was on an important job and members of the general public should respect that and keep out of his way. He shifted the stepladder more firmly into position on the porch and prepared to mount.

'Will you kindly let me pass!' Karina made it an order, not a question.

Mr H did a double take. 'You're speaking to me? No entry, miss. Why don't you use the agency entrance, down those steps at the side? They might let you in that way. Or better still, come back later, when we've finished.'

Karina recovered magnificently. She was indeed a splendid figure of a woman, tall and well built. 'If you would kindly move out of my—'

Mr H was having none of it. He was a big man, and when challenged seemed to swell. Together with the stepladder, he filled the doorway to capacity. 'Perhaps *you* don't realize, missus. If you'd used your eyes, you'd have noticed that something was amiss here.

'And not just amiss,' he said, his voice easily booming over her protests. 'Vandalism, that's what it is! The destruction of one of the finest fanlights in this part of London. The fanlights in this street are in the architects' books on the beauty of the past. Ask me, and I'll tell you, the man who built this fanlight was a genius! Look at the delicate tracery of the one next door.

Look at the colour of the glass, the depth of colour, the perfec-
tion of it . . . and weep at what some vandal has done to this
one here!'

He kicked and shifted the dustsheet to cover the porch floor
better. 'You come back tomorrow, right? And mind how you go,
now! You don't want any pieces of broken glass cutting into your
feet.'

Karina threw back her head, seeming to grow another two
inches. 'You don't seem to realize who I—'

He turned to mount the ladder. 'There's a good girl. You leave
me to get on with the job, though it's going to take some doing,
mind, replacing that fanlight. Most of the tracery we can repro-
duce, maybe, though it means going to a proper blacksmith to
do it and . . . No, missus, no one's coming in the house this way
till I've finished and I'm not going to be done in ten minutes,
nor an hour neither, I daresay.'

Karina tried another tack. Shrinking back to her usual height,
she put her hands together in a pathetic plea which would have
gone down well in a silent film. 'You don't seem to understand.
Perhaps you are too young to remember me, but—'

'I don't care who you are, ducky. There's broken glass all
over. Me, in my big boots, I'm not likely to get hurt, but you in
those itty-bitty sandals—'

Karina tried flirting. 'A big strong man like you could carry
me into the house, couldn't you? You see, I have an appointment
with—'

'Can't be done. Rules and regulations, see. Members of the
public have to be protected from themselves.'

The two boys abandoned their filming. 'Mother, we're wasting
time. I thought you said we'd be in and out in five minutes.'

Husband number three was staggering under the weight of the
picture. 'Look here, Karina; I can't hold on to this picture for
much longer. It's doing my back in.'

The foreman took another step up the ladder. 'You see how
much trouble these vandals have caused? They smash and crash
and don't care how much they put other people out, ordinary
people like you and me. If I were a cursing man, which I'm not,
though I must admit, seeing this damage, I wouldn't mind sitting
the man who did this down, and giving him a right going over—'

'Will you please let us in!' Karina, full throttle, full power to the eyes.

'Ah, the magic word, "Please!" Well, now. The people that live here say that two young lads kicked the fanlight in last night. It wouldn't by any chance be those two with the camera, would it? You agree with me that if it was them, they should pay to put the damage right?'

Karina raised her eyebrows to show she hadn't had a face lift. 'Why look at my boys? I've no idea who your vandals were.'

And maybe she didn't know, at that.

'And if they were to be identified by the house owners . . .?'

Karina hesitated. She might or might not have realized that her sons had done the damage beforehand, but she was becoming increasingly uneasy by Mr H's questions.

Handsome husband – number three – intervened. 'Look here, son; we've no idea who did the damage to your window, but it's nothing to do with us. We've an appointment to see the people here. If you don't believe me, just ask them.'

Bea thought that calling Mr H 'son' was probably a mistake, but he evidently decided he'd protested enough, and stepped down from his ladder, saying, 'An appointment? Why didn't you say so?' He folded the stepladder and laid it against the wall. 'Watch out for broken glass!'

One by one the visitors stepped and stumbled over and through the dust sheets into the hall.

Bea and Piers exchanged glances and abandoned their post at the window.

It was not the grand entrance Karina had planned but she made the most of it, sweeping through the hall to come face to face with Bea in the doorway to the living room.

Karina said, 'Mrs Abbot, I presume?' She did not hold out her hand or even smile. She expected to be welcomed in and given the best seat.

Bea declined to bend her knees in a curtsey. 'Yes, I'm Mrs Abbot. To what do I owe the pleasure of your company?'

Karina's entourage managed to squeeze themselves over the dust sheets and into the hall, but got no further as Mr H yelled, 'Hang about! There's one more to come!'

Sure enough, the third or fourth attempt to set up the stepladder was foiled by yet another visitor, calling out to Mr H to hold the door open for him.

Ah, to add to the general confusion, Mr Fletcher had arrived by taxi. He hobbled along the pavement and up the steps into the porch with the aid of two sticks. He did have some difficulty negotiating the dustsheets in the porch so Mr H offered him an arm to get into the house.

To complete the cast Molly appeared at the head of the stairs. She looked down on the assembly in the hall and struck a pose. 'Ta-da!'

Bea smoothed out a grin. Molly had discarded her persona as a biddable working girl. She was wearing false eyelashes and blusher. Her hair had been fluffed out and, what's more, she'd undone the top buttons on her very tight jumper. She was making a statement that she was a personage in her own right.

Behind Bea, Piers smothered a laugh. 'What on earth is she up to now?'

The two boys looked up and gaped.

Alexander cried out, 'Tally-ho! Teddy, look who's here! Our naughty little puss! So this is where you disappeared to, is it? Well, that's saved us from tracking you down.'

Bea invited Karina into the living room. 'Do come in. And would the rest of you please allow Mr Fletcher to come through and sit down? He's only just out of hospital.'

Karina swam into the living room with a gracious smile on her face and, as of right, enthroned herself on Bea's favourite chair. She ignored Mr Fletcher, who manoeuvred himself past the rest of the entourage and subsided on to a seat nearby. Mr Fletcher was looking grey and seemed to be in considerable discomfort.

Bea was worried about him. 'Mr Fletcher, I can see you're in pain. Did the hospital give you anything to take?'

He nodded.

Piers said, 'I'll fetch you some water,' and disappeared into the kitchen.

The handsome third husband put the portrait down beside the fireplace and eased his back. The canvas was indeed an awkward thing to carry around. He concentrated on Karina, ignoring everyone else. 'Would you like a footstool or a cushion at your back?'

Bea looked at the portrait. She'd thought it would be good because Piers always did his best, but the impact of the real thing was shocking. The eyes in the portrait met hers and Bea knew they would follow her around if she moved.

Meanwhile the two boys closed in one on either side of Molly and would have ushered her to sit between them on the settee, but she twisted away and perched on the dining table in the front window instead.

Karina's eyes followed Molly, who didn't seem worried and who wore the smug expression of one who held all the trump cards.

Piers oversaw Mr Fletcher taking some painkillers and retired into the background, frowning.

Bea was the only one left standing.

Karina waved at Bea. 'Do take a seat, Mrs Abbot. You are looming over me.'

The nerve of the woman, acting hostess in Bea's own house!

Bea took a chair and drew it up beside Mr Fletcher.

Karina rapped on the floor with her stick to attract everyone's attention. 'What a sweet little doll's house you have here, Mrs Abbot! So delightfully cosy! Dear me, there's hardly enough seating for all of us. Now, we won't take up much of your time. We are on our way to my publishers to deliver the portrait and the manuscript which dear Molly has been taking down at my dictation. Such a splendid portrait dear Piers has produced, though I'm sure I'm not nearly as, well, as *fearsome* as he has made me out to be, do you think?'

Karina twinkled at him. 'What a naughty boy he is, running away before he's signed my portrait!'

Bea said, 'Is that why you've come? To get Piers to sign the portrait? How strange! I thought you'd come to pay for the damage your sons have done to our property.'

'What nonsense is this? You cannot be serious!'

'Very serious. Perhaps they didn't bother to tell you that they had smashed their way into our house last night by breaking the fanlight? When challenged they fled, only to send your handyman and chauffeur to make a second attempt to break in again in the middle of the night? I suppose Bernard forgot to tell you that he was apprehended and photographed in the act of trying to clamber through the broken fanlight?'

'What!' She hadn't known about this. Nor, judging by their shocked expressions, had either of her husbands. 'Boys, you wouldn't . . .? You couldn't! No, I can't believe—!'

'It was just a prank!' said Alexander, laughing.

Teddy grinned, sure of himself. 'We were trying to retrieve stolen property. We had right on our side.'

'In his haste to get away,' said Bea, 'Bernard the Burglar left his jacket behind. It contains his ID and some money which we can only assume was payment for doing the job.'

Karina's eyes spit fire. 'This is the first I've heard of it. It's got nothing to do with me.'

'We will let you have the jacket and everything in it when you give us a cheque to cover the cost of the damage. Alternatively, we will hand the evidence over to the police. The choice is yours.'

'I . . .!' Karina turned to her current husband. 'We absolutely deny—'

Husband number four pinched in his lips. 'I'll see that the boys pay up.'

Bea thought, *That was easy*. She tried for the jackpot. 'Good. Now, you've brought Piers' portrait for him to sign. Have you also brought a cheque for him?'

A shifting of arms and legs around the room. Karina's smile became fixed. 'No, no. We have no intention of . . . After what he's done . . . stolen my wonderful . . .' Two large tears appeared in her eyes but didn't fall. 'He cannot expect payment, unless of course he can return my lovely jewels . . .'

Bea watched the older, bald husband with the paunch put his hands behind his back and rock forwards and backwards on his toes. It wasn't clear to Bea whether it was Karina herself who would sign the cheque, or the current husband.

Bea sighed. She looked at the clock. Karina could no doubt keep up her elegy for her lost jewels till the cows came home, but this was a working day for Bea, and she ought to be down in the agency at this very moment.

And what about the dead girl? Surely the police would be sending someone round soon to make enquires about Jolene?

Bea would make a bet that someone in that room knew more

than they were telling about Jolene's death and, for that matter, about Molly's pregnancy.

'. . . So you can understand,' Karina intoned, 'that this loss has wounded me deeply. It has stabbed me, a knife to the heart, a wound which—'

'Enough, my dear. Remember why we are here.' The fourth husband had spoken.

Karina stopped in mid-flow and touched her fingers to the corner of her eyes. She wouldn't wish to disturb her eye makeup, would she?

Suddenly Piers sprang to his feet. 'We're wasting time. Mr Fletcher drew up a contract for me to produce and deliver a signed portrait of Karina, which will be featured on the cover of her forthcoming book. I signed that contract in good faith. I had thought of doing another hour's work on it, but if you're happy to regard it as finished now, then . . .' He shrugged. 'Yes, I'll sign it here and now.'

Bea checked with Mr Fletcher but he had closed his eyes and seemed to be dropping off to sleep.

Husband number four produced a tetchy little cough. 'Ah, well. That is what we like to hear, definitely. We accept that the portrait is finished. We do agree that, my dear, don't we?'

'Well, yes,' said Karina, 'but we don't agree about—'

The little man flowed over her speech. 'But we have, naturally, to make certain adjustments to the promised payment, due to recent unhappy circumstances regarding the loss of certain jewels and involvement with Little Miss Ghostwriter here and her shenanigans.'

Bea expected Piers to object, but he merely picked up the portrait and walked off with it, saying, 'I'll set up my easel downstairs, get my oil paints out and sign it. It should take me no more than an hour.' His voice tailed off as he descended the inner stairs to the agency rooms.

Bea wondered what Piers was up to. He usually signed his portraits not on the front, but on the right-hand stretcher. Even if he had to set up his easel and sort out his oils, it would normally take him no more than, what, fifteen minutes, maybe less? Not an hour. So what was he playing at?

Fourth husband was pleased. He rocked up and back on his heels, fingering his smartphone and smiling gently. 'You see, my dear. There was no need to get in a state. The young man understands the situation.'

Karina patted away the last of her crocodile tears and grinned a crocodile grin. 'So, now all we have to do is get Molly to give us the memory stick and we can be off.'

Molly sat on the table and swung her legs to and fro. 'Chance would be a fine thing. You get nothing till I'm paid what you owe me . . . and we're not talking the money for the book only. We're talking about a paternity suit and who's going to put a ring on my finger!'

NINE

Friday morning, continued

What! Molly was going to claim she'd got pregnant by one of Karina's sons?

Shock! Horror! Now there's a turn-up for the books!

Voices exploded in protest.

'Well, don't look at me!' Alexander shot upright. He reddened with anger . . . or fear?

Teddy said, 'Nor me!'

Did Mr Fletcher's eyelids flutter? Was he, perhaps, not as fast asleep as he'd pretended to be? How would he like the news that his nephew was about to sire a child? More importantly, how would Karina like to have a grandchild?

Alexander appealed to Karina. 'She's lying, honest! She said she was on the pill! And it was only once or—!'

Teddy rounded on his half-brother. 'Oh, come on! You told me you'd had her five times! If you hadn't said that, I'd never have—'

'And you said she climbed into your lap without . . .!' Alexander's voice faltered and died away.

Karina's mouth stretched into a different shape. The snake became visible as she took on board what Molly had said. 'You're telling me, boys, that you allowed yourselves to be seduced by that . . . That piece of dirt? How could you!'

Molly frowned at her nails. And then smiled. 'Hm, hm. Chickens come home to roost. Of course they did. Why wouldn't they? And if I forgot to take the pill every now and then, why . . . they are old enough to know what they're doing, aren't they? Either of them could have fathered my child. Perhaps it was Alexander, perhaps it was Teddy. Perhaps it was the man in the moon. Who's to say?'

Molly's eyelids fluttered and she threw a meaningful glance at someone outside Bea's line of sight. Bea could feel that someone had reacted, but couldn't make out who it was. Alexander? Possibly.

The two lads looked stricken. 'No, Mother, I—!'

'Mother, she's lying!'

Karina put her hand to where she thought her heart was. 'My sons! Oh, my sons! How you have betrayed me!'

Molly laughed. 'Well, Karina, are you going to welcome your new daughter-in-law or are you going to pay me to have an abortion?' Her eyes glinted with amusement.

'She's just a slag who—'

'She knew what she was doing—'

The voices rose. Karina thumped the floor with her cane but the boys took no notice. Mr Fletcher was definitely not asleep. His mouth shifted into an expression of distaste, but he didn't open his eyes.

Husband number three was in shock; round-eyed, pressing a handkerchief to his mouth. His eyes switched from the boys to Karina to Molly and back again. Bea assumed he was trying to work out how this might affect his cosy life with Karina.

Number four's eyes were narrowed, computing the odds and finding them unacceptable.

Bea was struck by a nasty thought. Could Molly have tried it on with the husbands as well? Oh, surely not! Husband number three had no money, and Karina was unlikely to continue to support him if Molly claimed him as the father of her child. So Molly wouldn't have bothered to try it on with him. Or would she? And what about husband number four? Was he the cold fish he appeared to be?

The boys, on the other hand, were earning something, if not much as yet. They had a future with Karina to back them. That worked both ways, of course, since they were furthering her own future with their activities.

Karina might rant and rave now, but on reflection she wouldn't want to disown either of them . . . or would she? At the moment she was in shock, but when she'd calmed down, surely she'd accept Molly as a daughter-in-law? Or would she want to pay her off? Perhaps.

Husband number four lifted his hand and the shouting abated. He said, 'Karina, it's a try-on, can't you see?'

Karina's colour subsided, and she relaxed. 'Of course it is! My boys would never . . . No, not with that . . . that creature!' She laughed, a strangely metallic sound. 'Oh, what a wicked, wicked girl she is!' She projected such hate that Bea shivered.

Molly didn't lose her smile but waved both hands in the air. 'You can do better than that, Karina. Now which tabloid paper would like to have the news first, I wonder?'

'Enough!' said husband number four. Quietly, but with authority, he continued, 'Molly, by your own confession, you are a girl who sleeps with anyone who offers. I don't think that would sound good in court, do you?'

'You want me to splash a paternity suit all over the papers? Fine by me.'

That went down like a lead balloon.

A stir at the doorway and Piers entered, putting his smartphone away. 'Well, that's done. Duly signed and delivered.'

He wasn't carrying the portrait.

Husband number four looked wildly around. 'So where is it?'

'I phoned the publisher and asked if they were expecting the portrait today. They said they were, so I signed it and got a friend to take it over there. He's getting a receipt for it. All done and dusted.'

Number four gaped. 'But the contract stipulated you deliver it to us.'

'No, it didn't. You should read the small print. It states the portrait should be delivered by the end of next week, in order for it to be featured on the cover of the book. It says nothing about who it should be delivered to.'

'But our intention—'

Piers allowed himself a fleeting smile. 'You agreed the painting was finished. I have signed it. It has been delivered on time to the publisher. My agent will send you a bill. I wouldn't advise you going to the courts citing my alleged misdeeds. That would be expensive, and I could bring many a VIP as a character witness. You'd lose.'

Husband number four said, 'We could hold up payment indefinitely.'

'Sure,' said Piers. 'But if I say so myself, that portrait is likely to bring me a lot of publicity and even more clients. You'll pay up eventually, and in the meantime I'm not short of a bob or two. Plus I have other clients waiting for me to paint them.'

Karina wasn't happy. 'Cecil . . .!'

Was number four's name really Cecil?

Karina threw her head back and stretched out her arm in a theatrical gesture which brought everyone's attention back to her. 'I don't need this. You know what the doctor said. I mustn't be put under stress. I feel my blood pressure is going through the roof. I need to lie down in peace and quiet. If the portrait's gone, well, we know where it is. We can get hold of it when we want and he can whistle for his money. I'll deal with the boys later. Clearly they've been seduced by an older woman who knew exactly what she was doing, and if she thinks I'm going to allow her into my family, she's got another thing coming. Take the memory stick off her and get the car round to take me home.'

Molly laughed. Perhaps the laugh was not quite as merry as it might have been, but she did laugh. She held up the blue-and-white stick in one hand, and chanted, 'Oh, no you don't. I'm holding on to this until I have something in writing as to my future. And if you want to descend to fisticuffs, well, the first one who touches me gets my pepper spray in his eyes!'

And yes, she was indeed holding a can of pepper spray in her free hand.

The boys halted halfway across the room.

She chanted, 'La, la, la. Come and get it!'

Alexander and Teddy hadn't practised being a double act for

nothing. A quick glance between them, and Alexander feinted to the left while Teddy sprang to Molly's side. He knocked up the arm holding the spray, which shot into the air and discharged its contents into the air . . . but not directly into Teddy's face. He closed his eyes but retained his hold on her arm, while Alexander wrenched at her other hand . . . but only managed to snatch off the top of the stick.

Molly screamed.

So did Karina.

The husbands leaped into the fray, complicating the situation. Arms and legs went everywhere. There was a lot of grunting and squealing. A chair was knocked over.

Bea cried out but was not heard.

Molly was dragged off the table, kicking and screaming. Alexander said, 'Wuff!' and fell out of the scrum, doubled over.

Husband number three made an ineffective grab for Molly, who evaded him with ease, but this allowed Teddy to seize Molly's hand. He managed to wrestle the base of the stick from Molly, but she got an elbow to his midriff which made him, too, double over.

The memory stick shot into the air.

Alexander tried, oh how he tried! He was still in pain from Molly's well-aimed kick, but he nearly, oh so nearly, managed to get the stick. He did make contact but only to deflect it, high into the air and away from the duo . . . who scrambled after it as it descended, slowly, slowly . . .

The two husbands got in one another's way . . .

As did the boys . . . trying to catch it . . .

Molly tried to shove them apart so that she could retrieve the stick . . .

One of the boys surfaced with it in his paw, only to be knocked sideways by another of the contestants. The stick shot into the air once more and . . .

Mr Fletcher opened his eyes and reached for his jug and glass of water.

The memory stick fell, plop! Into the water jug and sank to the bottom.

Everyone froze.

Mr Fletcher blinked. 'What . . .?'

Number four – Cecil – swore under his breath.

Alexander yelled, 'Get it out, get it out!'

Teddy grabbed the jug from Mr Fletcher's hand and scrabbled around in the liquid to get the memory stick. Water sloshed everywhere. He held the stick up, looking as if he were about to burst into tears. 'It's ruined! Water ruins memory sticks!'

Alexander yelled, 'No, no, *no*! It can't be! There must be some way . . . if we take it to a professional . . .?'

Teddy said, 'Yes, yes. Of course. We have to deliver the book today. There's just a chance!'

Molly whispered, 'You bastards! If you hadn't interfered!'

'What . . .?' said Mr Fletcher, trying to catch up on what was happening.

Alexander danced around. 'It might be all right. We must try it! There must be a laptop here. Try it, Teddy. Try it!'

'Give it here.' Piers took the blue-and-white stick and dried it carefully on a tissue. He said, 'It wasn't in the water for long. What we have to do now is put it in a bag with some uncooked rice grains and let it dry out over a couple of days. It's quite possible that we can recover most if not all of what's there.'

'We can't wait that long!' Alexander snatched the stick from Piers and, over his protests, inserted it into the laptop on the table, and waited.

Everyone else held their breaths.

Molly moaned, 'I can't bear it!'

Alexander's shoulders slumped. 'It's no good.' He removed the stick and tossed it on to the table. 'What do we do now?'

Molly wept. 'All that work!'

Karina said, 'Impossible! It can't be true!'

Teddy said, 'She recorded everything Mother said on her smartphone. She'll have kept notes, so we can cobble something together.'

Molly said, 'I deleted them each day when I'd transferred what she'd said to the laptop. There are no notes.'

Alexander said, 'There's her laptop. I know it got damaged, but the hard drive from that . . . what have you done with it, Molly?'

Bea remembered that they'd copied the book on to her own red memory stick last night, and she'd left it on her dressing table. Should she offer to get it? She looked her query at Piers, who shook his head at her.

Piers said, 'Well, it's lucky we took another copy ourselves, isn't it? I had that delivered to the publishers this morning along with the portrait, so you can all relax.'

'What!' That was Cecil, rearranging his tie which had become loose in the recent fracas. 'You mean, they've got everything? The book and the portrait?'

Piers was smiling. 'Both. As per the contracts arranged by Mr Fletcher. No need to thank me. I believe that concludes our business today, and I suggest you make yourselves scarce before the police arrive to interview the agency staff about the dead girl, Jolene. Unless, of course, you wish to stay and tell them what you know of her?'

Glances of mystification from Karina and her entourage.

'Jolene? Who's she?'

'Never heard of her.'

Cecil said, 'Nothing to do with us, so we'll be on our way.'

Piers said, 'Very well. There's just one more thing. We need to arrange how Alexander and Teddy are going to pay for the broken fanlight.'

Alexander shrugged. 'It wasn't us. We were out at the pub. We were nowhere near here.'

Piers said, 'But we saw you!'

A grin. 'Not us. Nowhere near here.'

'So we are to give the police the jacket your chauffeur left behind?'

Cecil narrowed his eyes and looked to Karina for a lead. 'What, what?' Karina tossed her head. 'Nothing to do with us. If Bernie's had his coat stolen by someone who wants to burgle your premises . . .'

Cecil became wooden-faced. He was not going to admit that someone from their household might have attempted a burglary. He said, 'Yes, of course. I expect the police will find the jacket was stolen and was being used by someone else. Some career criminal.'

Teddy brayed a laugh. 'Well done! That gets us off the hook nicely.'

Cecil almost smiled. 'Shall we go, Karina?' He used his smartphone to summon Bernard and the car.

The two boys made a lot of noise, brushing themselves down and collecting their camera and other impedimenta. They seemed to be daring Bea and Piers to tangle with them. They exclaimed loudly that they were oh, so sorry that they must leave, but they were late for an appointment elsewhere and would pick up a taxi on the corner of the next street.

There was a flurry of movement as Karina and her entourage managed to trample over the dustsheets and circumnavigate the stepladder to reach freedom and then, suddenly, the room was quiet.

Bea reclaimed her big chair and sank back in it.

Molly collapsed on to the floor like a spineless cloth doll, but Mr Fletcher was now all bright and bushy-tailed.

Piers picked up the depleted water jug. 'Some more water, Mr Fletcher? You fielded that memory stick rather well. On purpose? Did you happen to play cricket at some time?'

'Thank you, dear boy. I'm afraid it was an instinctive reaction to reach for something falling out of the sky. Yes, for many years I turned out at weekends for our local cricket club. Happy days! And call me Christopher, if you will.'

'And you are able to sleep through anything?'

'I was resting my eyes.'

Molly moaned. She made no attempt to get off the floor. 'What's to become of me?'

Christopher Fletcher said, 'I left you a cheque to cover the loss of your laptop when you sign a release indemnifying Teddy from doing the damage. I'll do my best to see to it you get paid for writing the book. Now, where did I leave those papers?'

'Under the right-hand cushion on the settee,' said Bea.

'Ah, I remember.' He signed to Piers. 'Could you get them for me? Save me getting up.'

Piers fished the papers out of their hiding place and handed them to Bea to sort out.

'Is that the best you can do?' asked Molly. 'It's not much, considering . . . Oh, all right, then. It'll do for the present. Where do I sign?'

Bea found a pen in her handbag and lent it to Molly to sign the indemnity. Satisfied with the transaction, Molly pocketed the cheque and Christopher stowed his release in his breast pocket.

Bea said, 'Molly, before you go. Do satisfy my curiosity. Did you really sleep with both the boys in that household?'

'All the men except Cecil. He wouldn't.'

'One husband and both sons? Which one of them is the father of your child?'

Molly wailed, 'I don't know! How could I? They all followed me around, they pinned me against the wall, they came at me whenever they could get away from Karina! They never gave me a minute's peace. I should have cried "rape" when the first one cornered me in the kitchen, but I thought . . .' She sobbed loudly. 'I thought—'

'You thought you could make some money out of it.'

Molly went all pathetic. 'I wanted . . . I wanted someone to love me . . . someone who would give me a chance to settle down and . . . You don't know what it's like to be cast out on the world without friends, to hunt for jobs that will give you more than the minimum wage!'

Bea and Piers exchanged rueful smiles because they did know. In their younger days, they'd been there, done that, and bought the T-shirt.

Bea said, 'Piers and I both know all about that life, Molly. Now by all accounts you left your family to come up to London, and have been living with Jolene and her family rent free—'

'I deserve something better than having to share a room with Jolene, and being questioned every time I got back late—'

Bea was sharp. 'You repaid their kindness by leading Jolene into a trap.'

'I never! How can you be so unkind! I was very fond of Jolene and would never have led her into danger if I had known! Now she's gone and I don't have any friends at all, and you've got to help me!'

I'd like to shake some sense into the girl, but I fear she's too far entrenched in her vision of what life owes her. I suppose I ought to feel some pity for her. Well, I do. A bit. When Piers and I parted after a few short years of marriage, I was in a similar situation as a single mother, adrift in the world, looking for work, anxious and afraid . . . until I came to work here and I found myself being looked after by a kind man who picked me

and my son up and gave us a home. I loved him to bits, my
darling Hamilton. Oh dear . . .

So where is the difference between me and Molly?

Well, I wasn't pretending to be something I wasn't. I paid my
way; I didn't cheat anyone and I didn't sleep around.

Am I being a self-righteous prig?

Possibly.

Bea looked to Piers for a lead. 'Can we throw her out? She
said last night that she had a friend somewhere at the far end of
the Piccadilly line. When the police come to ask about Jolene,
we could give them her new address.'

'I'd prefer her to go, too,' said Piers. 'But . . .'

They both looked to Christopher for advice. The gentleman
sighed. 'We all know it's no good throwing good money after
bad. We know that promises to reform are meaningless from
those who habitually lie their way out of embarrassing situations.
Mind you, I'm no role model. I've been far too indulgent with
Teddy over the years. I've made excuses for him time and again,
and each time I tell myself he will change. And he doesn't. I'm
weak as water where he is concerned, and yet I know that my
weakness is not helping him to grow into an adult who takes
responsibility for his actions. I can't help you decide what to do
about Molly.'

Bea understood where he was at. Teddy was family and family
came first.

That was, however, a different case from Molly, who was not
related to Bea and Piers and who didn't seem to have a conscience.
There was only one way in which she might persuade Bea to
help her, but it didn't seem likely that the girl would think of it.

Molly slapped the carpet, hard. 'If you won't help me – and
I suppose there's no reason why you should – you might at least
find out what happened to poor little Jolene.'

Bea caught herself up in a sigh. Oh dear, Molly did know how
to press the right buttons, didn't she? 'How can we do that,
Molly?'

Molly rubbed her eyes. 'I admit I told Jolene tales of Karina's
household, of the boys doing these podcasts of the big house and
the servants, and the luxuries they took for granted. Jolene wanted
that lifestyle, too. And why shouldn't she? She wasn't going to

sit in a basement and make tea and run errands for some agency girls for ever, was she? She could see that your lot downstairs were never going to holiday in the Maldives or live in a penthouse in the city. I opened her eyes to a different sort of life and she wanted it, too. I didn't ask her to help me. She wanted to do so. It was all so exciting—'

Bea wasn't having this. 'Until it stopped being exciting and became dangerous? I imagine she got into that car expecting you to join her any minute. It wasn't very clever of her to do so, was it? Surely you'd warned her there was an element of risk involved?'

Molly was sullen. 'She was supposed to wait for me. She shouldn't have got into the car herself. She was stupid. She thought she could handle anything that came her way.'

Piers said, 'And who was she supposed to meet?'

Perhaps Molly considered telling the truth for once? She ducked her head and her shoulders drooped, but then she put on a brave little smile and lied. 'Dunno. I had this phone call, a man saying he'd like to meet me. I thought it was from the dating site. He sounded all right. Educated, you know? Said his name was Hermann. He said he wasn't German but that his parents had named him after a great uncle or something.'

Bea didn't believe a word of it. 'So now we can contact the dating site and find out more about this Hermann?'

Molly's colour rose. 'Yes, well. I tried that last night, when you said Jolene was missing. We had a bit of a row and I told them to take a running jump and they said they'd delete my details from their records.'

Christopher shifted in his seat. 'Young lady, you may have studied the art of lying but so have I. There is no doubt in my mind that you have achieved a master's degree in fiction, but then so have I in detecting subterfuge. There are tell-tales to look for when you are truthful, and when you are not. That story of yours – pardon me – was a load of old bollocks.'

Bea said, 'Molly, we know you were supposed to meet someone from Karina's household. Not her. No, she would have got the chauffeur to drive her around in the Rolls-Royce. So it was someone else from her household, wasn't it? Three of the four men in that household have had sex with you. I believe you were prepared to meet one of them for the purpose of blackmailing him to keep your liaison secret. So, which one was it?'

Molly managed a light laugh. 'Nonsense. Blackmail? Me? I was to meet a man from the dating site. Of course Jolene was intrigued that I should be so daring. She would have liked to go on a dating site herself, but the ones where you meet rich men are expensive to join and her job here didn't pay her enough for that. Is it any wonder that she was curious enough to shadow me on my first date with this man? Unfortunately for her, she must have come across the serial attacker instead who mistakenly thought Jolene was a prostitute like the others. Poor little Jolene. How surprised and distressed she must have been when he made it clear what he wanted. She would have demanded he let her out of the car, he became distraught and . . . and . . .'

'Stabbed her with a kitchen knife? He'd come prepared for a date with a mature woman, arranged through a dating site, and had brought a kitchen knife to the car just in case? Why did he do that, do you think?'

'Well, he was obviously a serial rapist. Jolene stepped into the wrong car and he killed her, just like that! I can hardly bear to think about it. Poor Jolene. She didn't stand a chance. But the police will trace him and lock him up for good.'

'Through the non-existent dating site?' Christopher's tone was dry. 'Never mind. When the police check your phone, they'll soon find out whether you have any record of signing up to a dating site . . . or not.'

Molly flashed an evil look at him. He took no notice of that but tried to shift his position again.

Piers said, 'Christopher, you're not comfortable. When can you take some more painkillers?'

There was a low whistle, and Hari walked in, holding some papers. 'Here I am, safely back. Piers, the Heritage people want you to look at the temporary job they've done. They've cleaned out the remains of the old fanlight and put a plain piece of glass over where the original used to be. It should hold till they can get a replacement made. Here's a receipt from the publishers for the portrait. Molly, the publishers said the book's editor will be in touch with you shortly, when she's had a chance to read it, and they want an address where you can be contacted. Bea, there's a bit of a situation downstairs and they could do with you.'

Molly started up. 'It's the police! They've arrived to talk about Jolene. I'll need to speak to them, won't I?' She began to button her top and fluff up her hair. 'I must change, have a wash and brush myself up.' She snatched the paperwork from Hari, disappeared into the hall and ran up the stairs.

Hari shook his head. 'It's not the police. But Bea, you are needed down below and it's not good news.'

TEN

Friday, late morning

S ure enough, miserable faces turned to Bea when she entered the big office. One girl was sniffing into a handkerchief.

Lisa was red in the face. 'We have a thief here, Mrs Abbot. She's stolen the tea money from the cashbox.'

'It wasn't me! I didn't!' sobbed the girl who was using her hankie. 'I wouldn't.'

'You were short of money this week,' said Lisa. 'You told us so.'

The girl wailed, 'Yes, but I wouldn't steal! I wouldn't!'

Lisa said, 'A likely story. Mrs Abbot, do you want me to call the police? There was nearly twenty quid in the tea money, and we wouldn't have known anything was missing only that we were short of biscuits this morning and I opened the box and there was nothing there.'

Bea felt a trickle of icy air pass down her spine. She shivered. She knew exactly what had happened. She had a mental picture of Molly getting herself locked into the office the previous night, unable to get out through the door to the street. Hari had rescued her eventually, but Molly had had plenty of time to look around. She'd known where the tea money was kept, and that Lisa often forgot to lock the drawers in her desk.

What a brat Molly was! Selfish, amoral . . .!

Bea said, 'You've picked on the wrong girl. I'm afraid Molly got locked in down here last night and went looking for money. We allowed her to stay the night upstairs because it was late and she said she had nowhere else to go. I'll have a word with her in a minute about it.'

She moved closer to Lisa and said in a low voice, 'Lisa, you keep the tea money in your top desk drawer, don't you? It doesn't look to me as if that drawer's been forced open. Was it locked up properly last night? Did you leave it open by mistake?'

'I . . . yes, I always . . . Well, perhaps . . . we're all at sixes and sevens.' Lisa washed her hands over and over.

'Quite!' said Bea. 'It would be a good idea to double check in future.' And to the room at large: 'Now, I'm going up to have a word with Molly. There was no thief here except for her. All right?'

They were not mollified. An older woman said, 'This is all very upsetting. When we heard about Jolene . . . She was only a child, really . . . and now she's dead! It's a shock. She was very silly in lots of ways . . . Oh yes, she was!' She overrode objections from one of the more soft-hearted women. 'But no, she didn't deserve this, and it's only natural that we should be upset that a girl we knew has lost her life.'

Bea liked that. She marked the woman down as someone to watch. Bea accessed the computer in her mind. Vera, that was her name. She'd come to them a month ago. She was married, had had various part-time jobs over the years, but was now looking for something more permanent as her grown-up children had departed for university.

They all looked at Jolene's empty desk and chair.

Another woman blew her nose. 'Jolene was always so full of life. I don't live that far from her and we used to come in on the Tube together sometimes. She shouldn't have died. It makes me feel as if I'd like to smash something, I really would.'

'Agreed,' said Bea. 'It's horrible. It looks as if Jolene got into a car that was waiting to pick up Molly and, well, we don't know what happened next. I hope the police will find out soon. In the meantime, I'm going upstairs to have another word with young Molly.'

They were not happy about it, but as two phones rang at that moment, they did turn back to their duties.

Bea started back up the stairs only to be find the front door open and Hari looking up and down the street. He said, 'I thought I felt a draught, and found the door wide open. Piers is with Mr Fletcher in the sitting room. So who—'

'Molly.' Bea was grim. 'She thought the police were coming and she didn't want to face them.'

Bea ran up the stairs to throw open the door of the guest room . . . which was in disarray, as was the en suite beyond. No sign of Molly.

Hari was at her shoulder. 'She's taken all her things?'

'Pray God she hasn't taken my jewellery box with her.' Bea flung open the door of the main bedroom, but all was as it should be. She'd left a pair of earrings on her dressing-table, and they were still there. Her valuables were kept in a small safe Piers had installed at the back of her big built-in wardrobe. That was untouched.

Hari prowled around. 'I'm furious with myself. I was meant to be safeguarding you and look what happens? She slips through my fingers. Anything missing?'

'I don't think so.'

'Do you want to inform the police?'

'Yes. No. I don't know.' Bea sat on the bed to think about it. 'The girl's panicking. Where is she going to go? She's got the cheque from Mr Fletcher but that's to replace her laptop and won't get her far. She can't come back here to find another job and I don't think she'll be welcome at Jolene's place. I would be sorry for her if I weren't so angry! Now I find she's pinched the contents of the tea-money box, which isn't important compared to everything else that's happened but . . . Do I want to set the police on her for the sake of twenty pounds' tea money? No. But she knows who she was supposed to be meeting and won't say. When the police come round, I'll have to tell them that. Let them find her and sort out when she's lying and when she's telling the truth.'

The landline phone rang. 'Perhaps that's the police now,' said Bea, and managed to get off the bed and start downstairs.

Piers met her in the hall. 'Lisa has just rung through on the internal phone to ask you to come down. Some visitor . . .?'

Bea clicked her fingers. 'I'm on my way. It'll be Mrs Hennessey, the cook-cum-housekeeper at Karina's. Poor woman, I don't suppose she knows why they accused her of theft yesterday. We need to find her another job. Lisa could have done that, but . . .' She shook her head. Lisa had gone to pieces, hadn't she? Lisa was like wet cardboard. She was about as much use as loo paper would be in a gale.

Bea explained to Christopher, who seemed to have settled himself down to drink coffee and read the newspapers, that she had to deal with Mrs Hennessey.

At which he said, 'Remember to get that release! Oh, and if you could sort Karina out another housekeeper, I'd be obliged.'

Bea nodded before realizing that no, the last thing the agency wanted was to steer another poor woman into Karina's household. What's more, Mrs Hennessey might be coaxed to talk about what she'd seen and heard at Karina's . . . but not, of course, if she signed that release. Ah, problem.

Thinking hard, Bea collected the cheque and the release and made her way downstairs.

This time most of the staff were at work, but there was a sense of uneasiness. Backs were stiff, and side glances were being thrown at a very solid newcomer in a heavy tweed coat. Mrs Hennessey? She was seated beside an unattended desk, a desk which should have been occupied by one of the younger members of staff.

Lisa said, 'Oh, Mrs Abbot. We don't know what to do. The girl who usually deals with Mrs Hennessey has gone home sick. I thought you'd prefer to deal with her yourself.'

So that girl had gone off sick? Or walked off the job? Were more of the agency staff going to leave because of the mess that Molly had got them into?

Bea's glance collided with Vera's. Vera could have dealt with Mrs Hennessey, but couldn't override Lisa.

Bea took charge. 'That's fine, Lisa. And, Mrs Hennessey? I'm so glad you could come in this morning. There have been developments. Perhaps you'd like to come into my office? Vera, can you see what we've got on our books which would suit Mrs Hennessey? Bring the paperwork in to me. Mrs Hennessey, would you care for a cup of tea or coffee?'

'Tea, thank you. Milk but no sugar. Strong.'

Mrs Hennessey followed Bea into the back room overlooking the garden and seated herself, unbuttoning her coat but not removing it. Bea sized her up, thinking that Piers had got her right: middle-aged and competent. Mrs Hennessey would know all about Sunday roasts and have excellent pastry skills but would have no time for such fripperies as sushi. Honest as the day is long, she would have been shocked and horrified at being accused of theft.

Mrs Hennessey wasted no time. 'You heard what happened yesterday? They accused me . . . Me! I have never in all my life! I still can't believe it!'

'I know. Ridiculous! My husband saw it all. They accused him of theft, too.'

Mrs Hennessey looked puzzled. And then she got it. She said, 'Your husband? Who . . .? You're married to the painter chap? Well, I never.' She gave Bea the once-over, re-evaluating her. A tinge of red appeared on her cheeks.

Bea also felt herself redden.

Were they both thinking about Molly and what that silly girl had told them about Piers and her? Oh dear. Embarrassment! Bea didn't know what to say.

Vera brought in the tea, and Mrs Hennessey accepted a cup. She tasted it, spent two seconds considering it, and set it back down. 'A decent brew.'

Vera put a couple of files on Bea's desk and withdrew. Vera was discreet. Vera was worth her weight in gold.

Bea said, somewhat stiffly, 'I can only apologize for the agency sending you to Karina's. We will not be assisting them to find staff in future.'

It was time to speak of Christopher's cheque. Bea reminded herself to refer to him as 'Mr Fletcher' to Mrs Hennessey, who might or might not call him by his first name. She said, 'Mr Fletcher has given me a cheque for your back pay.'

'Ah, Mr Fletcher. An honest man. I trusted him on sight and accepted the job on his recommendation, only to discover . . . well, well. It wasn't his fault. I took the job as a cook and it turned into a lot more than that when I got there. Mind you, I've been in that position before, hired by one person that I liked, but in the end having to work for someone that I didn't. When I calmed down last night, it did occur to me that if I appealed to him, he might see me right.'

'He has,' said Bea, handing the paperwork over, 'but he wants a release from you to say you won't talk to the press or anyone else about what you've seen or heard at Karina's.'

Mrs Hennessey put on some half-moon glasses. She took her time reading the release. She looked at the cheque long and hard, and seemed to be involved in some mental calculations before putting her glasses away. She picked up her cup and drank. And stared into the distance.

Bea sat back in her chair. Mrs Hennessey was no fool. She'd added up what she was owed and subtracted it from the total amount of the cheque. She'd weighed up the pros and cons of signing that release and wasn't convinced it was in her best interest to do so.

Bea chose her words with care. 'I believe it's normal practice to sign such a release to cover payment of wages due when employment with a well-known person has been terminated, especially if a bonus has been included. Such releases are normal and both parties are usually happy with the result . . . unless there are exceptional circumstances.'

Mrs Hennessey had small, sharp, grey eyes. 'What do you mean by "exceptional circumstances"?'

'Well,' said Bea. 'We should be able to get a first-class reference for you from Mr Fletcher, we can set you up with interviews for another job, you can cash that cheque and the police would never know you had anything to say about the matter.'

'Police? Why should the police want to interview me? I don't want to make a fuss about what happened yesterday. They've compensated me for it, as they should. And, once I'd calmed down last night, I realized I'd not been happy there for a while, and if they'll give me a good reference and you can find me another job then I'll put it down to experience.'

Bea was disappointed. She'd hoped for some gossip but no, Mrs Hennessey was discreet and sensible. She was not going to be drawn into saying anything bad. Bea was surprised at how angry she felt about, well, everything that had happened.

She said, 'Mrs Hennessey, I'll be straight with you. It's Karina's boys. They came here looking for Molly and kicked the fanlight in over the front door. It's going to take time and money to replace that.'

Mrs Hennessey was indulgent. 'Did they? Well, I never. I wonder why they did that? Perhaps they set it up as a joke so that they could film it and put it out on those podcasts or whatever they call them.'

Bea said, through her teeth, 'It's caused us considerable inconvenience.'

'I'm sure it can be put right. A harmless prank.'

'Would you say that Molly was harmless, too?'

Mrs Hennessey was jolted into giving a slightly rude laugh. 'Man mad. I wouldn't trust that one as far as . . .' She stopped herself from completing that sentence. 'Well . . .'

Is she blushing? Oh, no! She's remembering that Molly has told her she was shagging my husband!

Mrs Hennessey recovered herself sufficiently to say, 'Well, Molly is a different matter. Is that what they want me to keep quiet about?'

Bea picked her words. 'Let me tell you a story. Molly came to London to find a good job. She stayed with an old friend of the family whose young daughter, Jolene, worked here in the agency. Molly may have told you that she was living in a mews cottage down the road from here, but that wasn't true. She was sharing a bedroom with Jolene in a tower block in Acton.'

Mrs Hennessey froze. Yes, Molly had told her she was living in the mews. She said, 'Silly girl. What did it matter?' And managed an indulgent smile. But there was unease in her manner which told Bea that Molly had indeed been telling lies about herself and Piers.

Bea soldiered on. 'Molly made herself useful in the office here and through the agency managed to get the job to ghostwrite Karina's memoirs. She continued to lodge with her "auntie"– who was her mother's old friend – and to amuse her "cousin" Jolene with tales of the high life she was leading. She had pretty well finished the book when all hell broke loose yesterday morning. First, Karina accused you of theft. After you left she first accused Molly of the same thing, and then my husband.'

Mrs Hennessey narrowed her eyes. 'Did she now!'

Bea went on: 'It has crossed my mind that she did this to avoid paying what she owed you. All three of you.'

Mrs Hennessey opened her eyes wide, digesting this news. She said, more to herself than Bea, 'No, I've always been discreet. And I need that money.'

Bea continued. 'Last night Molly took refuge here. She told me a number of lies but the truth of the matter seems to be that she'd arranged to meet up with someone who was going to help her get the money she was owed for the book. She arranged for Jolene to join them, for backup. Only, when Molly was nearing the meeting place, she saw Jolene get into a car which then drove off. Molly waited. No one else came to meet her. She became distressed but not enough to call the police . . . and came round here hoping we'd help her. Only, well, Alexander and Teddy came after her, demanding the memory stick which contained the book she'd written for Karina. Molly managed to evade them and disappear. No more was heard of Jolene until she was found dead – from a knife wound – early this morning.'

Mrs Hennessey gasped. 'What! You mean . . .? She was killed by . . .? But by who? You don't mean someone from the family? No, that's ridiculous. You can't be serious. I've never heard the like.'

'Some people would say it's nothing to do with you. You didn't know Jolene. Or did you?'

'No, never heard of her till now. I thought, we all thought, that the painter man was . . . pardon me . . . well, *seeing* Molly, if you get my meaning, and that he was keeping her in this mews cottage she kept talking about. That was what she told us. But you say she wasn't . . .?' Her colour had intensified. She was aware of how embarrassing this situation might be for both of them.

Bea told herself to keep going. 'No, she wasn't *with* my husband. She tried it on, but it didn't work.'

Mrs Hennessey took that with a pinch of salt. 'Of course.' Only half convinced but being polite. Then she frowned. 'Come to think of it, Molly did mention a cousin a couple of times. Someone she met after work. Yes, I remember that. But I never met the girl – she didn't come round to the house. I didn't remember her name or anything. She's dead, you say? That's . . .!' A change of tone. Mrs Hennessey had made up her mind who to believe. 'Molly lies.'

'Yes, she does. Social lies like saying she lived in a mews in

Kensington are absurd but understandable in a way. A knife to the heart is another.'

Bea sat back in her chair and let Mrs Hennessey think through the options that faced her.

Mrs Hennessey picked up the cheque and looked at it, hard. She said, 'I could do with this, and I earned it. Well, I earned nearly all of it. There's one hundred and fifty quid more here than I've earned. I suppose it's to compensate me for being falsely accused of theft. Nobody can say it's wrong for me to have it, and I know nothing about this Jolene.'

Bea nodded.

Mrs Hennessey picked up the release and read it through once more. 'I could tear up the release and put the cheque into the bank today. Only they'd find out and stop the cheque, wouldn't they?'

Bea nodded. 'Mr Fletcher drew the cheque on his personal account. He's upstairs talking with my husband, waiting for you to sign.'

Mrs Hennessey explored another possibility. 'I could put the cheque in the bank and at the same time I could give him a cheque for the one hundred and fifty quid which I haven't earned. How would that work?' She shook her head. 'It takes too long. He could still stop the cheque on this ground or that. If I had internet banking it would go through and they couldn't stop it . . . but there, I've never had the head for computers and this is the first time I've wished I had.'

Bea nodded.

Mrs Hennessey sighed. 'I could sue them for my wages through the small claims courts but it would take for ever and the rent on my place is due.'

Again, Bea nodded.

Mrs Hennessey said, 'I've a bit put by in the building society and I could manage if I get another job straight away. This release is meant to shut my mouth which means they think I know something they don't want trumpeted to the media or to the police. I don't know what that would be, but I don't like being pushed around so I'm not signing. Would there be another cuppa in the pot, do you think?'

'Thank you,' said Bea. 'And I know a good solicitor who can help you if there's any trouble getting your money.' She went to the door to ask for a freshly made pot of tea for two, and some biscuits.

Mrs Hennessey declined a biscuit. 'If I'd thought, I'd have brought you some of my shortbread.' Another change of tone. 'I don't understand. You really care what happened to that girl?'

Bea told the truth. 'Jolene was a silly little girl, rather young for her age, but she was one of my team. I feel some responsibility for her even though she didn't behave particularly well in this matter. Then again, my husband has been accused of theft, manhandled and refused his fee for the portrait. And finally, the boys broke our fanlight, they set their odd-job man to burgle us in the small hours—'

'What? You mean Bernie?'

'He left his jacket and ID behind him when he fled. My remaining staff are in shock. Above all, Molly has told me so many lies, her behaviour is so destructive . . . She's made me so angry that . . . Honestly, I can't remember ever wanting to physically hit anyone before. I'm convinced she's covering up for whoever killed Jolene, that she's trying to play both ends against the middle. I wouldn't be surprised if Molly ended up dead, too.'

Bea realized she was shaking. She said, 'Sorry. Sorry. I seem to be . . . I don't usually . . .' She tried to laugh at herself. She couldn't possibly be breaking down in front of someone she was supposed to be interviewing, could she?

It was no use. She needed to weep. She stood up, forcing out a word of apology, thrust open the doors to the garden and stood there, sobbing. Uncontrollable. Hating herself for being so weak. Despising herself for breaking down, especially in front of someone she was supposed to be trying to help.

How stupid was this!

The clink of china brought her to herself. She mopped herself up, and returned to her chair, muttering an apology.

Mrs Hennessey had poured them both a cuppa, and had put a biscuit in the saucer of Bea's cup, too. 'There, now. Sometimes you just have to have a good cry. It was her making eyes at your old man as got to you, right?'

Bea nodded. She blew her nose and ran her fingers back through her hair. 'Right. But poor little Jolene . . . she didn't deserve a knife in the back.'

'You said it was to the heart before.'

'Did I? Actually, I have no idea where or how she was killed, except it was with a knife. I'm probably not making a lot of sense. Apologies.'

Mrs Hennessey put her empty cup down. 'I don't know anything about this Jolene, or what happened to Molly and your husband after I left, but I've kept my eyes and ears open while I was there and come to certain conclusions. You want me to tell you what I know? Where do you want me to start?'

Bea said, 'Thank you. With the people, I suppose. I really don't understand who's top dog in that household.'

'No, you'd think it would be her, wouldn't you? I thought so too, when I first went there. On her good days, she can put on a wonderful show. She plays her part well, is gracious and smiling, provided of course that it doesn't cost her anything. She indulges the two boys, tells everyone how much she loves them, but can turn on them in a flash if they annoy her. She can charm the shoes off your feet, but if displeased she spits poison.

'She believes, quite sincerely, that she is a power in the land, that she is rich enough and well-connected enough to destroy anyone who dares to do her wrong. That's an illusion, fostered by the men. She never reads a newspaper or a book. She mostly watches re-runs of her old films on the telly. It makes sense that she needed Molly to get the book written. She'd never have got a contract with a reputable publisher without employing a ghostwriter.'

Bea said, 'What of her fabulous jewellery? Real or fake?'

'I can't say. There is a safe in her bedroom and she does keep some things in it. The rest are strung over a stand on her dressing table or are half in and half out of a lockable jewellery box. She's careless about where she leaves her things. I thought some must be copies, but how would I know?'

'You don't know whether the ones she accused you of stealing were real or not?'

Mrs Hennessey shook her head. 'I'm beginning to wonder if they wanted to make out I'd stolen the stuff so's they could claim on the insurance.'

Bea pounced on that. 'That household must cost a lot. You think she's running short of money?'

Mrs Hennessey gave a grim little nod. 'The latest husband –

Cecil – had to cut up her cards last month. She'd get on the phone and order stuff like there was no tomorrow and he had to send things back.'

'Is the current husband, Cecil, the power behind the throne? I notice she defers to him now and then.'

'Not much to look at, but handsome is as handsome does, as my mother used to say.

Now, Simon – that's her third – we used to call his sort a "matinee idol". I hear he was in films, too, playing bit parts, doing quite well but no way was he star billing till they got married and she put money into a film where he was playing the lead for once. The film laid an egg and they fell out in spades, divorced, the lot.'

'That's when she met Cecil and married him instead? So why is this Simon still hanging around?'

A shrug. 'Don't ask me. I suppose he's useful. He cooks for them sometimes.' A sly glance. 'He keeps her warm in bed, and don't say I can't know about that, because of course I can, her sheets being as good evidence as you could hope not to find, and Cecil having his own bedroom and not being active in that direction any more.'

'You mean she keeps one for fun and the other to sort out her finances?'

'Pretty well. I've a lot of time for Cecil, he's doing his best to keep her afloat, but she won't face the reality of age and a diminishing income. He was in business before they married, but then he retired and there doesn't seem to be much left in the kitty nowadays. I reckon it's only the promise of big book sales that's kept them going recently.'

'What do you think now of the attempt to get rid of you, Molly and Piers without paying what's due?'

Mrs Hennessey moved uneasily. 'I don't know, I really don't. Except . . . when I met Mr Fletcher and he outlined the job to me, he did say that I could live in if I wished, but I didn't want to do that, having my own little place that my husband and I'd lived in for nigh on twenty years till he died, poor man; smoking, you know? And I've got it just so. I arranged to go in early, nine o'clock each day, order the food, prepare the meals and leave about six in the evening.

'I was told there was a handyman to do the cleaning but I soon found that Bernie doesn't do anything inside the house if he can help it. He'll drive the cars and wash them, and do some odd jobs if they pay him extra, and that's it. So I said I'd have to have a cleaner every day, and they argued about that, but finally they saw sense, and one comes in now . . . or did, till they sacked her last week.'

Bea raised her eyebrows. 'Sacked? For what?'

'Stealing. I was shocked but didn't question it. Then that Bernie, he started saying the household was jinxed and I'd better take care because I'd be next. He said the previous cook and the housekeeper had got the sack for selling off some wine that had been laid down by her first or second husband that was long gone. The wine was supposed to be worth a mint and it's true that there is a wine cellar there and there's nothing much in it. I didn't listen because Bernie was no saint, skiving off when he was supposed to help me in the house and running little errands for the boys that made me think . . .'

She shook her head at herself. 'No, I shouldn't say that.' She thought about it, and then blurted out, 'I thought he was getting drugs for them for their Saturday night parties. They didn't have parties at *her* house but went out to one of their friends. Karina couldn't have borne their making a noise in her house, you see.'

'What do you make of the boys?'

'Spoiled rotten. Selfish. Aiming to be media stars. Influencers, they call it. Maybe they'll make it. Dunno.'

'Mr Fletcher? What do you think of him?'

'I liked him. He does a lot for the household. I thought at first he was in love with Karina, but I don't think it's that. I think he's got a bad case of duty and responsibility. That boy of his winds him round his little finger. If there's any problem that Cecil can't deal with, they send for Mr Fletcher and he writes them another cheque. But lately he's been making noises about not being a bottomless well of money.'

'So they really were short of money. Hence the pattern of getting rid of staff without paying them?'

'Seems so. But that's hearsay and may not be true.'

'What about Molly?'

ELEVEN

Friday lunchtime

Mrs Hennessey shrugged. 'Molly? Like I said. Man mad. I used to wonder if she ever put on any pants in the mornings. Likely as not, if she did they'd be shed by lunchtime.'

'How many of the household did she . . .?'

'All the men. Well, perhaps not Cecil. I think he's past it.'

Bea made herself smile. 'And not my husband, I assure you!'

Mrs Hennessey acknowledged with a tiny smile that Bea had made a joke.

Bea continued, 'How about Mr Fletcher?'

There was something about Mr Fletcher which itched at Bea's mind. He came across as something of a saint, but she wasn't sure . . . though she really didn't know why she doubted him.

'Him?' Mrs Hennessey was shocked. 'No, never! She wouldn't appeal to him. He's . . . Well, I reckon he's still in love with his wife that died a while back.'

'Bernie, the chauffeur and odd-job man?'

A nod. 'Just the once, I think, when she first arrived. She'd asked him to mend something for her and he tried it on, recognizing what she was. She said, "All right, then! Just this once!" She clipped him round the head when he tried again. And he did try again, many a time. But no, she was after bigger game.'

Mrs Hennessey hesitated, then said, 'I think she's pregnant and it did occur to me to wonder which of them she'd try to pin it on. Whichever she decides to name, I'd advise him to ask for a paternity test.'

Bea was amused. 'In case Bernie was the father? Yes, that would be a bummer, wouldn't it?'

Mrs Hennessey folded her lips. 'It wouldn't be right.' She settled back in her chair. Her fingers twitched. Her eyes were on the files. She said, 'So, what job have you got for me now? Whatever it is, they'll want references.'

'Mr Fletcher is upstairs now. I'm going to ask him to tear up that release and to give you a shining reference.'

'Will he do it? He's so protective of the family.'

'He seems to have done his best for them over the years but now that the police are involved, secrets are bound to come out. I think I can put enough pressure on him that he'll forget about that release form.'

'I don't really know anything.'

'You know enough to show the police what questions to ask. Let me recap on what I've gathered. The family were running out of money. Mr Fletcher helped out but was getting increasingly stressed. Molly was brought in to write the book, which she did, but she was also the catalyst who upset the apple cart. She intended to use blackmail techniques to extract money and possibly a wedding ring from the family. She probably doesn't know herself who might have sired her unborn child, but each one of the men in that household would have been vulnerable to her demands. She made arrangements to meet whichever of them she fancied best as a prospective husband and planned to take Jolene along with her. And Jolene died. Don't tell me you think that wasn't cause and effect. Jolene died because Molly tried to blackmail someone in Karina's family.'

'Them's harsh words.'

'I know. But you follow how I got there?'

A nod. 'Which of them do you think . . .?'

'You know them better than I.'

Mrs Hennessey's eyes switched left and right, and she frowned. 'It's possible she accused the wrong one? Someone who was not in fact the father, but who was afraid he might be? In which case, it could be any one of them.'

'If she'd tried it on with the boys, might they have alibied one another?'

Mrs Hennessey didn't like that idea, either. 'I suppose that whoever she rang and arranged to meet, *might* have killed in a panic thinking they *might* have been responsible for her child even though he wasn't. If you see what I mean.'

'There are many possibilities, certainly. But whoever it was

– and the police will find out – this can't be covered up. That's why Mr Fletcher won't object to tearing up that release. Now I'll get Vera to sort out those interviews for you.'

Mrs Hennessey got to her feet. 'I'll put my cheque in the bank this afternoon.'

Bea saw Mrs Hennessey safely into Vera's hands and went round the office, having a quick word with everyone in turn. She noted that Lisa was sniffling . . . going down with a cold . . .?

Feeling the need for a spot of quiet reflection, Bea made her way back through her own office and out into the garden.

It was quiet there, except for the muted noise of London traffic in the distance. The high brick walls helped give the impression of this being a place set apart. Trees, bushes, flowers . . . a tiny fountain in the pond . . . the cat Winston sunning himself on a bench . . . a couple of sparrows flew down to investigate the bird-bath but didn't stop to drink after they'd caught sight of the cat.

Bea reflected that the sparrows were wise to avoid a space controlled by a predator. They were wise birds, those sparrows.

Jolene hadn't been wise.

Molly had thought herself wise but might well end up ruing her mistake.

Where was she, anyway? She was the elusive key to the puzzle. She'd set out to better her lot in life and had spread disharmony wherever she went.

Perhaps if she'd gone to work in a different household, temptation wouldn't have led to pregnancy and Jolene's death?

Bea lifted her face to the sun. She was cold to the bone and needed to feel the warmth. Thinking of Jolene made Bea's throat ache. That poor, misguided . . . no, *misled* child!

The kitchen door above opened on to the cast-iron balcony across the back of the house. Piers was in the kitchen, brewing coffee by the sound of it.

Bea didn't want coffee. She felt out of sorts. She looked up and up, checking that the windows for her ward's rooms at the top of the house were closed, which they were. Everything was as it should be, but nothing was right. Poor Jolene!

Bea shook herself. Jolene's death was nothing to do with her, really. She had pried some sort of story out of Mrs Hennessey but it was not her business to take the matter further. The police would ferret out the truth and justice would be done. Piers would get his money in due course, Mrs Hennessey would get a new job, Bea would find a replacement for Jolene and Bob's your uncle. All would be for the best in this best of all possible worlds.

No, it wouldn't.

Dear Lord, what would you have me do? I'm not equipped to be an examining magistrate. I haven't witnessed any crime. I have no idea which of those men has fathered Molly's child. I don't think she knows, either.

The man Molly was to meet might well have silenced the girl lest she jeopardize his cushy life in Karina's household.

Why didn't he throw her out of the car when he realized Jolene was not the person he expected to see? Did Jolene say something like, 'I know who you are!' Or 'Fly, all is discovered!' What excuse could he possibly have made to keep her in the car till he was able to deal with her?

Then again, whether he was the father or not, he might have recruited someone else to silence Molly for him while he created an unbreakable alibi for himself elsewhere.

Oh dear, I can see that happening. One of the boys might have asked the other to help him out.

Or if you take the men, Bernie might have got some lowlife to help him out . . .?

Or Cecil . . .? No, Cecil is too canny to get involved, and there's no reason why he should act as an assassin for anyone else in the household.

Or husband number three, whose name she couldn't remember. No, no. He was a nonentity, wasn't he? A pretty face, that's all.

Or Mr Fletcher – Christopher – himself? No, Piers had taken him to hospital by that time, hadn't he? And he was kept in overnight.

Christopher might have got someone else to do the dirty deed? Oh, that's ridiculous! And yet there is something not quite right about his support for Karina and her mad court. He's gone far beyond the call of duty in trying to help her.

He's upstairs now, with Piers. Why? Shouldn't he be booking himself into some kind of respite care if he can't manage the stairs to his flat? He can't really expect Piers to act as nanny for him, can he?

Bea shook herself back to the present. She was going round and round in her head and going nowhere. She had no proof that anyone in Karina's household was involved.

Come to think of it, if Molly had told Karina she was pregnant by a member of her family, then Karina herself could have organized that Molly be silenced . . . and killed Jolene instead.

No. Ridiculous. Karina had been surprised and disgusted by Molly's revelation, but not fearful.

Dear Lord God, help! I'm stuck.

If you want me to do anything, you'll have to give me a clue. I can't do this by myself.

She paced up and down. She was in no fit state to do any agency work. She was too het up. She wanted to hit somebody or something.

Winston leapt down from his seat and went to sit by the pool. Could he see his own reflection there? And how did cats perceive their reflection, anyway? If at all? Perhaps he was just watching a water boatman scull across the surface?

I have to put aside my own hurt feelings and anger. Piers was not unfaithful to me with Molly but I've allowed the suspicion that he might have been, to prejudice me against the girl. She's a liar, granted, but . . .

This affair is all about money.

No, it began with a shortage of money, which brought Molly and Piers into the house, and threw Mrs Hennessey out of it.

Start again: it began with money but moved on when Molly moved in.

Molly, where are you? You must know your life is in danger! Surely you don't think you can play both ends against the middle and come out on top of this particular heap?

Karina is the top of the heap. I can't see her allowing Molly into her family. So, how will she react to the situation?

Would she banish whoever it was who sired Molly's child? Yes?

Depends which member of the family is responsible. She wouldn't banish Cecil, would she? He's far too valuable. Husband number three? Mm, if she could find another toy boy, perhaps.

One of the sons? No, pride would prevent her doing that. I can see her excusing his 'little lapse' and blaming Molly for

*everything, saying, 'Boys will be boys' and 'What does the girl
expect? Such a tart! Let her have an abortion.' Oh dear. I don't
know.*

A cloud moved across the sun and the air chilled. Everything
changed. Winston decided he needed another snack and took
himself off to climb the stairs to the kitchen. The birds watched
him leave and descended to drink and splash around in the
birdbath.

The trees in the garden darkened. The splashing of the birds
in the water became louder.

It was an illusion that the sound became louder, of course. It
was like being colour-blind. People with normal sight could see
one thing in a picture, while those who were not saw something
quite different. Like those odd illustrations which showed you
either a young woman or an old, depending upon which way
you looked at it.

You could turn your preconceptions of people upside down
and they'd look quite different. Karina would be a heroine, struggling to keep her family together and Christopher Fletcher would
be a villain, scheming to get control of her fortune . . .

Bea laughed at herself, and then stilled. Piers had propped the
kitchen door open but she could no longer hear him. He must
have brewed coffee and taken it into the living room. He was
probably having an enjoyable time with Christopher, talking sport.
Cricket? Did their guest intend to stay for lunch? And why wasn't
he back at his own place? Ah, yes. The stairs. He really ought
to go somewhere with a lift.

Bea decided to point that out to him. She also decided that
she'd wasted enough time. There was something she could do
and she'd better get on with it.

She went back into her office. She knew now what to look
for. Wills and death certificates. Newspaper coverage of the lurid
lives of Karina and her courtiers.

She'd need help with this. Hari was in the office, checking
over a printer which was being temperamental. He looked up
when she came in and said, 'Piers has just been down to say that
unless you've got other plans, he's rustling up some lunch for
us all. Mr Fletcher is talking about going back to the flat after
he's eaten. He says he's sure he can manage the stairs by himself.

I doubt it, myself. Piers offered to help him which is all very noble of him but not sensible.'

Hari grinned. 'Piers says he can see Mr Fletcher's playing the "poor me" card, but doesn't know how to counter it. Piers also says that if we're busy down here, he'll leave something out for us in the kitchen.'

Bea was pleased. 'I'll eat later.' She wondered if she might ask Hari to help them in her search for background on Karina's family after he'd had some lunch. Well, why not? He'd be good at that.

She said to the office at large, 'Hari; everyone. Would you all stop what you're doing for a moment? I'd like you to join me in doing something for Jolene. I want to find out if her death had anything to do with Karina and her family's relationships. If any of you can set aside what you're doing for an hour or so, I'd be grateful. I'll give you each a name to research: births, deaths, marriages, divorces and gossip columns. Print out anything you find and bring it to me.'

Hari eyed the desk which was vacant because the girl using it had gone home. He said, 'I'm on it as soon as I've fed my face upstairs.'

Lisa said she was sure she was going down with something and might have to take the rest of the day off. It crossed Bea's mind that Lisa was going to report in sick and not return. It would, perhaps, be a good idea to check that the woman didn't take any of the agency's keys home with her, just in case.

The others liked the idea of being able to do something for Jolene. Each took a name and got on with it.

As did Bea. She'd reserved Lance Fletcher for herself as it meant going back into newspaper reports, as well as looking up his will. She discovered there was quite a lot of news coverage of his life and death.

Printers went into overdrive.

After nearly an hour, Bea collected everything that had been found and laid it out, collating the pages so that she had a time-scale of events. Eureka! One of the girls had found something which explained Christopher's behaviour.

Hari came into her office, fingering his smartphone. He said, 'You've missed your lunch. Piers would make a good short-order cook, wouldn't he? Soup and sandwiches. Look, do you need me this afternoon? Something's come up. The man I left looking after the pop star says I'm needed, sharpish. I'll be a couple of hours, back by six, probably. Everything's quiet here, isn't it?'

It was and it wasn't. Yes, superficially it was as normal. Only Bea's antenna was informing her that something, somewhere, had gone very badly wrong. She told herself that they were all waiting for the police to come and ask them about Jolene. Unfinished business. Oh, poor Jolene.

What about Molly? If the girl didn't tell the police that she'd arranged to meet Jolene, then how would they know her death wasn't a random knife attack? A nasty thought.

Hari was fidgeting to go. And surely . . . four hours or so? Not a problem. She said, 'Of course you must go,' and made herself look happy about it.

Once he'd disappeared, Bea checked that the girls were all right, back at work, some eating their lunches while they did so, some making a cuppa for themselves.

Lisa, however, said again that she thought she was going down with flu and went home. She took her personal belongings with her but left her office keys behind.

Bea wasn't sure whether to be pleased that Lisa was clearly leaving the agency, or annoyed that she'd done it when they were one person down already. Fortunately Vera seemed willing to step into the breach. Bea went over the office procedures with Vera, saying it was best to cover these in case poor Lisa were not able to return to work for a few days.

This excuse didn't fool anyone but everyone accepted it at face value. It seemed to Bea that the girls settled back down to work again with more enthusiasm. Evidently they liked and trusted Vera, as did Bea.

She was about to go upstairs when one of the girls signalled that a call had come in for Bea. It was Jolene's father.

Bea returned to her office to answer it.

'Mrs Abbot?' A voice thickened by catarrh. He'd been weeping?

'It's Jolene's dad here. I know you're a busy woman, but we thought you'd like to know they've caught him. The man. He was in the very act of attacking another girl. It doesn't bear thinking about. But at least this time the girl survived. Not like our Jolene. If they'd only caught him earlier! They said he'd killed three other girls he'd picked up. Raped, knifed and dumped.'

Bea sat down with a thump. *They'd caught one of Karina's men trying to kill another girl?* She said, 'That's good news!'

'I keep thinking, if they'd known he attacked women in the past, couldn't they have prevented this? They said he was in and out of care, in and out of prison since he left school, not that he attended that much, anyway. They say they'd had their eye on him for a while and they suspected some other girls' deaths were down to him, but they could never catch him in the act till last night. I reckon nobody cared enough because they was all black girls. But Jolene wasn't on the prowl, if you know what I mean. She wasn't like that.'

'No, she wasn't.'

'Jolene must have been in the wrong place at the wrong time. Ten minutes later and he wouldn't have seen her. The police say he used to pass that way going home from work, not that it was much of a job, hanging around the petrol station, supposed to be cleaning cars and such. He wasn't the type to appeal to my Jolene. Why she ever got into his car beats me.'

He said, 'I wish he'd admitted killing Jolene, but he's the sort that's learned to say "no comment" to everything. They've got all the evidence they need from the one he attacked late last night. She survived and is willing to testify against him. They'll charge him with her assault and rape and leave the other cases on file. This means they won't be charging him with Jolene's death. I'm not clear in my mind whether that's a good thing or not.'

Hang about! Is this really something to do with Karina and her family?

Bea said, 'If they don't want to name Jolene, at least there won't be so much publicity.'

A deep sigh. 'I tell myself that. And they'll let us have the body for burial after the inquest.'

'Let me know when the funeral is to be. I'd like to attend and I'm sure some of the others would, as well.'

Another deep sigh. 'Sure. You'll think it strange I'm ringing you up like this—'

'Not at all. I'm glad you did. We were all worried sick about her.'

'The thing is . . . It's awkward like . . . I wouldn't mention it but it's going to cost an arm and a leg . . . Can you get Molly to cough up at least some of what she owes us? It's been months now, and she said she was nearly at the end of her contract and would be able to repay us in full. Not that we didn't take her in gladly, for her mum's sake. They go back a long way and we was that proud that Molly was getting on so well.'

Molly owed them money? Yes, of course she did! That girl deserves . . . I don't know what! A good shaking, for a start.

Bea said, 'I believe her contract has finished, but there was some confusion about how she was to be paid. The book has been delivered to the publishers. If I see Molly, I'll tell her you rang and—'

'What! Isn't she staying with you? In your mews cottage? She told us she was moving into—'

'I'm sorry to tell you this, but Molly was not always truthful. She is not staying in the mews. I gave her a bed here last night, but she left this morning and I don't know where she is now. And frankly, I don't want to know.'

Long, heavy breathing at the other end of the phone.

Bea said, 'I'm so sorry. It must be one more worry for you to—'

'The wife's in pieces. She can't stop crying. She can't go in to work and nor can I. I've tried phoning Molly but she doesn't pick up. I feel so helpless. Molly knows we find it hard to make ends meet sometimes and our other daughter got married last year which cleaned out our savings. Are you sure you can't get hold of Molly?'

'I'm in touch with someone who's been involved in the arrangements for Molly's work at Karina's. I'll ask him to contact you about the money she's owed. Jolene's also owed some wages for her work here at the agency. I'll look into that.'

Another long silence. And then what sounded like a gulp . . . and the phone contact was broken.

Bea picked up the file of paperwork and threw it down into the wastepaper basket. She dusted off her hands. Well, that was that!

Jolene had stepped into the wrong car and been killed for her pains. Her death had nothing whatever to do with Molly and her shenanigans. Nothing!

The police weren't going to take the matter of Jolene's death any further. They would prosecute the man who'd been going around attacking and killing young black girls on the evidence of the one that had got away. The killer would go to prison and that would be that.

Nobody was going to take up Jolene's case. The matter was settled. Full stop. Done. Jolene stepped into the wrong car. Her misfortune.

It was nothing to do with Karina and Molly and someone getting the girl pregnant.

Molly would waltz off into the blue, Karina would get all the kudos for her book and Jolene would be forgotten by all except for her parents, who would miss her for all sorts of reasons, not least of which was her wage packet.

Bea remembered the tiny teddy which Jolene had taped to the top of her computer screen. Lucky teddy. Lucky for some but not for Jolene.

Bea could clear out Jolene's desk now and advertise for another operative.

She wanted to scream and stamp her feet and break something. Oh, Molly! What harm you do to everyone you meet!

Mind you, if Molly hadn't told us that she'd arranged for Jolene to meet with her to discuss bringing pressure on someone in Karina's family, then Bea wouldn't have wasted everyone's time on digging up the dirt on Karina and Co.

The fact was that Jolene had stepped into a car expecting Molly to join her. Molly wasn't far off down the road and had seen what had happened. If Molly hadn't confided in Jolene about her problem at work, then Jolene wouldn't have been on that road, waiting for a car to meet them.

Jolene wasn't a tart. She didn't sell herself for money. There was no way she would have stepped into a car with a view to giving sex.

Did that mean Jolene had not been attacked by this serial rapist and killer? Her case did not fit into the rest of the list which the police were ascribing to the man they'd arrested . . . or did it?

The police are not going to do anything about it because they think they have the killer already. Nobody except Molly is going

to upset that comfortable conclusion, and Molly won't because
. . . because she wants to blackmail the person concerned . . .?

And now she's conveniently disappeared.

And nobody is going to do anything about it, unless . . .

Well, there is one person who might be persuaded to take
action, if only she could prod him into doing so.

Bea made up her mind. She retrieved the file from the wastepaper bin and took it upstairs. She was starving, had missed
lunch. So first she would eat, and then she would see what she
could do to even up the odds.

TWELVE

Friday afternoon

Three hungry men had been in the kitchen before her.
Mr Fletcher – Christopher – probably didn't have a big
appetite but Piers and Hari had made up for him.

There was hardly anything left: half a cup of soup and the
heel of a loaf of bread, only two eggs and a scrap of cheese.
She'd have to organize a food shop tomorrow.

To make matters worse, Piers hadn't bothered to take another
loaf out of the freezer to defrost, he'd left their used crockery
on the table, the cutlery drawer had been ransacked and left open,
and her best kitchen knife was missing from the magnetic strip
above the chopping board. Also her favourite mug.

It wasn't like Piers to be so messy, but there; it happened.
Even though the door into the living room from the hall was fast
shut, she could hear the telly was on next door, with the volume
turned up high. Perhaps Christopher was a trifle deaf?

She scrambled the eggs and brewed a cuppa, then went through
the papers again to make sure she had the sequence of events
clear in her mind. Something jumped out at her. A date. The date
of one of Karina's divorces, followed closely by the date of the
next marriage.

Bea looked for the date of Teddy's birth. Ah, yes. Interesting.

She checked forward and then went back and . . . Gotcha! How had Molly treated that event in her book?

Bea put the used crockery into the dishwasher, turned it on and went through to the living room to find the men perfectly relaxed and enjoying themselves. There were yet more used coffee cups here. Piers' travelling chess set had been in use and left open on a side table and the two men were watching a cricket match on the telly. Christopher's foot was up on a stool, and his tie was undone, indicating he was in a relaxed mood.

Bea, however, was not in holiday mood.

Piers straightened up in his chair, recognizing storm signals. 'Sorry. Bit of a mess. We were discussing where Christopher might take a holiday. He hasn't been away since his wife died.'

Bea had more important things to think about than holidays. She said, 'Sorry to interrupt, but this is important.' She switched off the telly and sat down with her bulging file of papers on the coffee table before her.

Christopher wasn't as quick as Piers to recognize an amber alert. 'There's a problem?'

Bea said, 'Christopher, I don't think you've been entirely frank with us. You appeared to be very open when you told us about your connection with Karina, but I've been doing some research and what I've found has caused me to consider what you've said in a different light.'

He wiped the smile off his face and sat more upright. He knew what she'd found, didn't he?

Piers also stiffened to attention. He fumbled in his pocket for something . . . his smartphone and laid it on the table beside her papers. To remind him he had to make a call later?

Bea said, 'To recap. Karina's first marriage was to a businessman. At that time she was an up-and-coming star in great demand and her husband didn't like playing second fiddle to her career. She had various well-publicized affairs, but none were serious till she met your brother Lance. She obtained a divorce from her first husband and their son Alexander went to live with his grandparents on his father's side. I can't find any mention of alimony for Karina and I don't think any was agreed on because of her affair with Lance.

'Now this first husband of hers died of drink a couple of years after their divorce. Here's a copy of his death certificate – natural causes – and one of his will. After probate, newspapers publish details of how much a deceased's estate amounts to. Karina's first husband didn't leave much, did he? And neither did Alexander's grandparents when they also died a couple of years ago, but at least they'd lived long enough to see Alexander go to university and be theoretically capable of earning his own living. My interpretation of these events is that Karina didn't come out of her first marriage with a fortune. Rather the reverse. She had very little to show for it. Do you agree?'

She held out some papers to Christopher, who waved them away, saying, 'Yes, yes.'

Bea handed the papers to Piers, who leafed through them and nodded.

Bea continued, 'So much for the first marriage. Now for the second. When Karina met Lance Fletcher they fell for one another big time. He was the darling of the tabloids; he was landed gentry with a country estate and a good income while she was the most famous, most beautiful, most daring of starlets. What could possibly go wrong?'

Christopher put his handkerchief to his lips. 'They were well matched. A handsome pair.'

'Indeed. But according to the gossip columns of the newspapers this second marriage was tumultuous. One minute the couple were all lovey-dovey, and the next at one another's throats. They had a child, Teddy. They separated, they reunited. Lance bought a big house in Belgravia and they partied the nights away. She worked hard but still that invitation to Hollywood eluded her. He wanted to beat world records in flying solo, climbing the highest mountain, racing the fastest car, and diving in the deepest oceans. They lived life in the fast lane, but somebody, somehow, managed to get him to make a will, which turned out to be fortunate indeed. Was that someone you, Christopher?'

'Er, yes. I worried for him, and for little Teddy. I couldn't see it ending happily.'

'It didn't. Did you help your brother decide what to put in his will?'

'No, I knew nothing about it until—'

'He died. Fair enough. Here is your brother's death certificate. Accident. I heard a rumour that he was pushed to his death down the stairs but I see no reason to believe it. Do you?'

Christopher shifted in his seat. 'He got into a shouting match with Karina. She threw something at him, he ducked but in doing so he slipped and fell down two flights of stairs. The housekeeper witnessed it, as did the nanny. I spoke to both of them. They were shocked but quite clear that both Lance and Karina were drunk at the time.'

Bea said, 'I've seen newspaper pictures of her at the inquest. She looked ravishing in black. Now, I've a copy of your brother's will here. He appointed you as his executor and as Teddy's guardian in the event of his death. You told us that the country house and estate were left in trust to Teddy and that the balance of your brother's estate went to Karina. In fact, that didn't mean much because he owed money everywhere.'

'Yes. His debts were staggering.'

Bea said, 'He could trust you to do your best for the boy. From what I have observed, that guardianship has been a thankless task.'

'Well, yes. But he's young . . . and I'm feeling older by the day.' He tried to make a joke of it, but he did indeed look old and tired.

Bea said, 'What you omitted to tell us was that Lance also left you the London house, heavily mortgaged but potentially valuable. Was it his way of repaying you for everything you were going to have to do for Teddy? Or was it his way of making sure you'd keep an eye on Karina?'

Christopher managed a painful smile. 'Both. I asked Karina if she wanted to take on the house and pay the mortgage, but she'd finally got a contract to go to Hollywood and she wanted a clean break with the past. I've been paying the mortgage all these years. Thankfully, it was up last month.'

'Did you ever think of declining to clean up the mess your brother had left?'

Christopher shrugged. 'How could I? He'd asked me to look after Karina and Teddy. He knew she'd no idea how to handle money. She was paid enormous sums from the time she went to America and she spent even more. I advised her to invest some portion of her earnings but she preferred to let various boyfriends handle her money. I don't think any of them knew what they were doing. She didn't want Teddy with her any more than she'd wanted Alexander. My wife and I had our own place in Wimbledon so it made sense to rent out Lance's big house to cover the mortgage and the maintenance of the house in Belgravia. It also went some way to repaying Lance's debts.'

Bea said, 'I suppose you yourself covered Teddy's school and university fees? With careful husbandry I imagine you've managed to pay off Lance's debts and have kept the country house and estate in good nick. Yes?'

He nodded. 'True.'

'Ah, yes. According to the gossip sheets, Karina remained single for many years though she had a number of "escorts". But then' – Bea waved another piece of paper – 'she succumbed to the charms of Simon, a handsome if second-rate British actor. They had a splashy Hollywood marriage costing the earth. Simon had done well in character parts but then he persuaded Karina to put money into a film which would give him a starring role. The film bombed, leaving them in debt.'

She handed Piers a review of the film and its leading man. 'Suddenly, Karina was forced to face reality. Her new husband was a liability instead of an asset and, perhaps worse still, fashion had moved on and her type of looks were no longer in demand. She was ageing and her reputation for being temperamental was not helping matters. So . . .'

Bea handed over more paperwork. 'She divorced Simon and married a visiting British businessman, Cecil, who had no charisma but had recently retired with a nice big pension pot. He promised to look after Karina for ever and ever and probably had no idea what he was committing himself to. So the couple came back to England where she demanded you turf your tenants out and allow her to move back into "her" house. And you did. Major mistake, if I may say so.'

Christopher said, 'She was supposed to pay the mortgage. Cecil managed the first six months but . . . it was impossible.'

'I can only imagine,' said Bea. 'How did it go? She ran up more debts. He struggled to clear them. Her sons moved back in, and then Simon turned up needing a bed and she invited him in, too. The question is, why on earth did she do that?'

He reddened. 'I believe . . . he's good in bed. And he's useful to her in a thousand little ways. He's a reasonable cook. He fetches and carries for her.'

Bea rolled her eyes. 'All right, I suppose. Provided Cecil doesn't mind.'

'Well . . .' He guested helplessly. 'I've never quite understood how they can share . . . But she does need a lot of attention and perhaps Cecil . . . and he has done his best to rein in her lifestyle. Only she takes no notice.'

Bea said, 'So the problem, instead of being far away on the other side of the Pond, was now living on your doorstep, and to make matters worse, Teddy got involved. Bills for the household came in and were left unpaid. Housekeepers came and went. How long did it take you to realize Karina sacked people to avoid paying their wages?'

He grimaced. 'I couldn't believe it at first. When it happened a second time—'

'You made up the difference to the servants she'd abused and took over the hiring and firing yourself. I suppose it was you who came up with the idea of the book to earn some money?'

'I thought it might help. I drummed it into her that she needed to downsize or to kickstart her career somehow. She liked the idea of telling her story to the world. I negotiated the contract with the publisher, who were doubtful at first because she's been so long out of the limelight but they agreed in the end, provided she took on a ghostwriter. So then I had to find one. Molly had a degree but was inexperienced and therefore charged less than the professionals. I thought she was worth a try. Fortunately Karina took to her, so she seemed a good choice.'

'Was it Molly who came up with the idea of Piers painting Karina?'

'Yes. I had some idea of how much he charged and tried to divert her, but once Karina got the idea into her head . . .!' He spread his hands in resignation.

'Piers' charges are high.'

'I realized that. Karina couldn't afford him. She threw a tantrum . . . Oh, my poor head! In the end I agreed pay for it, on the

understanding it would have to be sold immediately the publishers
had finished with it. When I told her that, she threw a vase at
me and I left in a hurry. It solved a big problem for me when
Piers took the portrait direct to the publishers. And from there
it will have to go to be sold. Quick thinking on his part, and I'm
grateful.'

'Which bring us,' said Bea, 'to Molly, who strolled into Karina's
toxic little circle thinking it would be her passport to a starry
lifestyle. I'm hoping she did a reasonable job on producing the
memoirs. The publishers will no doubt be getting back to her with
all sorts of queries, but if she's done the job reasonably well, the
market should open up for her. If she'd only confined herself to
being a ghostwriter, she'd have been all set for the future.

'Unfortunately, she couldn't keep her pants on. She says – and
I have no reason to doubt it – that she's slept with all the males
in Karina's household, excluding Cecil but including the handyman. Do you think sleeping with the men was part of her plan
from the beginning to forward her career? Did she see an opportunity to entangle one or more of them in her net? Or is she
simply man-mad?'

Christopher blushed. 'She . . . er . . . I couldn't believe . . . I
had to tell her that I was old enough to be her grandfather!'

Bea was amused. 'You turned her down, too? I gather Cecil
did the same. And then Molly found out she was pregnant. Now
she really did have something to sell. She had no idea which
of the men had fathered her child, but she decided she was going
to blackmail her way into a big pay-off. A wedding ring or a
ticket for life. I don't think she understood that what the world
saw – a famous film star living in a big house with servants and
a possible bestselling book to her name – was a false picture.
She didn't understand that money was short. No, she set up a
meeting with whoever it was she'd decided was the father of her
child, planning to bargain her way to a brilliant future.

'She shared her plans with her "cousin", poor, star-dazzled
Jolene, who'd put Molly on a pedestal and would do whatever
she wanted. Now Molly had enough sense to take precautions
about meeting with her lover, and asked Jolene to go with her
to the rendezvous. How excited Jolene must have been! From
making the tea and taking messages here at the agency, from

being the youngest and least regarded of the staff, from living in a high-rise block of flats and facing a future in which the high spot would probably be marrying a low-paid worker in similar circumstances, she was being given a glimpse of the Never Never Land of film and television stars, of podcasts and riches galore.

'Molly was late to the tryst. The man drove up and looked out for Molly. Jolene, thrilled to dip her toe into this world of intrigue, stepped into the car. She must have said that Molly was just coming, and that sealed her fate. She was whisked away, killed and dumped like so much garbage.'

Christopher winced. 'Why? Why did this man – whoever he was – kill a girl he'd never seen before?'

'Because he'd admitted to being the father of Molly's child simply by turning up at the prearranged spot at that time. Whoever got into that car with him could now recognize and identify him. I don't suppose for a minute that he had any intention of making a deal with Molly. None of Karina's men had the money to buy Molly off, and I don't think any of them were prepared to marry her. The man in the car had come prepared with a knife. He'd intended to use it on Molly but found himself confronted by Jolene instead.'

Christopher wagged his head from side to side. 'No, no! That's too appalling to contemplate. You really think that it was Teddy who might have . . .? No, I can't believe it. I won't believe it.'

Bea said, very gently, 'Teddy is one of four people who had sex with her. It might not be him. It might have been Alexander.'

He nodded, much relieved. 'Yes, Alexander. Of course. It must have been him. Teddy wouldn't have known anything about it.'

'How do you think Teddy will react if Alexander asks him for an alibi?'

Christopher gaped. He hadn't thought of that. 'No, surely not. He wouldn't, would he? But Teddy . . .! No, we've brought him up to respect the law. I can see how difficult it would be for him to refuse Alexander but . . .' His voice shook. He'd no faith that Teddy would refuse.

A girl had died and his nephew might have been responsible. It was a lot to take in.

There was a long, long silence.

Piers sat so still that he might have been a statue.

Christopher stared into the future, not liking what he saw. What would he decide? He'd gone along with everything Teddy had thrown at him in the past. If he ran true to form, he'd say that Teddy couldn't possibly have tangled with Molly, could never have carried a knife or used it, and that he would undoubtedly have an innocent explanation as to where he'd been the previous night. Blood ties trip you up and hamstring you for life.

But he was a fundamentally decent man and to cover up a murder might be one step too far.

Bea waited. The police had closed the case on Jolene. If Christopher decided to back Teddy, then there was very little hope of the truth ever coming to light.

He surprised her. 'What does Molly say? Perhaps she can identify the car and clear Teddy of all involvement.'

'She's gone missing.'

'Has she been killed, too?' There was horror in his voice.

Piers said, 'God forbid.'

Bea felt a chill run down her back. 'I hadn't thought of that. I hope not. That's a dreadful thought.'

Piers said, 'Christopher, it's understandable that you don't like to think Teddy has fathered a child on Molly. You can't bear to think he'd carry a knife and use it. But you realize that if Teddy has killed one girl, he won't feel safe till he's silenced Molly as well? You say he's not to blame. You're almost sure of it. You'd like to be a hundred per cent sure, but that's not possible unless we can find out who really did it.'

Christopher said, 'It's all too much. The last straw. You never stop worrying about children, do you? I feel we failed, my wife and I. I can't think Teddy's murdered anyone but yes, he's turned into someone I don't recognize. I blame Alexander. When they first met up, Alexander was the leader because he was older and knew more about the world. Recently this has changed because Teddy is going to inherit a fortune, and Alexander only has what he earns. So now they're more equal.

'Even so, I think it would have been Alexander who had sex with Molly first. And surely . . . No, I'm lying to myself again. Making excuses. I'm tired and disappointed and want shot of the whole business. My wife and I did our best with Teddy but it's no use deceiving ourselves. He's not going to settle down in the country. He'll probably sell the old house and estate to fund his cockamamie ideas.'

He choked and put his handkerchief to his mouth for a moment. 'You've been so kind, listening to me. You've made me see that this situation can't go on however unpleasant it's going to make life in the immediate future. If he killed that girl, then I'll see that he gets a solicitor to defend him, but for the rest, I have to make a stand.'

Piers said, 'We understand that you feel battered and defeated by events. But if you've served twenty years of martyrdom to the family, it doesn't mean you have to serve another ten or twenty – or even another one. You've fulfilled the task which your brother laid on you, at a high cost to yourself. You say you want to draw a line under the past. How do you want to do that?'

Christopher made a restless movement. 'You mustn't think I've been unaware of the way things have been going. I've spent hours worrying about it, considering various scenarios, making tentative plans . . . and then putting off the day when I need to put them into practice. I know what I ought to do; I should stop giving in to Teddy. Nothing else will help him to develop into a man who takes his responsibilities seriously. I know the consequences of any such action on my part are going to be unpleasant. To tell you the truth, I have one great weakness: I dislike people shouting at me. It dates back to childhood, when my father . . . I learned to put up with it at work but Teddy has been so dear to me that . . .

'I see clearly enough that I should have stopped him in his tracks before this.' He tried to smile but couldn't hold it. 'You'll laugh. Just over a week ago we had yet another confrontation. He wanted me to back him in an application to borrow money to produce a film! Simon was to direct and Karina to star in it. He's no idea what it would entail, or the amount of money required. I turned him down, of course, so he said he was going to sue me for mismanaging his estate. I was so angry, so shocked that I acted in haste. It's not like me. I usually mull things over and take advice, but this time I was so incensed that I actually did something about it.'

'What did you do?' asked Piers.

'I went to see my partner in the law firm we ran together for twenty-five years or more. I discussed the matter with him; not for the first time I might say. He thinks I've been weak in not acting sooner. And he's right. So I asked him to prepare a new will, disinheriting Teddy. I also asked him to start the process of evicting Karina so that I could put that big house on the market. And then, of course, I went home, calmed down and had second thoughts. The papers are ready for me to sign but I've been putting it off day by day.

'And now . . . the situation has got out of control. If Teddy is arrested . . . I'm sure he didn't do it, but I know I'm biased. If he did . . . No, I can't believe it. But if Molly is dead, too? I can't ignore what's happened. I only wish I could. No, I do see that the time has come to take action. It will force Teddy to face reality. Or will it? If he turned on Alexander . . . but what if Alexander turned on him? Would he give in? Or would he step back, give himself time to rethink?'

There was silence. Bea thought that only Christopher could make a decision in this case. She knew what she'd have done in his place . . . Or would she? The ties of blood are stronger than common sense.

His eyes were a little brighter. 'Yes. It's time to act. If only my dear wife were here to hold my hand and tell me I'm doing the right thing. I miss her. Well, now. What do I do first? Ah, how about if I can get an appointment to see my partner today and sign those papers?'

He fumbled for his smartphone. His hands shook, but he managed to make the call. His voice grew stronger as he said what he wanted done. And then he listened to his friend's voice . . . and listened.

Finally he clicked the phone off, saying, 'He'll see me at five. He's also going to see what steps we have to take for someone else to take over Teddy's guardianship. I must admit, it would be an enormous relief to be rid of the responsibility. One thing, he suggests sending copies of everything round to Karina's place tonight. I think he's afraid I might change my mind again. He also advises I make myself scarce this evening, drop out of sight for a while, let Teddy come to terms with the future before we meet again. He suggests I go to a hotel where no one knows me for the weekend. Actually, that's not a bad idea because of my ankle. I need somewhere with a lift. My partner's gone all cloak and dagger on me, saying I mustn't answer my smartphone but get a "burner" phone and only give him the number.'

He passed his hand over his forehead. 'I'm exhausted. I know he's right, but . . . ah, if only my dear wife were here to make the arrangements for me. In the old days, I'd say that we should go away for the weekend or a holiday and she'd make all the arrangements; packing up; organizing someone to look after the flat; everything. Pathetic, isn't it?'

Bea said, 'You've come to the right place. I have people on my books who can make all the arrangements for you. They often have to arrange travel and accommodation for overseas businesspeople. I can get someone here within the hour who would take care of everything. You have your cards on you? Good. All you have to do is instruct me to find someone to take on the job for you. She can pack a bag for you, book you a hotel and a car to take you there. She can also buy you a new phone, whose number you will keep to yourself.'

A flicker of amusement. He said, 'And someone to cut up my food when I eat?'

Bea smiled. 'You'll do. Remember the only person who gets your new phone number is your partner.'

'Would you mind if I kept in touch with you, too? Oh, the relief! But there's guilt, too. Tell me I'm not running away from my responsibilities?'

'You are only running away so that you can fight again another day and flush out a murderer.'

'Ah,' he said. 'I can see that that's your priority. I regret that it's not mine. I feel slightly guilty about that but no, I can't believe that Teddy was involved in any way with that girl's death. What was her name, JoJo? I wish you well with that, and I hope that Molly turns up alive and well and . . .' He managed a faint chuckle. 'Ready to take on all comers. Would you allow me to stay here till you can find me a chaperone? And perhaps I may visit the facilities again?'

Christopher was recovering as he saw his heavy burdens slipping away from him. And of course he needed to visit the loo.

Bea said, 'Of course.' She switched the television back on. Christopher was going to be around for a couple of hours at least. She said, 'Make yourself at home and I'll sort you out a nice, old-fashioned nanny who will look after you beautifully.' She signalled to Piers and went out to the kitchen to access the internal phone. *Who would be best to deal with Christopher?*

Piers followed her, shutting the door behind him. He said, 'Well done. It doesn't get us far with Jolene's murder, but—'

'It'll stir things up nicely.'

'I'm with Christopher; anything for a quiet life. What you've pushed him into doing is like stirring a wasps' nest with a stick. He's right to run away. I suspect the whole boiling lot of them will descend on us when they can't find him. I suggest we decamp to foreign parts, too.'

'An attractive proposition, but we can't run away. Too much to do,' said Bea, getting through to Vera on the internal phone. 'Vera, I'll be down in a minute. Can you find out if one of our tour guides is available to babysit a retired solicitor who's been through a hard time and urgently needs to get away from a nasty situation at home?' She detailed what Mr Fletcher needed.

Vera said, 'I think Marina's just finished shepherding a group around. Shall I ask her?'

'Brilliant. A bonus if she can get here within the hour.'

Piers busied himself taking clean crockery out of the dishwasher.

Bea clicked off the phone, saying, 'I'd better get downstairs. We're two people short. Can you organize something for supper? Will Christopher need something to eat before he goes? Oh, and what did you do with my big carving knife?'

'Mm? Haven't touched it.' He reached for the stack of menus from local restaurants. 'Shall we have a takeaway tonight? Do you fancy Greek for a change? We seem to be short of cheese. I thought we'd got enough for the weekend, but . . . Whatever's the matter?'

Bea clasped her arms around herself. Was that a chilly breeze coming from the open back door? 'You haven't seen my knife?'

'You told me that the only crimes worthy of death in this household were to remove your scissors or the big knife. I haven't touched either.'

Bea's mouth was dry. 'Piers! I know where Molly is!'

THIRTEEN

Friday, late afternoon

Bea said again, 'I know where Molly is. Don't you see? Food's gone missing. And my knife! She was with us on Thursday night when Hari asked if the top floor had been locked up and I said yes, because Bernice wasn't due back this weekend. Molly overheard, so she knew no one was living on the top floor and that the door to it was locked. She stayed last night in our guest room but this morning when I told her to leave I didn't stand over her to see that she actually did go, which was a big mistake. Because what did she do?

'She left me in the office and came upstairs into the hall. There she'd have heard you and Christopher happily chatting away to one another in the living room. She didn't have anywhere to go. She would have remembered that the top floor here was empty. Perhaps she looked for the key to Bernice's quarters? She didn't find the key because I keep it in a box on the wall in the hall. But she grabbed some food from the kitchen and took my large knife, not to use on anyone – God forbid! – but to prise open the door to the top flat.'

'Molly is upstairs? Armed with a knife? When's Hari coming back?'

Bea reached for her phone and got him on the line.

Hari sounded grim. 'Sorry. Ought to have got back to you sooner. My faded rock star says he's actually been attacked by his stalker. He's not badly hurt but there's a lot of blood and he's ging to have to go to A & E for a stitch or two. He's yelling for twenty-four-hour protection. I'm toying with the idea that he's set the whole thing up as a publicity stunt, but I can't get away just yet. I don't want to let you down. How desperate are you on a scale of one to ten?'

'We think Molly's taken my big carving knife and broken into Bernice's rooms at the top of the house. If I sound wobbly, it's because a knife was involved in Jolene's murder. I don't think for a minute that Molly killed Jolene, but the thought of her going around with my knife is alarming. I tell myself that she wouldn't use it. Of course not, but still . . .' Bea tried to laugh. 'How on earth are we going to get her out of the house?'

'Don't tackle her. She might not think of using the knife ordinarily but if driven into a corner . . .'

Bea was silent. That's what she'd been thinking, too.

Hari said, 'Look, I'll try to get my pop star stabilized and get back to you soonest.'

'Yes, please. As soon as you can.'

She put the phone down. Piers looked a question.

Be said, 'Dealing with an emergency. I don't think Molly took the knife to use as a weapon. No, no. She wouldn't!'

Or would she? Hari clearly thought she'd use it if cornered.

No need to pass her panic on to Piers. She said, 'Molly needed a place to hide. She's not got enough money to go to a hotel, and I don't think she'd be welcome back at Jolene's. She's stolen enough food to keep her going for a while, and no one's going to look for her up there, are they? It's a safe house for her. From this house she can contact anyone she likes by phone. She can dictate her terms to whoever she decides is to be the father of her child.'

Bea went on with gathering confidence. 'If she's after money and isn't bothered about a wedding ring, she can ask for cash to be transferred to her bank account and if she's got internet banking, she can check on her smartphone that it's been done. She can then book herself into an abortion clinic and summon a taxi and hey presto! She picks a moment when we're otherwise occupied, waltzes down the stairs and out of the house to freedom. With money behind her, she can then go wherever she likes. Perhaps apply for a live-in job somewhere. We'll probably never hear from her again.'

Piers said, 'And if she's after a wedding ring?'

'I think she'll go for a lump sum. Getting a wedding ring would pose greater risk of discovery. Remember that someone in Karina's circle has already murdered once to avoid detection and she's got to be careful.'

The murderer must be one of the boys, with the other one backing him up. Christopher is well out of it.

Piers stared down at his hands. 'It's ridiculous to be frightened of Molly.'

Bea attempted a smile. 'If Bernice were here, she'd make short shrift of Molly.'

'So she would. It's sobering to think that a fifteen-year-old schoolgirl can cope with Molly better than two adults. I must admit I don't fancy my chances against an angry woman armed with a long knife, so I've decided to think of this as a hostage situation. Molly can't have taken enough food to see her through the weekend. Surely I should be able to lure her out with the promise of a hot meal and a return to the guest room? Or yes; an appeal to her vanity should do it.'

The internal phone rang. It was Vera, advising that Bea had a caller waiting downstairs. Marina, the tour guide who'd been summoned to look after Christopher.

Piers set off up the stairs. 'Send an ambulance if I'm not back in an hour's time.'

Christopher appeared from the downstairs loo, looking agitated. He said, 'When will my minder arrive? Do you know her well? Is she reliable? Can she keep her mouth shut?'

Bea managed a smile for Christopher. 'I think your protection officer has arrived. I'm just going down to check.'

She took the stairs down, wondering if Piers was being fool-hardy in trying to tackle an armed Molly on his own. Ought they not get the police on to it? But on what grounds? Trespass? Maybe. But how to explain that her presence was not welcome without raising the subject of Jolene's death, which the police had written off as solved?

Personally, Bea would like to chain Molly to a chair under harsh lighting and give her the third degree. If only Molly could be treated like other uninvited guests such as rats and mice! There was a Trace and Despatch team at the town hall which could be called upon to deal with vermin. And yes, it helped a lot to think of Molly as a rat, scrabbling around, always on the lookout for the next meal . . .

However, Vera had come up trumps, and a cool, fortyish blonde was even now waiting for Bea.

'Marina!' said Bea. 'Good to see you again.'

'Likewise.' A faint American accent even after all these years of living in the UK. Marina was a comfortably-off widow who kept herself amused by acting as a tour guide on occasion. She spoke five languages fluently and looked like a catwalk model. She would have Christopher eating out of her hand in five minutes.

'Come upstairs and be introduced to your charge.' Bea filled Marina in on some details as they went up to the ground floor.

Marina nodded. 'Families! I'll let you know where he'll be staying, and his new telephone number.'

'Brilliant. If we act quickly enough, there should be no need to fear family intrusions, but when they do find out he's gone missing there may be ructions. I suggest he puts a message on his smartphone directing all queries to his solicitor, right?'

'Good idea. I'll see to it.'

Christopher was in the hall, shifting from one foot to the other. 'I've just realized that if I'm away for more than the weekend I'll need to get my post redirected and advise my cleaner. There's so much to be done. This running-away business is making me feel quite shaky.'

'No worries,' said Marina, extending her hand to him. 'I'm Marina and I'm your personal assistant for as long as you need me. Shall we be on our way? I expect you'd like to go home and show me what you need to pack before we arrive at your solicitor's at five? I've a taxi waiting for us outside and you can fill me in on which part of the UK you'd like to holiday in as we go along.'

Her manner was, Bea noted, exactly balanced between friendliness and authority. Christopher put his hand in hers, and visibly allowed his fears to slip away and something else to take their place. Shedding ten years, he said, 'Nice to meet you, Marina. Perhaps you will allow me to treat you to supper one day when the dust has settled?'

Bea tried not to laugh at the thought of the tough chick Marina being treated to supper by this retired solicitor, and then it was her turn to have a rethink, for the tough chick in question was going all fluttery and lowering her eyelids at the idea. Was this one of Marina's ploys for dealing with awkward customers, or was she actually taken with Christopher's charms?

Bea set that problem aside. Meanwhile, the taxi was waiting.

Christopher remembered his manners, saying to Bea, 'I hope I haven't left anything . . . Do give Piers my thanks, and you, too, for your hospitality and for, well, everything. You've been so kind; I didn't know which way to turn . . .'

Still talking, he was wafted out of the front door and down the steps into the waiting taxi which drove off straight away.

Ah, the relief! Christopher was in safe hands.

Bea set her back to the closed front door, noticing as she did so that a shard of broken glass had been overlooked on the skirting board. The hall did seem strange with plain glass where there used to be a delicate fanlight. Ah, well.

What next? She was needed downstairs. She'd hardly done any work today, and she needed to check everything was in order. Vera was coping well, praise be! And if Lisa didn't return, well, it would be easy to replace her.

There was something Bea felt she'd overlooked, something to do with Karina's circle. She'd collected information on all of them, hadn't she? What had she missed? She couldn't think what it might be.

She hesitated, her foot on the stairs leading down to the agency. Piers was still upstairs.

Bea listened hard but couldn't hear any cries of anger or distress. Instead, there was a murmur of voices from above. He was talking to Molly through the broken door? And what Bernice was going to say about the intrusion into her sanctum was nobody's business? Perhaps it would be best not to tell her?

Bea thought of going up the stairs to see how Piers was getting on, and to reinforce any arguments he might be having with Molly. But what man likes to be backed up by their wives? Well, Piers wasn't so insecure as to think that he couldn't manage by himself, but still . . .

Bea was so afraid Molly would turn violent and use that knife . . .

Dear Lord Almighty; please, please, please!

Distracted, she put a foot on the staircase leading up . . . and then took it down again. If Piers had needed her to help him, he'd have said so. He was right to think of this as a hostage situation, and in those circumstances you never interrupted what the mediator was saying.

Also, she was supposed to be running an agency and she hadn't been down there much that day, when they were short-handed and in shock because of Jolene's death.

Yet the threat of Molly doing something stupid underlay everything . . .

And how annoying it was that the light was so much brighter with plain glass in the fanlight over the front door . . . and when would Mr H be returning to replace what had been lost? And what were they going to have for supper?

Business first.

She went down the stairs, noting that it was Friday afternoon. Lisa and one other girl usually came in on a Saturday morning and after that phone calls would be directed either upstairs for Bea to deal with, or to Lisa's mobile. If Lisa was going to opt out, Bea had better have words with Vera about that, too.

But that would all have to wait, for they had another visitor. Another dark-skinned girl with cornrowed hair. She was sizzling with emotion and grief.

'I'm Maybelle, Jolene's sister. I came round to ask if anyone knew why she would have done something so stupid as to get in a passing car, and to get her wages, if you can make it up in cash, please. We could do with the cash and they'll close her bank account, won't they? And I'm taking her little teddy bear that I gave her last Christmas for a good luck charm.'

Maybelle looked to be some years older than her sister had been, and her complexion was not as good. She was holding Jolene's little teddy bear.

Bea made calming motions with her hands. 'Vera, could you check that Lisa sorted out Jolene's wages yesterday, and if not, can we manage cash?'

Bother, Molly's cleaned out the petty cash, hasn't she? And anyway, that wouldn't be enough, would it?

Vera opened her mouth to point out that there was a difficulty and Bea got there first.

'If Lisa did it, fine. If not, could you do so? Make a cheque out to cash and I'll sign it. Maybelle, come and sit down in my office while you wait for it. Would you like a cup of tea?'

'No, I would not!' Almost shouted. But she did follow Bea to her office, though she refused to sit down.

Bea closed the door to the main office. 'We are all so shocked to hear about Jolene. So young, so full of life.'

'So stupid!' The words burst out of Maybelle. She was dry-eyed. She was in shock. 'The police say she got into a car driven by a man looking for a prostitute! Why would she do such a thing? She had a boyfriend, not that he was much of a catch, but she could have got someone else, easy. We've been brought up to know what's what, and getting into a stranger's car is a no-no.'

Bea said, 'Molly is saying that she'd arranged to meet a man through a dating site and—'

'Dating site, indeed. Doesn't she know how much some of those people charge? Phooey! Codswallop! Worse! I've never heard the like!'

'Me neither,' said Bea.

'I'm so angry I could . . .!'

'I agree. You'd worked out already that Molly tells lies?'

'In a heartbeat! I warned Mum not to trust the woman, but she and Dad were always anxious to give her the benefit of the doubt for old times' sake. They took Molly in thinking she'd make up for the rent I was paying before I married last year. I did check once and they said it was early days and Molly was having a hard time and . . . They said they could understand it if she wanted to better herself and . . . I could kill Molly, I really could, leading my little sister up the garden path and for what? So she could feel all superior like?'

Tears came at last.

That was good. Bea coaxed Maybelle on to the settee at the back of the office and sat beside her with an arm round the girl's shoulders.

Maybelle shook and wept, stamped her feet and pushed Bea away. And then she allowed her to come closer and to hold her . . . And finally reached for the box of tissues and mopped up.

'The police told Dad that young girls are always getting them-selves into situations where they can't cope. They're thinking about men who use knives and drive cars and go after prostitutes! And she wasn't a prostitute. She wasn't!'

'Agreed.'

'So why did she get into that car?'

'She was looking for adventure. Molly had fed her this idea of living the high life and she wanted a part of it.'

'Molly! If I could only get hold of her. Do you know, Molly said she was going to introduce Jolene to some people who were making a film and might find a small part for her! Can you believe it? How could she be so silly as to believe that!'

Bea felt a chill settle on her shoulders. 'I suppose Molly might have promised to do just that. Molly was working for Karina, the film star, whose two sons have been talking about making a film. Alexander and Teddy are already involved in some podcasts, and I'm told that Teddy has been trying to raise the money to make a film, but—'

'You mean that was for real? Molly really might have offered to introduce Jolene to them?' Maybelle thought about that. 'So that's why Jolene got into the car. She thought she was going to meet someone in films?'

Bea sighed. Yes, it was a possible scenario.

Molly, oh, Molly! Everything seems to hinge on you and your lies. The damage you've done! How to work out what is the truth?

Maybelle blew her nose and generally put herself back together again. She was not as pretty as Jolene had been. Her eyelids were swollen and she'd bitten her lipstick off. But she looked good to Bea. Solid. Grown up. Unlike her younger sister.

Bea asked, 'How are your parents coping?'

'They're in pieces. One of my aunts lives nearby. She's moving in till they're able to shop and cook for themselves. The phone keeps ringing. You've no idea how many people have rung up to ask about Jolene. Mum and Dad just can't cope. My husband and I are in a flat just down the road and we plan to go over and spend a couple of hours there every evening after work. And the pastor of our church has been good. I don't know whether it makes it better or worse that Jolene was following her dream when she died. Maybe it's better. She'd have been good in films, wouldn't she? So . . . sparkly. I always envied her that.'

Maybelle had something better than sparkle. 'You have integrity,' said Bea. 'And common sense. You have a child on the way?'

Maybelle managed a tiny smile. 'How did you guess? Yes, I wasn't sure but this morning I took time off work to go to the doctor to see if it was true. When he said it was, I sort of went crazy thinking that Jolene would have loved to be an aunty and to spoil our child. Then I thought I couldn't tell our parents at the moment, because they're grieving so hard.'

'Tell them,' said Bea. 'It's the best thing that could happen to your family at the moment. And congratulations.'

A watery smile and a nod. 'Thank you for letting me have Jolene's money. The rent's due for Mum and Dad, and they were going frantic because they were short and we didn't have enough to give them to cover it. They'd lent Molly some money, you see. She'd promised . . . I don't suppose we'll ever see her or their money again.'

Bea thought of Molly hiding away on the top floor and shook her head. It would do no good to send Maybelle upstairs to talk to Molly. But she said, 'If I see her again, I'll remind her.'

Another watery smile. 'Chance would be a fine thing. She's a bad apple.'

Bea didn't normally go around hugging people, but this time she did. 'Take care of yourself, my dear. You have something precious to look after, now.'

Maybelle returned the embrace a little awkwardly. 'God bless you.'

'And you, too.'

Friday, late afternoon, continued

The end of a perfect day. Lisa had rung to say she wouldn't be able to manage cover for the office the following day; the printer which Hari had been looking at had definitely gone on the blink; there'd been a no show for someone who'd made an appointment to see one of the girls, and it was raining. And it wasn't just raining but chucking it down.

The only good thing that happened was that Piers rang to say that he'd coaxed Molly down from the top and she was having a cuppa with him in the kitchen.

Bea said, 'How did you manage that?'

'I said I was thinking of doing an oil sketch of her if she

agreed. Which she did. She wants feeding. Shall I get a Greek takeaway?'

It could only be good that he'd coaxed her out of Bernice's flat, but if he'd really promised to paint her . . .? That was a hefty bribe, but if it worked then Molly would have to stick around for a bit – or would she? Perhaps he could do it from the sketches he'd made of her already?

Bea oversaw Vera closing down the office and redirecting phone calls. Then Vera was gone and Bea stood at her office window, looking out at the dripping trees and bushes in the garden and wondering what it was that she'd forgotten to do.

Nothing came into her head that was helpful, so she switched off the lights, checked that the agency door to the street was locked, and went up the stairs to the ground floor, careful to lock the door halfway up so that Molly couldn't get out that way.

Friday, supper time

Bea wanted to hit Molly. Hard. Ah, if only she could!

Perhaps it would be more satisfying to slap her, first this side and then that? Anything to take that supercilious grin off her face. Everyone else in this tangle was in a bad way, but Molly was coasting along, high as a kite.

Bea thought longingly of picking up her rolling pin and clocking the girl over her head . . . and then was horrified at herself. She'd never, ever resorted to fisticuffs. All aggressive action was anathema to her.

Well, normally she wouldn't have allowed such thoughts to enter her mind. She would have told herself to keep calm, that it wasn't worth worrying about, and so and so forth.

That line of thought failed to calm her.

There sat Molly, bright as a button, munching her way through a large portion of Greek food with a side order of salad and talking at the same time about how she'd never imagined that dear Piers would ever have time to paint her portrait, and how all her dreams were coming true and wasn't it wonderful how brilliantly life turned out in the end!

Bea considered putting poison in the yoghurt and honey dishes which Piers had ordered for dessert. What poison did she have in her cupboard that she could use? Something tasteless and non-detectable? If only she had a properly equipped medicine cabinet available for emergencies such as this!

Piers gave her a long, searching look. He knew when she was about to boil over and do something stupid. Sensible Piers, who hadn't let his emotions govern his actions . . . as she had been about to do.

Bea reminded herself that Molly, however annoying, had been working closely with Karina for months, and probably knew the answers to various questions.

So Bea interrupted Molly's sickly-sweet praise of Piers' talent, to say, 'I expect you learned lots of secrets when you were with Karina. I don't suppose all of them will make their way into her book, will they?'

Molly giggled like a teenager. 'Wouldn't you like to know?' She wagged her forefinger at Bea.

I am not going to be sick. I am not going to kill her. I am going to disembowel her, slowly. After I've dug one or two secrets out of her.

Bea managed a smile. 'Oh, I don't need to know anything which Karina wouldn't want spread around. It just occurred to me that Cecil must be hiding his lamp under a bushel. I mean, he took Karina away from Simon, but he doesn't look a romantic figure, does he?'

Molly put her finger on her nose and giggled some more. 'I wondered about that, too, and we talked about how we could write about it in the book. It really was romantic, in a way. Who'd have thought it, to look at him? Dried up, desiccated, losing his hair and with a waist measurement you wouldn't want to boast about. But there it is.

'The thing is, he was desperately in love with Karina all the time she was married to Simon. Cecil used to send her flowers and gifts. She showed me some of the poetry he'd written her. A bit blush-making, to be truthful. We did think of putting a couple of quotes from them in the book. I know one got left in, but the others we had to take out because he didn't want them made public, which I perfectly understand because they're quite childish, you know?'

'Really?' Bea was interested. 'So was he stalking her, do you think?'

'Oh, no. She liked it. Every time he went over to America on business – he only retired a couple of years ago – he'd take her out for a meal and maybe leave her with a little something in the way of a pair of earrings or a bangle, or something. Oh yes, she loved that.'

'Didn't Simon object?'

'Well, yes. He did and he didn't. She told me he'd make a scene after she'd been out with Cecil, but she knew how to deal with that. Two strings to her bow. Isn't that what they call it?'

Bea said, 'Then what went wrong? I don't understand the relationship between the two men. She was married to Simon, then ditched him for Cecil, and then allowed Simon to come back to live with them. I mean, isn't that weird? How did you deal with it in the book?'

Molly preened. She knew all the answers, didn't she? 'I couldn't possibly say.'

What she meant was ask me again!

'Come on! You know you're aching to tell me.'

'Mm. Well, she told me that Simon had been indiscreet, spent the night with another woman, that she'd found out and been dreadfully upset and told him to leave the house. And there was Cecil, just retired and ready to step into Simon's shoes and, well, it was all over within weeks. She was on the rebound, as you might say.

'She got a quickie divorce and Cecil offered her a lifetime of devotion and . . . and, well, stability. He brought her back to London, and they were terribly happy together. Then poor Simon turned up. He'd bitterly regretted his one-night stand with another woman and had had a bad time with his last film crashing and all that. He said he'd never stopped loving her and begged to be allowed to see her every now and again, so she forgave him.'

There were stars in Molly's eyes as she said this.

She really is quite an actress.

Molly touched a fingertip to each of her eyes in turn. 'Poor Simon. He couldn't get any more work in America and he had nowhere else to go. She was so sorry for him. I mean, it was all

over really, but she did take him in. Cecil doesn't mind because
he knows he has her love for ever and ever.'

Bea tried not to let her eyebrows rise to her hairline. She didn't
believe a word of it. She hinted, 'But there was more to it than
that, wasn't there?'

Molly shook her head but smiled. 'Oh, I mustn't say, and it
isn't in the book. It wouldn't be kind, you know.'

Piers said, 'Oh, you know you can tell us.'

'We-ell, I did overhear Karina shouting at Simon once, saying
that he'd brought ruin upon them all, and from what I can make
out, I think he put a lot of her money into that last film of his,
and when it flopped there was nothing much left. They had a
terrible row and that's really why she divorced him.'

'Nothing to do with his playing away?'

'She made that up. It sounded better for the book. Poor Simon,
he was so out of his depth with Karina.'

'And Cecil was there to pick up the pieces, pay her debts,
bring her back to London, set her up in style. Realistically, do
you think Cecil can keep her?'

Molly giggled. 'I know they have separate bedrooms. Mrs
Hennessey told me that. He appears to be a cold fish, but he still
adores her. Imagine that! At her age! I've seen him grind his
teeth when Simon has been paying her too much attention. And
she loves it. She's got everything exactly as she wants it. Two
men at her beck and call, and her sons are going to make a film
with her and life is going to be beautiful for ever and ever, amen.'

So there it was. The whole picture laid out before them. Karina
imagining that she will have fame and fortune again. Cecil
hanging on to her like grim death, unable to satisfy her in bed
and running out of money. Simon feeding her vanity by paying
court to her . . . was that lip service or was he still in love with
her? Then the boys had moved in, dreaming of a future based
on Teddy inheriting money enough to bankroll their future.

Bea pondered, 'It costs a lot to make a film.'

Molly shrugged. 'Teddy's coming up with it, and they're going
to mortgage the house. I'm to write the screenplay and Simon
thinks that maybe, just maybe, he can get me an audition to play
Karina when she was younger.'

What's this? All of a sudden Molly seems to know a lot about

what Simon felt and did. Has she been in contact with him, too?
Has she actually fallen for the old casting-couch trick of getting
girls to have sex with older men?

Bea sighed. It seemed to her that the whole darn lot of them
had built a castle of dreams but the foundations were laid on sand.

Bea reflected that Karina's house had been due to come
tumbling down even before Molly had got herself pregnant and
started blackmailing the family.

Bea was, almost, sorry for Molly. The family would be
receiving the letters from Christopher soon, giving them notice
to quit and saying he had changed his will. And then all hell
would break loose. What would Molly do then?

Piers was not sorry for her. He'd had enough of being pushed
around by Karina and Molly and Uncle Tom Cobley and all. He
decided to spill the beans, so to speak. He managed a conversational tone as he said, 'Molly, the house doesn't belong to Karina.
And Teddy doesn't inherit for a couple of years and is already
in debt. It's highly unlikely he can raise enough money to finance
making a film.'

Oh boy, yes! Light the touchpaper and retire to a safe distance!
Molly is going to explode!

FOURTEEN

Friday, supper time, continued

Molly didn't explode but the colour left her face and she
swayed on her stool. In a hoarse voice she said, 'That's
not true.'

Piers said, in the same conversational tone, 'We have a copy
of Karina's second husband's will in which he left the house to
Mr Fletcher. Would you like to see it?'

'No! You lie! He bought the house for his wife.'

'Lance bought it, mortgaged it and kept it in his name. By the
time he died in that unfortunate accident, he'd realized Karina
hadn't the faintest idea how to manage money or look after

children, so he very wisely made his brother Christopher Fletcher executor of his will and guardian of his baby son Teddy. He left Teddy his ancestral home and estate, which the lad will inherit when he reaches twenty-five but not a day before. Lance had been spending money like there was no tomorrow, so the country estate was encumbered with debt. Lance left the London house to Christopher, which was a poisoned chalice considering how heavily it was mortgaged. He left the residue of his estate to his wife, but that wasn't much considering he owed money left, right and centre.'

'No, no,' protested Molly. 'Lance was a wealthy man.'

'Who spent money like water. By careful management Christopher has managed to clear the country house and estate of debt. What of the children? Well, Karina didn't want Teddy any more than she wanted Alexander—'

'That's not true, either! She was left penniless and distraught when her beloved Lance died. She had no option but to take up the offer from Hollywood. It devastated her that she had to leave her babies behind.'

It was time for Bea to intervene. 'Nonsense! Didn't you check the birth and marriage certificates, Molly? Perhaps you didn't bother but took Karina's word for everything.' She shook some papers out of her pile and held them out. 'Want a look?'

Molly tossed her head. 'If you mean did she tell me why her first marriage broke down? Of course she did. She was exhausted after having Alexander and her husband was so unkind, wanting sex at all—'

'She wasn't interested in the baby. She'd met Lance Fletcher and fallen for him. Didn't you realize that was why she lost custody of Alexander when she divorced, and why she wasn't awarded any alimony? Didn't you realize she must have been at fault?'

'It wasn't like that at all. He made up lies about her, and she couldn't fight him in the courts because she was exhausted.'

'Look at the dates.' Bea held out the papers to Molly, who refused to take them. Bea said, 'She married for the second time within a week of getting a divorce from her first husband and she produced Teddy four months later. She was already pregnant when she married Lance.'

'Teddy was premature.'

'I bet she gave you a different set of dates to make them fit her halo.'

Molly's eyes filled with tears. 'She suffered terribly over the whole affair.'

'Alexander was handed over to her first husband's family to rear, and she asked Christopher and his wife to take Teddy. It's her husbands' families who've paid to bring the boys up, with little by way of thanks. Christopher, for instance, has found himself deserted and vilified since Teddy fell under the spell of Karina and Alexander. Now Teddy wants to raise money to make a film when his only asset is a country estate which he doesn't inherit for another couple of years. Christopher is not going to help him with a loan and is changing his will to exclude his nephew.'

Molly grabbed her glass of water and downed it in one. She set the glass down awkwardly and it rolled over. 'You're lying!'

Piers caught the glass and set it upright. He said, 'Karina hasn't paid a penny towards the upbringing of either of her two sons. Her career has stumbled to a halt. When she came back to London, Christopher very kindly allowed her to move into the London house on condition she paid the mortgage, which she has failed to do. Are you surprised that he's had enough of it and is about to issue her with notice to quit? He has also refused to back Teddy's application for a loan to make a film. And I don't blame him.'

Molly gasped something. 'But . . . he can't throw Karina out! It's her house. She told me so.'

Piers was implacable. 'It's payback time, Molly. Karina lives in Cloud Cuckoo Land. She persuades herself that she deserves the best and ignores any inconvenient facts to the contrary. What about the way she sacked Mrs Hennessey to avoid paying her wages? What did you think when she turned on you and accused you of stealing from her?'

'Well, I . . . I was shocked. I couldn't believe . . . Then Simon explained to me that it was all playacting and that Mr Fletcher would see me right. He will, won't he?'

Simon again! Molly has definitely been keeping in touch with him, hasn't she?

Piers said, 'Mr Fletcher is an honest man. Check your contract to make sure it's with him and not with Karina. Whose idea was it to accuse staff of theft in order to avoid paying their wages?'

'I don't know. Cecil's, I suppose. Not Simon's. Simon is, well, a gentleman.'

'Are you hitching your star to Simon now? Is that a good idea? For a start, how does Karina explain their strange arrangement? One minute he's married to her and all is going well, and the next he's out of favour and divorced. She marries Cecil, they return to the UK . . . and then she takes Simon back into her bed.'

'No! Not into her bed.' Molly was getting agitated. 'He told me. He thinks she's an ugly old hag nowadays. Yes, he loved her to distraction at one time, but the scales have fallen from his eyes and now he sees her for what she is. He's a gentle soul, rather out of his depth where Karina is concerned. He stays with her now out of pity. He does what he can to help her but he hasn't visited her bed for months.' She tried on a coy look. 'Not since he met me.'

Bea interjected. 'Wrong! Mrs Hennessey told me he spends most of his nights in Karina's bed.'

Molly coloured up. 'That woman. She'd say anything to make Karina look bad. I tell you, he loves me now.'

Piers leaned forward. 'I see where you're heading. You've made your decision and chosen to say that Simon is the father of your child. You think the youngsters are too young for you. You rather fancy Simon's fading charms. He has no money. You realize that, don't you?'

Molly was eager to explain. 'He's got connections; he's worked with so many people. I know his last film bombed, but he's had offers since to do television work. He's in discussion now, this very minute, with Netflix about a series. What's more, he's going to direct the film Teddy and Alexander are going to make.'

Piers said, 'You can't really believe that will happen!'

Molly put her nose in the air. 'You're just jealous because everything's going well for me. You'll laugh on the other side of your face when my name is up there in lights and I'm walking down the red carpet with photographers shouting out my name to make me look their way. You're a pair of has-beens and I'm on my way up to the stars!'

She stormed out of the room. They heard her pound her way up the stairs . . . and then slow down . . . and stop right there.

Piers shook his head and sighed. 'She's realized she's nowhere else to go.'

Bea tapped her papers into a neat bundle and got to her feet, looking at the clock. 'It's getting late. I'll draw the curtains.'

Piers produced Bea's knife from where he'd hidden it behind the bread bin. 'Molly forced the door with this but didn't seem to see it as a weapon. We'll need a locksmith to repair the damage. I'll ring round for one in the morning.'

'Did Molly make much of a mess upstairs?'

'Not really. Bedclothes awry, bathroom needs a clean.' Piers started to clear the table. 'What are we going to do with her?'

Bea didn't have an answer to that, any more than Piers did.

They both heard footsteps slowly coming down the stairs, into the hall, and pause in the doorway.

Molly said, 'I suppose I can stay here the night? I've nowhere else to go.'

Bea wanted to say, 'No way!' but couldn't bring herself to do so. 'Why don't you ring Jolene's parents? You could go back there. They're very distressed. You could help.'

For a moment it looked as if Molly might do so, but then her mouth sagged and self-pity took over. 'I can't go back there. I owe them rent, and I've nothing, no money . . .' Tears rose in her eyes and threatened to spill over.

Actually, she might indeed have a career as an actress.

'If only,' Molly gulped, 'I had the money due to me for writing the book! Then everything would be all right. You said Mr Fletcher would see me right. If you give me the money for a taxi I could go and see him. Perhaps he could give me my fee in cash and I'd be off and away.'

Mr Fletcher had gone without leaving a forwarding address, or payment for Molly, or for Piers, too.

Piers said, 'Let's have a look at your contract. If it's with the publisher, then you can ring them up and ask for an advance. I suspect the contract says you get paid on delivery of an accept-able manuscript, which means you won't get anything till they've read it and may want you to revise this and that before they pass it as good enough. But, under the circumstances, they might play ball. If your contract is with Mr Fletcher, I'm afraid you'll have to wait. He's gone on holiday and isn't contactable.'

Molly said, 'What! But he can't! No, you're lying! He wouldn't do that to Karina, or Teddy. They all rely on him, you know they do!'

'Sorry,' said Piers. 'Not my problem!'

Molly swung around and stamped off to the stairs. And stopped right there, drooping with exhaustion? Or defeat?

Piers started to load the dishwasher.

Bea said, in a low voice, 'We can't turn her out, can we?' And then, remembering her favourite mug: 'Have you seen my mug, the one with the forget-me-nots on it?'

'It was here when I made coffee for Christopher and myself this morning. I remember that because I thought of taking a cuppa down to you but decided to wait a while.'

He looked around, then lifted the lid of the bin bag in the corner. 'Ah.' He picked out fragments large enough to be able to identify them as Bea's favourite mug. He said, 'Molly must have wanted to make herself a cuppa and broken it. I'll get you another.'

Bea felt her own eyes brim with tears. Stupid to cry over a mug, but she had had it for many a long year and she'd really liked it. It had been a birthday present from an old friend, with a chocolate Easter egg in it. The egg had long been eaten, but the mug had been something she'd used every day since. She tried to pretend its loss was unimportant and reached for a tissue to blow her nose.

Piers put his arm around her. 'Molly wreaks destruction wherever she goes. What else will she break if we let her stay?'

Bea told herself to be brave. 'Then let's think how to get rid of her.'

From the hall they heard the murmur of someone speaking softly into their phone. Molly was ringing someone. Who? Was she passing on the bad news about Christopher giving them notice to quit and changing his will? And that he'd gone on holiday?

Piers said, 'When did you say Hari was able to get back to us?'

'As soon as he could.' She checked her smartphone to see if there were any text messages on it. There weren't. She wondered how Marina was getting on with Christopher. Was he really taken with her? Maybe she wouldn't mind chaperoning him around for a while?

Winston, the cat, wandered in from the great outdoors and sized up the situation. Bea looked as if she could do with a spot of attention so he wound round her legs and purred. She reacted just as she should, by picking him up and giving him a cuddle. As a reward for being warm and affectionate she gave him a serving of his favourite tuna.

Winston got down to it. Ah, but then his ears went back. Someone was invading his territory? Ugh, she smelt nasty. Winston was very particular about the company he kept. He finished the tuna in record time while keeping an eye on the newcomer, and then hared it out of the back door into the lowering evening sunlight.

Molly looked pleased with herself as she grabbed a seat at the table. 'I told Simon what you've been up to. He was really annoyed. He said I shouldn't listen to a word you say, that you make things up all the time. He says you're trying to destroy Karina by accusing her of theft! He says the next thing will be you saying that Karina is a murderer.'

Bea laughed. 'Who is she supposed to have murdered? Jolene?'

Molly was shocked. 'Of course not. How would she know anything about Jolene? No, it's her second husband Lance, of course. I suppose you remember me telling you about that? Karina was blameless, I can assure you.'

Bea and Piers said nothing to that. Bea wiped the central island down and laid it for breakfast.

Molly fidgeted. 'Well, what did you hear, then? Karina told me that he slipped and fell down the stairs. She was all alone in the house. She was shattered.'

Piers said, 'There were witnesses to what happened. Mr Fletcher spoke to both of them. I recorded what he said.'

Piers got his phone out and set it to play back some of the recording he'd made. Mr Fletcher's voice came over clearly enough. '. . . He got into a shouting match with Karina. She threw something at him, he ducked but in doing so he slipped and fell down two flights of stairs. The housekeeper witnessed it, as did the nanny. I spoke to both of them. They were shocked but quite clear that both Lance and Karina were drunk at the time.'

Piers clicked his phone off. 'Well, Molly? Did that version go into the book?'

Molly stared at him. 'No, of course not. Karina wasn't drunk, she was all alone in the house and she didn't throw anything at him. What nonsense! *He* had been drinking, that's true. He slipped and fell. He was the love of her life and it was tragic that he died so young. You're making it all up! And no one's going to believe you because I've painted the real portrait of her, kind and generous-hearted and always loving too much and being betrayed by these men whom she trusted.'

'Suit yourself. So you told Simon what Mr Fletcher's done? Has everyone in that household received a copy of his letters yet?'

'No. So I told them what was in them.'

'Who did you tell? Simon, of course. What about the others?'

Molly smirked. 'Simon is such a lovely man. So understanding and so clever with people. I texted the others.'

'Were you relying on Simon to help you get a settlement out of Karina? Was it he whom you arranged to meet on Thursday evening?'

No reply. Molly set her lips in a thin line. 'No comment.'

Piers said, 'You've decided that he's your best bet but you can't be that sure of him or you wouldn't have contacted the others as well. Did you really think you'd get a proposal of marriage out of this, or were you really in it for the money?'

A toss of her head. 'None of your business.'

'When you arranged to meet whoever-it-was, you were sensible enough to realize you needed a backup, so you got Jolene to be there by saying you were going to get her an introduction to someone in films.'

'You're right. I wasn't sure that it would be Simon who would turn up,' said Molly, casting her eyes down. 'I should have had more faith. So yes, I did text the others as well.'

Bea was, almost, amused at Molly's audacity. What, Bernie Sanders included?'

'I wouldn't give him the time of day. Of course not. The very idea.'

'We heard you'd allowed him your favours once.'

'I allowed him to kiss me. Once. That's all.'

Perhaps it was. But Mrs Hennessey had no axe to grind by saying that Bernie had had his wicked way with Molly at least once.

Piers said, 'But you were late to the venue and Simon – or whoever – had brought a sharp knife with him intending to rid himself of you. Only it was Jolene who got into the car and Jolene who died because she could identify your lover. Don't you feel even the slightest tinge of guilt? And won't he – whoever he is – come after you next?'

Molly shivered, then tossed her head. 'It wasn't Simon. He's sworn to me that it wasn't. He really truly cares about me. We may not be able to marry for a while since he's got to keep Karina sweet till she gets used to the idea that he loves me now. But—'

'What was the car like? The one that Jolene got into?'

'I . . . It was too far away to . . . It was black, just like any other car on the road. It wasn't the Rolls-Royce, if that's what you were thinking. Anyway, Karina doesn't let anyone but Bernie drive the Rolls. It wasn't one of those really huge new cars. Sorry, I'm not good on cars. It was too far away. I don't know! Honest! I have thought about it, because naturally I'm worried that Jolene . . .'

Molly stopped here, and then restarted. 'The truth is it was getting dark, and there was a tailback of cars all going in that direction and one of them stopped and, honest, it was too far away for me to see anything but Jolene getting into it. When I saw her do that, I was angry, thinking she'd been given a lift home by someone she knew instead of waiting for me. She'd long gone by the time I got to the corner, and I waited and waited . . . No, I reckon it was just some chancer seeing her standing at the side of the road and looking into cars. Then when he found out his mistake, he killed her. I mean, that's awful, and I'd give anything for it not to have happened, but it's *not my fault!*'

Piers said, 'So you really don't know which of Karina's three men might have been in that car? Simon, or one of the boys?'

Molly smiled. 'Well, it wasn't my darling Simon. He told me that he doesn't check his smartphone for texts very often. He said he did see it eventually, but he wasn't sure what to do about it and didn't respond. He likes to take his time to think things through, you see.

'Anyway, when I texted him the next day – that was after all that fuss and bother with the memory stick and getting the portrait signed and he'd seen me again – the scales fell from his eyes and he realized how much I meant to him. He'd been getting very fond of me for some time, you know? But he'd been fighting his feelings for me, trying not to realize how much he'd come to love me because he's still so fond of Karina, though not in a lover's way any more, of course. So now we know where we are.'

Bea blinked. Was Molly for real? Bea cast her mind back, trying to remember any sort of rapport between Molly and Simon when they'd been in the room together and couldn't come up with anything. Granted, they might have discovered their passion for one another after that, but . . . No, Simon wasn't going to leave his cosy quarters at Karina's for a penniless girl who was far too young for him and pregnant to boot . . . was he? A man of his age wouldn't want to take on a baby, would he? Especially if there was any doubt as to its paternity.

'Anyone like a coffee?' She made three cups. Bea switched the radio on because the silence had become too much for her. She had it on so low that they didn't listen to it, not really.

Molly received a text on her smartphone which threw her into a state. She said she'd decided to have a shower and change and disappeared upstairs.

Piers said, 'She's going out to meet someone? Simon, do you think? I hope she knows what she's doing.'

A text pinged into Bea's smartphone, but this one made her smile. She read it and reported to Piers. 'Marina's taken Christopher to one of the country house hotels which she uses when escorting important people around the country. Log fires, good food and even better wine. Christopher wants her to stay over, for company. He's offered to foot the bill for her. It sounds like he's enjoying himself. Oh, and here's his new phone number. Can you copy it into your phone under a false name? I'll do the same. We don't want Molly seeing it.'

She turned off the radio and they moved into the living room. Bea was restless. She went round the ground floor, drawing curtains, tidying up, plumping up cushions, straightening a picture which she fancied was tilting to one side.

Piers started channel-hopping on the telly.

They were both listening out for Molly to descend, which she eventually did. She'd done her hair and makeup afresh. She was excited. 'Simon's picking me up in five minutes. I look all right, don't I?'

She went to the front window and drew back the curtain to look out. 'He said parking around here is terrible, so he'll toot when he arrives and I'm to be waiting on the pavement to get into the car.'

Piers dumped the remote. 'You mean, like Jolene?'

'What?' Molly got it. 'Oh, no. Of course not.' An artificial laugh. 'Not like Jolene.'

Her smartphone pinged and she read the message. 'He's at the end of the road now. I'll just pop out on to the pavement and—'

'You'll do nothing of the kind,' said Piers, going to stand behind her so that she couldn't move away from the window. 'Not till you know who sent that text. Is it really from Simon? Has his number come up as the sender? Even if it has, someone else could have used his phone to send you a text. Have you and Simon worked out a code so that you know which message comes from him and not from anyone else?'

'Well, no. That's not necessary. Let me pass. He'll be here in a minute.'

Piers held her arm. 'Remember what happened to Jolene. She got into the wrong car. I suggest you text back or ring his number to say that when he gets outside, he must put the roof light on inside the car, so that you can be sure it's Simon out there and not a prowler looking for a quickie.'

'What? That's not in the least necessary!'

A car tooted outside. Bea hurried out into the hall. They kept a torch on the hall chest for emergencies. Yes, it was there. She turned the alarm and the hall light off. She opened the front door and looked out. The street lighting was not great. Yes, there was an anonymous mid-range car double-parked outside. It was dark inside, and out. A pale oval indicated that someone was in the driver's seat, but she couldn't make out who it was.

She could hear Piers arguing with Molly. 'Go on! Tell him to put the inside light on!'

Molly shouted, 'Let me pass! Look, there's another text come in from him! The traffic's building up and he has to move!'

Bea stepped out into the porch. She switched the torch on and aimed it at the dark car in the road. A sleeve came up and hid the man's face . . . it was a man, wasn't it? The car accelerated and took off.

Molly screamed, 'Wait for me!'

Piers shouted, 'Get off me!'

Bea went back inside, turning on the alarm and the hall light as she did so. 'He's gone. He didn't want to be identified, did he?'

Piers was bent over, gasping with pain. Had Molly hit him amidships?

Molly sat down and drummed her heels on the floor. First-class hysteria beckoned. How that girl enjoyed a melodrama!

Bea said, 'Do you want some cold water thrown over you?'

Molly gasped, held her breath, and allowed herself to relax. Tears came. 'What will Simon think of me?'

'That you're being careful. Did you check that message came from his phone?'

'Well, I . . . no. But it must have been. I didn't recognize the number, but . . . he's got a new phone, obviously.'

'A burner phone? Why would he use one of those? Why don't you get him on his usual smartphone and check whether he was in that car or not?'

Piers straightened up, holding one hand under his armpit. 'She bit me!'

Molly shrugged. 'You deserved it. I hope you get rabies.'

Bea held out her hand to see the damage. Molly had bitten him all right. There was a double circle of toothmarks imprinted on his palm. The skin had been broken in a couple of places. He looked pale. He was in shock.

Bea didn't panic, though she would have liked to do so. Piers needed his hands for his work. She said, 'The first-aid box is in the kitchen. Let's wash your hand and disinfect it.'

Molly said, 'Piers laid his hands on me. He restrained me from leaving. I can sue him for that.'

Piers said wearily, 'Molly, I was trying to stop you committing suicide. Why aren't you phoning Simon? Is it because you're afraid it wasn't him in the car outside?'

'I'm on it. I'm on it!' And she did get her phone out.

Bea pushed Piers towards the kitchen. 'Do you want me to call the police and charge her with assault?'

'We'd be up all night explaining. I did lay my hands on her to stop her leaving, so I'm in the wrong there. And she'll do her "poor little me" act and they'll fall for it and . . . I wish we'd never laid eyes on her! She's nothing but trouble.'

Bea dealt with the toothmarks. It was his right hand that was affected and he was very right-handed. Neither of them mentioned what that bite might do to his professional life. She thought he might need antibiotics to deal with the injury. She put a light dressing on to keep the hand clean and sent him off to bed. It wasn't ten o'clock yet, but it had been a long and tiring day.

Bea fed Winston again, tidied the kitchen and wondered if she could make Molly sleep outside in the garden shed. There was a lounger there she could use. It would be cold, of course. Tough! She could pull the garden cushions over her. Or freeze, for all Bea cared.

When Bea returned to the living room she found Molly chatting away on her phone, making no move to go up to bed. Bea supposed the girl was talking to Simon. Did Bea want to know what Simon was saying? She didn't. She would like the whole pack of them to fall into the sea and drown. Or walk into a burning building and fail to come out again. Or die horribly slowly of some long-acting poison. Or just disappear. Downwards, not upwards.

Molly was enjoying herself, gesticulating, laughing. She shut off the phone only to tell Bea that Simon wasn't picking up his phone at the moment, but she'd speak to him in the morning and explain why she hadn't been able to join him in the car, and she hoped he wouldn't be too cross about it. He was probably too busy to answer his phone, said Molly, because he'd have to cook for Karina and Cecil and then dance attendance on them all evening.

Molly said she'd just been talking to her friend who lived out East London way and it was just as well that Molly hadn't gone out there on the off-chance of getting a bed with him, as he'd just moved in a flatmate so there'd have been no room for her anyway. She waited a moment to see how Bea would react and then went off up the stairs, humming to herself.

Bea had said nothing at all. What could she say? If the man in the car had been Simon, then she was the Queen of Sheba. Her overall impression of the person in the car was that he was . . . smaller? Younger? She couldn't quite put her finger on it.

Oh well. She turned off all the lights and made sure the house alarm was on. She thought about phoning Hari to report and then decided she was too tired to talk to anyone.

Tomorrow . . . ah, tomorrow there was going to be the almightiest rumpus as Karina and Co tried to come to terms with the fact that their comfortable way of life was about to come to an end. What would they do about it? Answer: they would hunt for Christopher. Well, he was safely out of touch.

When they found out they couldn't get hold of Christopher, they would hunt for Molly – and Molly had been last seen at Bea and Piers' house. So they'd try that next. And what would Bea and Piers do about that? Hand Molly over to the clan to do what they liked with her? In a heartbeat.

I'll think about that tomorrow.

FIFTEEN

Saturday morning, a late breakfast

Neither Bea nor Piers slept well. At six they were sitting up in bed sipping an early morning cuppa and discussing the situation they found themselves in.

At half past six they had breakfast quietly, together. And then went their separate ways.

At half past nine Bea left her computer and went upstairs to make herself a cup of coffee, and heard the shower running up at the top of the house. Soon after, Molly came pounding down the stairs and bounced into the kitchen.

Winston, who had been laid out on the island twisting this way and that to attract Bea's attention, decided that three was a crowd and exited the kitchen.

Molly said, 'I don't like cats. Where's Piers?'

'Working.'

'Has he started on my portrait? He said I didn't need to pose for it as he already has some sketches he's made of me. I can't believe my picture could be hung in a gallery next to Karina's. How long will he take? How much does his work sell for? I suppose I'll have to sell anything he paints of me, which is a pity.'

Bea ignored all that. 'Help yourself to cereal and bread. There's coffee, too.'

Molly seated herself. 'I'd like a full English, and then some croissants.' She didn't bother to add the magic word 'please'.

'Tough,' said Bea, 'I'm working this morning. I've told you what's available. Help yourself to coffee. The rest is in the fridge.'

'You should be happy to prepare me a good breakfast,' said Molly. 'Am I not an honoured guest in your house? By the way, I like it up at the top of the house. I think I'll move up there permanently.'

'What? No, you can't. That flat belongs to my ward, Bernice, who is currently away at school, but comes back for the odd weekend. She'll be here next Friday.'

'She can stay in the guest room, can't she? Remember, I can call the police at any time and accuse Piers of manhandling me.'

'Go ahead,' said Bea, smiling a little. 'They'll probably believe you, at least at first, because you're such a good liar. They'll remove you, you poor abused creature, to a women's refuge. You may not have to share a room there, but I doubt if you'll find it very comfortable. And there you'll stay until you get tired of playing the victim. Don't worry about us. We'll survive. As Wellington said when a woman tried to blackmail him, "Publish and be damned".'

'Who's he when he's at home? Someone who podcasts about Wellington boots?'

'As a matter of fact, he did popularize them. A couple of centuries ago.'

Molly wasn't interested in the past. 'So is Piers working in the mews cottage? You'd better get him back here. Simon wants to have a word with you both about damages. You've been spreading lies about Karina, and Simon's organizing a solicitor to deal with it for her. I thought you'd like to know. He says it'll cost you this house and make front page headlines.'

'You terrify me,' said Bea, not sounding frightened at all. 'By the way, I've been trying to pin down the memory of the man I saw in the car, the one who was supposed to be collecting you last night. It definitely wasn't Simon. It was a smaller man. Not as tall.'

Molly didn't like that. 'Oh. Then I suppose it was the knife man on the prowl? The one who killed Jolene?'

'No, the police arrested him, remember? And would such a man have texted you on your phone, to ensure you'd hop into his car when he reached us? How did a prowler get your number? Come on!'

Molly thought about that while she grabbed herself a mug of coffee. 'Well, it was one of the boys, then. It must have been. Alexander, probably. He thinks everything is a joke.'

'A joke that killed Jolene?'

'That's different. That was a pervert looking for a victim.'

Bea sighed. 'Molly, hasn't it occurred to you that you've caused a lot of trouble to Karina and her court, and that your death would solve a lot of problems for them?'

'What nonsense you do talk. I'm quite safe. I've told them I've written everything down that I know about Jolene's death, and given it to you to hold for me.'

Bea raised her hands to her head. 'Molly, you can't have it both ways. Either we're the villains of the piece – in which case you wouldn't trust us with your testimony – or we aren't.'

'Oh. Well . . . it sounded good. Simon will be here soon. He's promised to look after me for ever, so—'

'You think he's prepared to lose his cosy place in Karina's orbit, and to offend her by taking up with a much younger woman who has no visible assets? A woman, moreover, who is pregnant and trying to pin paternity on him?'

'He's a slow starter, all right, but now he's got it all planned. Karina doesn't realize how much he's changed, but she'll come round in the end, because she needs him to look after her. She'll just have to share him with me in future, that's all. He gives her a head-and- shoulders massage every day, and cooks for her when there's no one else available. He doesn't want to leave her in the lurch so I'll move in with him. The house is big enough. Simon's looking forward to the baby.'

'Karina won't be, I can tell you that. She never nursed her own and she won't want the limelight to be transferred to a baby, not at her age.'

'Nonsense.' Molly produced a beatific smile. 'She'll love to be a granny.'

Bea rolled her eyes. She said, 'You had better get busy packing. Your stay here comes to an end today. My cleaner will be here first thing on Monday morning to put the guest room and the flat at the top to rights. I'll tell her to throw away anything she finds which does not belong here. Also on Monday we have the carpenter coming to mend the door you forced open. So you'd better get a move on.'

Bea went down to the office. There was still something she needed to look up.

At ten minutes to ten, she found the link. So that was it! And that made sense of everything that had happened. She lifted her phone to tell Piers about it. He sounded abstracted as he always did when he'd started a new piece of work, but he promised to be back soon.

Bea yawned. She checked that her skeleton staff was on duty and that nothing had come through that needed her attention.

The sun had come out. She opened the French doors and stepped out into the garden. And relaxed.

Only then did it strike her that if Molly was an embarrassment to Karina and Co, and they managed to get rid of her, then Bea and Piers were the only other people who knew of their connection to Jolene. And, Molly had told them she'd given proof of what she knew to Bea and Piers!

If this were so, then there was going to be an attempt to silence not only Molly, but also Bea and Piers.

Bea breathed softly, telling herself to keep calm. What a fool she'd been to tell Molly that her cleaner and the carpenter weren't due till Monday, by which time . . . oh dear! They might all three be dead.

No, surely not!

Yes! Remember Jolene! She was efficiently despatched from this life within hours of Molly making an assignation to meet the father of her child.

Such efficiency does not appear to be one of Simon's qualities. True. But it does make one think of his co-conspirator.

Now, given that the killer was efficient, how would he plan to get rid of those who threatened his way of life? It would have to be done straight away, in case one of his potential victims decided to go to the police with their suspicions. Or would he rely on the fact that there really was no proof that he could be linked to Jolene's death?

Ah, if only there were proof! To accuse someone in Karina's household of the murder of Jolene on the basis of supposition . . .? It would be laughed out of court.

In any case, how would the killer set about removing first Christopher, and then Bea and Piers? Fire? Poison? Knives? He'd used a knife before so why not again? He or his accomplice could remove Molly this morning and deal with her straight away. They would provide alibis for one another. Also, having an accomplice makes disposal of the body much easier.

So what would he do? Well, Christopher was out of the way for the time being, so after he'd dealt with Molly, he'd turn his attention to Bea and Piers. Would he make a double killing look like an interrupted burglary? Perhaps he would access the place that night, getting someone to kick in the fanlight in the hall for entry? It had been done before, so why not again?

Dear Lord above, you see how it is. They live in an alternative universe of false ideas, false hopes, and the wilful disregard of facts. I suppose we're all guilty of colouring our view of the world with fantasy now and then. We imagine that 'somewhere over the rainbow' we'll be able to live in peace and prosperity. The test comes when reality breaks in.

You understand how this situation has come to escalate from comedy into tragedy. I can't see that much comfort awaits the

players involved in this fantasy. They are their own worst enemies.
You will know best about that. I pray that you put the right words
in my mouth so that when we come face to face with one another
there will be no more killings, no more destruction. In Jesus'
name, I pray.

Bea looked up. Piers was back and had thrown open the French
windows that let on to the balcony at the back of the house. He
was standing there, talking to someone on his phone. Even as
she watched, he beckoned to her to join him.

Intrigued, she mounted the outside stairs.

There was no sign of Molly – presumably she was packing?
– but Piers was smiling, clicking off his phone. He put his arm
around her and said, 'You don't know what you've started. That
was Christopher. One evening in the company of a lovely woman
has rejuvenated him. Apparently he poured out the whole story
to her and they talked it over late into the night. He's even beginning to look forward to the future. For a start, he's going off on
holiday somewhere with Marina. A tour of the Scottish Highlands
was mentioned. He apologizes for getting us mixed up in his
affairs.'

Bea said, 'I found the link between the two men. You were
right. They were in cahoots all along. I feel sorry for Karina.
She may have behaved badly but she didn't deserve this.' And
then: 'You got Molly to come downstairs by promising to paint
her portrait. She wants to know how much she can sell it for and
how long it's going to take you. You started it this morning,
working from your sketches. So, how's it going?'

He made a restless movement. 'It won't take long. Just an oil
sketch. It'll be good, I think. I need to get back to it.'

When a sitter didn't inspire him he could, without too much
effort, produce a portrait that would always be saleable even
if he saw it as just another job to be completed and delivered.
Occasionally a subject proved to be difficult or inspired him
to produce something out of the ordinary. On those occasions
the drive to paint would take hold of him and not let go until
he'd finished. Those portraits would wear him out. Those
portraits were the ones that had made his name and which
were fought over in the rare event that they ever came up in
the sale rooms.

He was displaying all the symptoms of a fever for painting now.

She said, 'I can manage here by myself, if . . .?'

'No. I have a bad feeling about this one. I'll stick around. We have to deal with the killers before they do any more damage.'

The front doorbell rang.

'Here they come.'

Piers ran his fingers through her hair and kissed her.

She checked that the dressing on his hand was holding despite having collected a number of paint stains, and kissed him back.

'Once more into the breach, dear friends.'

He put his smartphone down on the coffee table, collected his sketchpad and a pencil and took a seat at the back of the room near the door to the balcony.

Bea turned off the alarm and opened the front door.

Yes, the Rolls-Royce was outside as before, but this time there was no camera, no long-drawn-out performance from Karina and her court, but a fast entry in which no time was wasted on pleasantries.

Karina swept into the house, pushing Bea back as she did so. She was carrying her cane but was dressed from head to foot in a black silk robe with a diamond necklet, and a black bandeau around her red hair.

'Where's Christopher? He's not at his flat and he's not answering his phone, so he must be here. Produce him! Now!'

Bea said, 'Christopher's gone away.'

Karina ignored that to sweep into the living room with the shadowy Cecil close on her heels. After them came the tall figure of Simon, looking apprehensive. Alexander and Teddy trod on his heels. The two boys were also looking worried. Teddy even looked harassed. Had the rest of the family turned on him because his fount of gold had dried up?

Karina seated herself in Bea's chair and thumped the floor with her cane. 'This is not to be tolerated. I want Christopher! Here! At once.'

Cecil fussed around her. Simon faded into the background, sending quick glances around . . . looking for Molly?

'Well, now,' said Bea, ignoring the command to produce

Christopher, and acting the hostess with all her might. 'To what do we owe the pleasure of this visit?'

Thump, thump on the floor. 'I said, where is he?' Karina was in no mood to be polite.

'Good morning, everyone!' A woman's voice, low and sultry.

Everyone swivelled round to see Molly, posing in the doorway. Another change, this time from mouse to mistress.

Molly had tinted her hair a bright red – even redder than Karina's wig – had she used one of those spray-on jobs? She wore a white dress which clung to her contours and revealed a lot of bosom. She had made up her face exactly as Karina did. She was a knockout and she knew it.

Bea realized that women like Molly knew precisely what they were doing. They'd been born to procreate and everything they did was to that end. Natural selection demanded that the Mollies of this world would push the ageing stars out of their way to take their place . . . only to be dislodged and discarded in their turn when they reached old age.

Molly had tried out all the males in Karina's household and was now prepared to go with the one who promised the best lifestyle for her and her baby. She kissed her fingertips to the boys, who avoided her eye and shuffled their feet.

Karina said, 'What? Who? *Molly!* I don't believe it!'

Molly homed in on her prey. She put her arm through Simon's and rested her head on his chest. Simon coloured up but let her do it, saying, 'Yes, my dear, but remember, we're taking it slowly.'

If you looked at it one way, what Molly was doing was admirable. But oh, dear! The damage done to everyone else!

Karina gasped. 'Simon! What are you doing? Tell that trollop to get lost!' She thumped the floor with her cane but lost her grip and it fell to the floor.

Cecil pounced on the fallen item and restored it to her, saying, in his usual soft voice, 'Now don't get too excited, my dear. You know it's bad for your heart.'

Uh-oh. Had Cecil realized that Simon had become the weak link in the chain that bound the courtiers to their diva? And if so, what was he going to do about it?

Simon was looking down at Molly as if he would like to eat

her, if he only dared to do so. Simon had done the maths and realized that Molly could offer him something Karina couldn't.

Molly looked up at Simon. 'My own dear love!'

Karina spat at Molly. 'You slut! You foul . . . you toad! You take your filthy hands off Simon! Tell her, Simon!'

'Well . . .' Simon looked down at Molly and tried, not very effectively, to shake her off. 'Oh, Molly! I told you to wait till I'd sorted things.'

Molly wasn't having that. 'I can't wait and you know why!'

He drew himself up to his full height and put his arm more firmly around her. 'Well, perhaps it is time to clear the air.'

Karina cried out, hand on heart. 'Simon, no! Do you want to send me to my grave?'

Simon was burning bridges. Quietly but firmly, he confronted his ex-wife. 'I'm sorry, Karina, but it's time for me to have a life of my own. It's not as if we were married any longer. You divorced me, remember? I admit that you did take me in afterwards when I was down and out, and yes, I was truly grateful for that. But I don't think you've realized how much you've changed since we came back to London. I never have a minute to myself. I always have to be at your beck and call and . . . well, frankly, I'm fed up with it.'

Karina patted the air. 'You don't know what you're saying. You swore you'd never leave me!'

Simon paled but remained firm. 'I'll always be there for you, but my life in the future has to include Molly, who is giving me something you refused to have, and that is a child. From today, Molly moves in with us. We'll take over the top floor of the house and she'll go out and get more work and you won't know she's there. And, if you can get the finance, I'll direct your picture and it will be a great success.'

Cecil said, in his quiet, reasonable voice, 'This is all a bit sudden. We'll have to take our time to think it over, won't we, Karina? As for the film, there won't be one unless we can get Christopher to help us. So, where is he?'

Alexander turned on Teddy. 'I told you to butter the old boy up! Instead, you had to knock him over!'

Teddy's fingers went into his mouth. 'It'll be all right, I tell you! He's never refused me anything I've really wanted.'

Teddy wasn't going to bite his nails, was he? Urgh!

Simon was gaining confidence with every moment that Molly clung to him. He said, 'Oh, I'm sure there'll be a film, eventually. It might be difficult now that we can't rely on Christopher, but perhaps later.'

Karina turned childish, mouth wide open. 'You promised me there would be a film, now!'

'Yes, yes.' Simon was embarrassed, caught between two powerful women but doing his best to satisfy both of them. 'And the future is bright. Karina, I didn't like to tell you in case it didn't work out, but my agent has been putting out feelers, I've been having discussions with people and it's on the cards . . . Well, in short, I'm being considered for a part in a sitcom for television. My background, all my years of experience have paid off. I wasn't sure about it at first because it's only a cameo part but if it goes well then they'll write me in for good.'

Molly reached up to kiss him. 'And you're going to help me get a part, too?'

Karina wailed, 'No, no! You can't abandon me, Simon! And you can't trust that promiscuous little tart. She's slept with both of the boys, and maybe half the neighbourhood, too.'

Molly grinned. 'Yes, your boys did force themselves on me, but then I had a period and I haven't slept with anyone but Simon since then.'

Was that true? It might be. Um. Not sure.

The boys looked doubtful, as well they might.

Karina put her hand to her throat, and in throbbing tones said, 'Simon, I know you better than you know yourself. You'd never leave me!'

Simon went all noble and sacrificial. 'Karina, can't you see it's time to part?'

Every line on Karina's face tightened. 'Let me be quite clear about this. There's no way I'm letting that bitch back in my house. And don't say it's not my house. It's mine by rights. Teddy, you said your uncle would be here and he isn't. I told you we needed to talk, so where is he?'

Teddy cleared his throat, his colour coming and going. He was dead afraid of Karina, wasn't he? 'I, er, he won't pick up. There's just a message saying to phone his old partner in an emergency and I did. And *he* says my uncle's gone away for the weekend, but he wouldn't say where. I keep trying uncle's phone but he's turned it off. I don't know what else to do!' He ducked his head and put his fingers in his mouth again.

Poor creature. He's collapsed at the first hint of something not going to plan.

Bea decided it was time to intervene. 'Christopher has gone away on a short holiday. He told us before he went that he was going to sign a new will yesterday, disinheriting you, Teddy, because he can't trust your judgement with money. He also said he was sending notice to evict Karina from his house and putting it on the market. I presume that you have all received copies of his correspondence and that that's why you're here. We haven't seen hide nor hair of Christopher since yesterday afternoon and I don't expect him to return to London in the near future.'

Teddy said, 'He'll come round, I know he will!'

Karina was unable to accept defeat. 'Yes, of course he will. He knows how much I've suffered and he won't turn me out. Will he?' She turned to Cecil for reassurance.

Cecil was soothing. 'I'm sure he won't. Christopher hasn't been himself lately. Perhaps he needs to see a doctor. I'm sure that when we speak to him, he'll realize his error, your film will go ahead, and as for turning you out of your home . . . No, no. Nonsense.'

Teddy was almost in tears, dabbing at his phone. 'He always picks up for me. Come on, come on! Pick up! If we can only talk! If he thinks I've spent too much, then I'll promise anything . . . of course the film will go ahead. I'll get the money, somehow, even if he . . . I've always been able to talk him into a good temper.'

Alexander had been thinking. He turned on Bea. 'You seem to know a lot about this. You know how to get in touch with him, don't you? Yes, that's it. He's left you his number. I don't believe he's refusing to speak to Teddy. Perhaps he's ill, and we ought to be out looking for him at this very minute. He mustn't die yet. I mean, not when he's signed a will which might destroy our future.'

Cecil was calming. 'Everything will be all right, just you wait and see. First things first.' To Simon: 'You've upset Karina. Why don't you take Molly away for the weekend to talk things over? When I've got things sorted here, we can work out a plan for the future.'

Oh, Cecil: I see what you're up to. You've decided there's nothing to be gained by continuing this discussion. You'll divide and rule. But first you have to clear up the mess left by Jolene's death.

Where to start? You have to remove the link between Jolene and Karina's family, which means you have to dispose of Molly. You'll get Simon to take her away to some nice quiet place and when you join them, you'll see that she never makes trouble again. Simon will go along with this because that's what he does. Oh, he might make noises this morning about going his own way, but Cecil only has to twitch his eyebrow and Simon will fall into line.

After Cecil has got rid of Molly and dragged Simon back into the fold, then what will he do? He'll turn his attentions to Christopher, that's what he'll do. And then to me and Piers.

'You can't let Simon go off with that trollop! I forbid it!' Karina screamed. 'He's mine! I need him!'

Simon made an instinctive move towards Karina but was unable to get far because of the fast hold that Molly had on him. He said, 'Karina, my dear . . . can't you see that everything's changed now? We can't go back to how we were.'

He's kidding himself if he thinks he can forget what he's done in the past and start a new life with Molly. And, if I read Cecil aright, he won't let Simon wriggle away from him.

Prompt on cue, Cecil said, 'Simon, remember our agreement.'

Simon wasn't a complete dum-dum. He knew what he owed Cecil. He must know he was a fish that had been caught by an expert angler, but he made another effort to get free. 'Cecil, it will only be for the weekend to let tempers cool down. We'll go away to a little place I know in the country for a long weekend. All right by you, Molly?'

'Of course!' she replied with stars in her eyes.

Karina produced her imitation of a snake. 'If you leave me now, Simon, you needn't bother about coming back. I mean it!'

Simon hesitated for a long minute, and then he shook his head.

'I'm sorry, Karina. I need the space to clear my head. I'll be back after the weekend.'

Such bad dialogue! Perhaps he would do well in a telly sitcom. So, Simon is the first rat to try to leave the sinking ship. Does he really think he can get clean away? Time to throw a spanner in the works.

Oh, dear, all these clichés! It must be catching.

Bea said, 'One moment, please. In all this talk of eviction and wills and breaking up long-standing arrangements, you all seem to have forgotten that a girl died because of the way you were carrying on.'

SIXTEEN

Saturday morning, continued

Alexander snorted. 'You said that before. It's ridiculous! Never laid eyes on her.'

Teddy stopped looking at his smartphone long enough to say, 'Nor me.'

Alexander said, 'I know you think she's connected to us in some way but I can't see how. Molly's been playing games. She says now that she's sure Simon's the father of her child, but on Thursday she texted me to say that I was——'

'Same here,' said Teddy, faint but pursuing. 'I mean, I thought I might have been, but no, I did use a condom. Always.'

'Same here,' said Alexander.

Molly said, 'Liars! You used nothing. No protection. And you both pounced on me every time you found me alone, up against the door, even in the bathroom. You were like pigs, snorting around. Animals!'

Simon tried to withdraw but she drew him closer. 'My darling Simon wasn't like that. He was just wonderful! And that's why I love him so much.'

'Yes, but,' said Alexander, 'you have to be lying. I had you early last week sometime. You were fiddling around with your laptop and the memory stick, and I wanted a quickie, knowing you were nearly finished with the book and—'

'Me, too,' said Teddy with a nod.

Molly maintained her smile. 'You are both lying through your teeth. Yes, you had me at your mercy when I first entered the house, but I soon learned how to keep you at a distance, both of you. You just like to boast about your exploits.'

And to Simon: 'I was yours and only yours from the moment you kissed me in the kitchen that day.'

Bea said, 'I suspect that you will need a DNA test for the baby to prove paternity, but in the meantime, let us agree that Molly texted the three of you – and possibly Bernie Sanders as well—'

'What! Bernie? Our Bernie?'

'You mean she had him as well?'

'Certainly not!' Molly's denial produced a hoarse laugh from Alexander and a long stare from Teddy, while Simon tried once more to release himself from her. And this time he managed to take one step away from her before she caught him again.

Bea said, 'Let me finish. Molly texted all the men she'd had sex with. Maybe she texted Bernie as well; I don't know. Possibly not, because he wasn't worth blackmailing.'

'She tried to blackmail my sons?' Karina was horrified. 'Oh, Cecil! Oh, my heart!' She put out her hand to Cecil and he patted it.

'You're kidding!' That was Alexander, but his voice sagged. He knew what Bea was getting at.

Bea continued, 'She texted each one of you, suggesting a meeting opposite a certain pub that evening. I don't know whether or not she laid out her terms in her text . . .' Bea waited for one of them to fill in the gaps, but they were all silent.

It was Karina who spoke up. 'What terms? Cecil, she's lying, isn't she? I mean, none of my boys would have bothered with the likes of her, and if she did offer them a quickie and they took it, they'd have taken precautions. So she's lying when she says she's pregnant!'

'Molly's pregnant all right,' said Bea. 'I don't know whether she'd planned the pregnancy or not. Probably not, because it didn't fit in with her original ambitions. Right?'

Molly pouted but didn't deny it.

Bea continued, 'In any other situation, Molly would probably have gone for an abortion although she might well have asked for some money from the man concerned to keep her till she'd got some more work. But that Thursday morning she was accused of theft, manhandled, her laptop seized and broken, and she was given to understand that she wouldn't be paid for the work she'd done on the book. She was understandably very angry and probably also rather frightened. She'd borrowed money from the family who had taken her in, she owed money for rent, and she was broke. I feel sorry for her, almost.'

Molly nodded. 'I was very frightened, yes.'

And maybe she was.

Karina flared up. 'Are you trying to make me feel guilty? She stole some of my jewellery to . . .' She looked at Cecil, then reconsidered what she'd been about to say. 'It was a misunderstanding. I did think she'd stolen from me, but then I realized that it wasn't her. I suppose I should have apologized, but she fled the house and . . . Well, I'm sure she would have been paid for what she'd done. In due course. If it was accepted by the publisher. She had no need to try to blackmail anyone.'

Bea didn't agree. 'Think of it from her point of view. I'm sure she thought of going to the police about the way she'd been treated, until she realized that it would have been her word against yours and she didn't think she'd be believed. So she decided to see what she could get out of you by other means. She texted all those who had had sex with her and asked for a meeting. For backup, she took her young friend Jolene into her confidence and asked her to come with her to the meeting place. Tell them what happened next, Molly.'

Molly spoke up. 'I was a little late. I saw Jolene waiting on the pavement opposite the pub. There was a stream of traffic going past. I saw one of the cars stop momentarily beside Jolene and she stepped in. Before I could catch up with them the car drove off. It was a black car, like so many others. I never had sight of the number plate and I was too far away to see who was driving.'

Karina said, 'I'm confused. We do have a smaller car which the boys use now and then, but are you really trying to say you think it was one of us who drove a car to meet her? Nonsense! I've never even heard of this girl. And I don't drive the Rolls-Royce nowadays.'

'No, it wasn't anyone in the Rolls-Royce. That car would have been too easy to recognize,' said Bea. 'And it wasn't you driving the car, Karina. You didn't get a text from her, did you?'

Cecil said, in his quiet way, 'Nor I.'

'I believe you, Cecil,' said Bea. 'So who is your alibi for Thursday evening?'

He said, 'Tut!' and shook his head. 'I can't believe you've asked that.'

'You're asking Cecil for an alibi?' Alexander was shocked. 'You mean . . . You think one of us . . .? Next thing, you'll be asking if we've all got alibis for that night! It was Thursday? The night before last?'

'From about five o'clock.'

'What?' He looked around, inviting everyone to laugh with him at the absurdity of his being asked to provide an alibi. Then reconsidered. He said, 'Well, I suppose there's no harm in telling you. The atmosphere at home was toxic – everyone shouting that it was their fault at everyone else. Mother had one of her headaches, and there wasn't going to be any supper since the housekeeper had walked out. Teddy and I opted for peace and quiet and a bite out at the pub. Which we did.

'Then we got the texts from Molly; first me and then him. How dare she! Well, it was a joke, obviously. We agreed on that. She'd gone plain off her rocker! Did she really think she could threaten us? As if we'd be stupid enough to meet her after all that had happened. Stupid cow! On the other hand, we were worried what she might do with the memory stick. We needed that. So we decided she needed teaching a lesson. We came round here looking for her, which is when we had that little accident with the fanlight over the front door.'

He guffawed with laughter. 'Your faces when you saw the broken glass! You crack me up, you really do. We caught sight of Molly but somehow she managed to get away, which was a right nuisance. So Teddy and I went back to the pub and had another pint or two, and then I went round to my friend's house. He'd come across something I thought I might use in my podcasts.

He's another influencer, but with a different range from me and . . . I can't believe you're asking us for alibis!'

Teddy chirruped up. 'I stayed in the pub for quite a while after Alex left. Had a coupla games of snooker. I was there till closing time.'

Bea said, 'So you two admit you came here and broke the fanlight and that you were looking for the memory stick. And failed to get it. So, which of you was it who phoned Bernie and asked him to break into the house to get it for you?'

Silence. Teddy looked at Alexander, who stared into space.

Bea said, 'Come on. We have Bernie's phone and I'm sure that when we hand it over to the police, they'll be able to track down the call one of you made to him. Bernie's phone records will tell us who made it. It was Alexander, was it? But you were both in on it, weren't you? If Alexander went on to visit his friend, it must have been Teddy who stayed on to meet Bernie and to give him his fee for doing the job. Unfortunately for you, Bernie is as inefficient at breaking into houses as you are. He was interrupted in his attempt to gain entry and left his jacket with all his identification behind when he left.'

Karina gasped. 'The boys got Bernie to break in here? Boys, whatever were you thinking of! I can't believe this is happening.' She had begun to panic. The situation was getting out of her control. Suddenly she looked a lot older.

Alexander put on a sullen look. 'Don't worry, Mother. They won't prosecute if we pay for the damage.'

Bea said, 'That's probably true. So you two boys alibi one another for the time Jolene stepped into the car? How about you, Simon?'

'Me?' Simon was taken aback. Then his eyes narrowed. He didn't look at Cecil, but it seemed to Bea as if one asked a question and the other answered it.

At last Simon said, 'I suppose I'm damned if I do and I'm damned if I don't. I think I'll say "no comment" until I've thought about it.'

Karina was losing it. 'Don't be absurd, Simon. I know what you did, even if you can't remember.'

Bea said, 'What was Simon doing, then?'

Cecil looked as if he'd like to interfere, but Karina brushed him aside without giving herself time to think. Her speech had become rapid, her breathing louder. 'Thursday, after we came back from visiting you? Well, there was a lot to discuss, wasn't there? One of my headaches was threatening. I couldn't find my pills and both Simon and Cecil had to look for them. It was Simon who found them eventually, between the cushions of my big armchair. I took one and soon felt better. Nervous exhaustion. And, I have to watch my health. It was only then that I realized that the cook had gone and there'd be no supper. I don't cook, of course. I never have.'

Cecil patted her hand, but she brushed him aside. 'The boys had gone out, and Cecil vetoed having something brought in, so Simon volunteered to put something together for the three of us. I had a little nap while he was doing that, and then we had supper and decided we wouldn't talk about the horrid things that had been happening. So we watched television, the three of us. It had been a tiring day. Simon gave me my neck massage and brought me a tisane and we all watched the telly. I fell asleep halfway through something. Was it a repeat on one of the minor channels? Do you want to know which one it was? I can't remember. Can you remember, Cecil?'

'Something mindless in black and white. I wasn't paying much attention.'

Karina shook her head, irritated. 'I know it was black and white. I asked you what it was. I know Simon dozed off and snored . . .' She shot a vengeful look at Molly. 'And that's something you haven't told your little bit of fluff about, is it? Your snoring, and the way you pick your nose in the morning.'

Bea said, 'You say you were all three together from five o'clock onwards?' She turned to Cecil. 'Do you agree with that?'

A deprecating movement of the hands. 'You can hardly believe that I . . . No, really. That's the outside of enough. Were we all three in the same room all the time? Well, probably not all the time. I believe I did go out to the loo and to make myself a cup of tea later. Oh yes, and we went all over the house looking for Karina's pills. No, I don't suppose we were all in the same room all the time.'

Bea said, 'Do you agree with all that, Simon?'

'I suppose so. Yes, we talked a lot about what had happened.

Karina did begin to have one of her headaches, and we did spend some time looking for her pills. Yes, I cooked supper. We ate together and then we switched the telly on for the rest of the evening. Really, I can hardly tell you what we watched. Some documentary or other. At intervals we talked about what had happened that day. There was much to think about. How to manage paying Molly; would she require a written apology; that sort of thing. And then we went to bed.'

Bea said to Molly, 'Are you satisfied with their alibis?'

Molly cuddled up to Simon. 'Darling Simon, I couldn't have borne it if you'd been the one to meet Jolene.'

Simon kissed her forehead. 'I didn't leave the house all evening.'

'No,' said Bea, 'you didn't. Molly, I know that you left two messages on Jolene's phone before she left the agency at just after six. Had you planted your time bombs on the men's phones by then?'

Molly shrugged. 'About six, I suppose. I wasn't looking. I was mad, believe me!'

'What time did you arrange to meet?'

'Seven, opposite the pub which is on my way home.'

Bea turned to Simon. 'What time did you receive the text from her?'

His eyes switched right and left. 'I'm not sure. I'd turned my phone off. I don't think I checked it until supper time, maybe later.'

Karina looked puzzled. 'Wait a minute. You got a text while you were looking for my pills. I heard it, and you did look at it. I asked what it was and you said it was nothing, an ad or some-thing. Then you found my pills and got me some water to take them with, and I rested till the pills had taken effect. And you left me alone then, for ages and ages.' She pouted.

'Only a few minutes. Till you were calmer.'

Bea said, 'And in those few minutes, Simon, you went to find someone you respected and showed him the text. That person told you not to worry and that he'd take care of it. He didn't specify what he meant by that, and you took care not to know.'

Alexander was affronted. 'He didn't come to me, I can tell you. Simon wouldn't ask me to do any favours for him. I've always said he was a gigolo and Mother could do better than him.'

Teddy chimed in. 'Definitely not me. What could I have done for him, anyway?'

Bea said, 'No, it was neither of you. This person arranged with Simon to take his place to meet Molly and said he'd deal with her. Only it wasn't Molly who stepped into his car but Jolene, who didn't know who she was going to meet and wasn't prepared for the knife which ended her days.'

A blank silence. Most of the company looked at one another, puzzled.

Only Cecil continued to look at Bea. He wasn't puzzled. He knew exactly what she was getting at. He said, 'And why would anyone want to kill a strange girl?'

'Because she could testify that a certain person had responded to Molly's text and had come to meet her with a view to making some kind of settlement. She could identify the man who was the father of Molly's baby . . . or rather, the man who represented him. I don't think you fathered her child, Cecil. But to protect your "family" situation, you were the one who killed Jolene and dumped her body.'

'What?' Alexander laughed.

'No! Ridiculous!' Karina, indignant. 'Cecil, I can't take much more of this.'

Cecil ignored Karina to concentrate on Bea. 'Why do you imagine I'd kill to protect someone else?'

'Not "someone else", no. To protect your cousin and your relationship with Karina.'

'Nonsense!' But his nostrils flared white. 'Total nonsense.'

Simon echoed that. 'That's ridiculous!' But his denial didn't carry conviction.

Molly swivelled to look from Simon to Cecil and back again. 'What? Simon, tell me she's joking!'

'No joke,' said Bea. 'When I started to research you lot, I concentrated on Karina's early career and I didn't go far into everyone's background. But the way Simon was shot out of the marriage and then welcomed back into Karina's household has always intrigued me. I could understand the divorce if Simon had been unfaithful, but not the return. So I did some more digging and I found a copy of your birth certificate, Simon. This gives the maiden name of your mother, which is the same as Cecil's. So I dug around in your complicated family background and found that you and Cecil were linked by marriage.

'Simon's mother, Colleen, had one older brother, who married young and produced one boy – Cecil. Colleen married late in life and had one son, and that was Simon. This means that Cecil is actually Simon's cousin, though the age difference makes it more like uncle and nephew.

'Now, some families drift apart but you two remained in contact with one another. Simon and Cecil each had something the other lacked. Cecil had money; he was doing all right in business, while Simon had the glamour of Hollywood and had managed to marry one of the brightest stars around. Did Simon introduce his relative to Karina on one of his visits to America? Cecil fell for her big time and gave her expensive presents whenever he visited America.

'Simon didn't mind that because he was the man in possession. Then, disaster. Simon had invested Karina's money into a film which bombed and left them both penniless. And there was Cecil, with his shoulder all ready for her to cry on . . . which she did. Cecil saw his chance. He was childless and currently at a loose end as he'd recently retired with a nice pot of money. He offered to bail Karina out but he exacted a high price. He wanted her to divorce you, Simon, and marry him. Simon was desperate for a way out of his money troubles and Karina was furious with him because he'd lost all her money. And so the deal was struck.'

Karina nodded. 'Cecil's always loved me to distraction. Always. And Simon had let me down, big time.'

'Agreed.' Bea continued, 'Karina obtained a quickie divorce on the grounds that Simon had been playing around. That was probably not true but Simon was not going to contest the divorce because he felt it was all his fault that things had gone wrong. He stood back and let Cecil marry the woman who had been his wife. Cecil cleared her enormous debts, not caring that that more or less broke him, too. He brought her back to London in triumph and only gradually did reality break through.

'You see, there were a couple of things wrong with the new arrangement: Cecil couldn't satisfy his wife in bed and Karina had passed her sell-by date so couldn't get any more work. She could no longer play young romantic leads while parts for older women were not easy to come by. Then again, she was accustomed to having servants and to giving elaborate parties. She couldn't rein in her spending. She had got Christopher to let her move into the London house, but never considered how the mortgage was to be paid.

'To make matters worse, Alexander and Teddy turned up with great ideas for the future. They proposed to use her fame to help their own careers. She loved that idea and invited them to stay, which made two more mouths to feed and less money coming in. At that point, when the gilt had begun to wear off the gingerbread, Simon bobbed up again. He hadn't been able to get any more work back in Tinseltown and wanted to return to the UK. Did he contact Cecil about returning home, or was it Cecil's idea to invite him in order to keep Karina happy?'

Simon shot a look at Cecil, who continued to look bland. Simon attempted a smile but was clearly uneasy at this exposure of what everyone could see was the truth.

'Either way,' said Bea, 'the new arrangement suited everybody. Simon kept Karina happy and cooked for the family when they had no help in the kitchen. If being Karina's love slave was the price Simon had to pay for board and lodging, then he was content to pay it.

'The money constraints continued, but Christopher Fletcher suggested Karina might rejuvenate her career by producing her memoirs and, sure enough, media interest was aroused and there seemed at last to be a prospect of some money coming in. Her son Teddy even promised to fund the making of a film for her. In the meantime, money was tight. I don't know whose idea it had been to sack the servants in order to avoid paying their wages. Cecil's? Or Simon's?'

Cecil said, 'Don't look at me.'

Alexander laughed, and said, 'No, no. Don't look at me, either. I might, in jest, have suggested we could accuse someone of theft in order to get rid of them, but it was our dear mama who put my idle words into practice. It worked for a long time, didn't it?'

Bea said, 'It worked to the extent that when Christopher Fletcher found out what was going on, he took over the hiring and firing himself. Unfortunately for you, that meant he was drawn further into your affairs when you decided to save the monies due to Mrs Hennessey, Molly and to Piers. It pushed Christopher into an outright refusal to back Teddy's application for a loan, it pushed Molly into threatening to make her pregnancy public and it killed Jolene.'

Bea looked hard at the boys, who didn't meet her eye and shuffled their feet.

Karina, incredibly, laughed. 'It was amusing to see the servants run for their lives when I'd got bored with them. I was quite scary, wasn't I?' Then she frowned. 'But I can't be held responsible for some tart getting herself knocked up.'

The boys hooted with laughter but Molly reddened and Simon winced. Cecil maintained his blank expression.

Bea thought that, given the chance, Karina and the boys would probably try accusing servants of theft again in the future, but next time Christopher would not be willing to bail them out and one of these days some brave soul would actually sue Karina for falsely accusing them of theft.

Bea continued, 'Once Karina and her family had run Mrs Hennessey, Molly and Piers out of the house, Cecil took stock and realized that everything he'd been planning for was in danger. How to claw something back? Well, the first thing he did was to send Christopher to us in the hope that he might recover the memory stick and also neutralize Piers, who was justifiably angry at being accused of theft and refused payment for his portrait.

'How much of your accusations of theft Christopher believed was immaterial; you thought he'd do his best for Karina, and he did, within his limits. But when Teddy was unwise enough to show his contempt for the man who had brought him up it was, finally, one insult too many for Christopher. He began at long last to count the cost of being Karina's brother-in-law and Teddy's guardian.

'And it was at this point that Molly – quite independently of Christopher's change of heart – made her move. She wanted revenge for the way she'd been treated, she wanted money and she wouldn't mind a ring on her finger. She didn't know which of the three was the father of her child so she played safe and texted them all, asking them to meet her to discuss the situation.'

Molly grimaced. 'I was playing it safe but all the time I knew it was my own, dear Simon.'

Bea didn't feel up to querying that. She went on: 'Cecil was not one of those she texted, but he learned about it soon enough. While the boys were at the pub plotting to break in here to retrieve the memory stick from Molly – and possibly intending to beat the living daylights out of her at the same time – Simon got his text and didn't know what to do. His cousin Cecil had always helped him out in the past, so why not ask his advice now? So he showed it to Cecil. Right?'

Simon looked at Cecil, and Cecil looked at the floor.

Simon said, 'Well, yes. I did. I was . . . conflicted. Molly's quite something. I'd become very fond of her, but I hadn't thought anything could come of it because I had nothing to offer. I had got myself an agent over here, but he'd not been able to find me any work until . . . Well, it was only last week . . . I couldn't believe it, but my luck changed at long, long last. I was asked if I'd be interested in auditioning for the part of a rascally estate agent in a soap. Quite a good part, actually.

'It would mean long days out of the house but the money was good and if I got the part then it would be six weeks' work and, if they liked me, the contract might be extended. For the first time for years, I could see that I might be able to afford a place of my own and maybe things would work out with Molly. It might be my last chance to have a child, if only I were brave enough to make the break. On the other hand, I knew Karina would be furious that I'd been offered work and she hadn't. She was accustomed to having me around and I didn't want to let her down. I didn't know what to do.

'So yes, I showed her text message to Cecil. I knew he wouldn't want me to leave, either, but I thought he'd understand. Cecil said I shouldn't jump into something I'd regret later and I should let things calm down before making a decision which would alter the course of my life. He said that he'd talk to Molly for me that evening and get her to hold off for a while, and I agreed that would be best. He asked me not to contact her for a while in case she talked me into something I really was not ready to do, and I could see the point of that.'

Molly looked sharply up at Simon. 'Is that what happened? You sent Cecil to meet me?'

Simon mumbled, 'He said he'd make sure you got your money, and that was only right. After all, we had behaved badly to you that day. Things had got out of hand, and I . . . yes, I'm ashamed about that. It had just seemed a bit of a lark before, with the others, though I must admit I had been thinking it was a bit steep, and when they did it to you yes, I did say something to Cecil about it afterwards and he said everything would be all right when the book came out.'

He was putting a fine gloss on his behaviour, wasn't he?

Bea said, 'So Cecil did go out that evening? Did he give you instructions to cover his absence, Simon?'

'I . . . No, not instructions. I do like to cook occasionally. The boys were out so it was only natural that I should throw something together for a late supper. Karina had been distressed by everything that had happened earlier, so I gave her a massage and I encouraged her to take a nap while I popped in and out of the kitchen and, well, Cecil wasn't that long. I heard the car leave – not the Rolls-Royce, of course, but the one we use for every day – and I heard him return and I woke Karina and laid the table and he came in and washed his hands. And I asked how he'd got on with Molly and he said she hadn't turned up and he'd ring her in the morning and arrange another meeting.'

Bea said, 'The person Jolene met had a knife with him. That means premeditation. What do you think would have happened to Molly if she'd got into the car first?'

'I don't like to think about it.' He twisted his hands. 'This is *not* happening! I mean, why kill anyone?'

Bea said, 'Cecil was all out of ideas. He was feeling beleaguered on every side. He'd run out of money. He was struggling to keep the household going. If you were to leave and shack up with Molly, then who would keep Karina happy? So he took a knife with him to the meeting. Perhaps he only meant to frighten Molly. Perhaps he didn't think things through. Cases have proved that if you carry a weapon, even if only for defence purposes, you will use it. And he did just that. By the time the girl got into the car, he'd worked himself up into such a state that using the knife seemed the only way forward.'

Molly objected, 'But it wasn't even me who got into the car.'

'No. But Jolene had seen him. Jolene could identify him as the man whom Molly had accused of being the father of her child. It didn't matter that he wasn't. His turning up was an admission of responsibility. And that, in his mind, was justification for killing her.'

Molly gave a little cry and put her hands over her mouth, asking Simon, without words, what he knew.

He whispered, 'I don't know. It never occurred to me at the time that anything was really wrong. I believed him when he said Molly hadn't turned up. So I did nothing.' He made an ineffective movement with his hands, pleading for understanding. He coloured up. 'I'm aware that perhaps I should have done.'

Molly looked as if she'd like to believe him but wasn't entirely convinced.

Bea shared Molly's feelings.

Cecil maintained his tiny, secretive smile. 'Proof?' he said.

Bea tried again. 'Simon, you say you didn't know what Cecil planned, but surely you suspected something afterwards? What about the day you all came here with the portrait for Piers to sign, when you tried to get the memory stick off Molly?'

SEVENTEEN

Saturday morning, continued

S imon spread his hands. Innocence personified. 'No, not really. Yes, he was out for about an hour before supper, and then afterwards, when I was feeding the dishwasher, he said the car wasn't running smoothly and he'd have a look at it while we were watching the telly. He wasn't away long that time. Maybe three quarters of an hour. Then we all watched the telly for a while and went to bed.'

Molly said, in a tight voice, 'I wish you had rung me that night.'

'So do I.' Simon seemed to mean it. He was a complex character, wasn't he? He was still tied to Karina, but shedding her influence to move into that of a younger, perhaps even stronger woman? And then there was the family link to someone he'd always looked up to.

Bea asked, 'So, Simon, when did you link Cecil with Jolene's death?'

Simon produced a pained smile. 'I didn't. Why should I? I'd never heard her name before. I had no idea that anyone else would anticipate Molly by stepping into the car. I did feel uneasy when I heard about her death yesterday morning when we came here to get the portrait signed, but honestly, it seemed so unlikely . . . Only, later . . . but the thought that Cecil might have killed a girl by mistake? No way! It didn't make sense, so . . . Molly, you must believe me! I had no idea!'

Bea reminded herself that Simon was an actor accustomed to delivering lines. He was surely not as innocent as he tried to make out. She said, 'Simon, Jolene was killed with a knife. Is one of your kitchen knives missing?'

'How would I know? Mrs Hennessey had her own knives, which she used all the time and took with her when she left. I admit I did have to rummage around for a big knife when I cooked supper, but I didn't think anything of it because everything was upside down in the kitchen. I hadn't cooked there for quite a while. I've no idea whether anything had been taken or not.'

'Have you examined the car for bloodstains?'

He shuddered. 'Please. No. That's enough.'

'It's going to have to be done. You realize that, don't you? And it's odds on that you'll be charged as an accessory to murder.'

It was time for Cecil to make his move. In his usual quiet way, he said, 'I really don't understand what you're making such a fuss about. I had nothing to do with this silly girl's death. You say her name was Jolene and the police have decided she got into a car with a man who goes around looking for prostitutes and leaves them dead. You think I enticed a strange girl into my car and knifed her to death without anyone noticing and without a struggle? As if I would do such a thing! No, no. No one's going to take your fantasy seriously.'

His air of authority took its effect. Doubt could be seen on most faces.

Bea said, 'Jolene got into the car because she wanted to. I think you intended to kill her when you turned up at the rendezvous, or you wouldn't have taken the knife with you, but no, you wouldn't have risked using it on her while she was sitting next to you in the car because a passer-by might have seen you do it. Also, you might have got too much blood on you.'

Bea turned to Molly. 'You have an active imagination, Molly. What would he have done?'

Molly said, 'I've been wondering what might have happened, too. I think he'd say that the plans had changed, that I was going straight to the house and wanted her to meet me there. Then, when he drove the car into the garage, he'd help her out, stab her to death and put her body into the boot to be disposed of later.'

Bea said, 'Yes, I think that's what happened, too. The only question is: did Simon know what he intended to do? Did Simon provide him with the instrument of destruction, or not?'

Simon blinked. 'No. Oh, no! I had no idea at all.'

And maybe he hadn't, at that.

'The police will work it out. That's not the only mistake Cecil made. What about the car? When the police examine it, they'll find traces of Jolene's blood.'

Cecil smiled. He was very sure of himself, wasn't he? 'The car? Oh, yes. Well, that's most unfortunate. Bernie reported to me this morning that our car has gone missing overnight. That's the worst of living in a crime hotspot. Someone must have taken it for a joyride, torched it and left it to burn. Remind me to contact the insurance people about it when we get home.'

Simon gasped. 'You torched the car?'

'Of course not,' said Cecil, with a touch of impatience. 'Would I do such a thing? And wasn't I up and down all night with indigestion?'

Karina leapt to his defence. 'Of course you were, you poor darling. In and out of my room looking for my pills. We had a cup of tea together at two a.m. and, since you weren't around, Simon, Cecil finished the night in my bed.'

Molly drew the right conclusion. 'Cecil got Bernie to take the car and set it on fire to get rid of it. So there's no proof that he did for Jolene . . . except the knife. What did you do with that, Cecil?'

Cecil's eyebrows rose. 'I imagine the man who killed your friend will have thrown the knife down a drain somewhere. If he tells the police where he left it, they may well be able to find it. Or not, if it's been dropped into a sewer and carried out to sea.'

Did that mean Cecil had disposed of the knife that way?

The little man drew himself up to his full height. 'I had nothing whatever to do with the girl's death and I feel cut to the heart to think that anyone here might harbour such an idea.'

He put a hand on Karina's shoulder. 'After all I've done for you . . .'

She smiled up at him. 'Darling Cecil. What would I do without you? I never doubted you for an instant.'

Now he has the whole boiling lot of them wondering if they've misjudged him. He's going to get away with it, isn't he?

Alexander and Teddy shot a quick look at one another.

They want to know what the other is thinking?

Karina flashed a look at them. 'Boys, I want to hear you say that you've never once doubted our darling Cecil, who looks after us so well.'

Teddy mumbled something.

Alexander crossed and recrossed his legs. 'That's all very well, Mother, but the police are pretty hot on finding clues in abandoned cars.'

Cecil said, 'Not when they've been thoroughly torched.'

Teddy mumbled something. He wasn't a happy bunny about this, was he?

Karina was sharp. 'Speak up, Teddy! I want to hear you say it.'

Teddy swallowed hard but managed to say, 'What's going to happen when they interview Bernie? I assume that's who Cecil got to do his dirty work.'

Cecil was smooth. 'No one's going to interview Bernie. Why should they? There's nothing to connect Bernie with a prostitute who plies her trade in cars.'

Bea fought back. 'We have Bernie's jacket from the break-in here.'

'Stolen from him,' said Cecil.

Molly had been working herself up to intervene. Face flushed, she turned on Cecil. 'Jolene was not a prostitute! You keep saying that and it's not true! She was a bit silly, I agree, and she thought she was clever, interfering with my plans, but she didn't deserve to die for it! I've tried and tried to believe that she was killed by a serial attacker on the rampage. Sometimes I've almost managed to convince myself that that was what happened, and I can forget about it and move on with my life, but then . . . when all is said and done, when I look at what's been happening, I can't keep it up! If no one else is going to go to the police, then I will!'

The doorbell rang.

Everyone froze . . . except for Cecil, who darted like a snake across the room to where Molly was. He whirled her away from Simon and clamped himself to her. He said, 'Don't move, Molly. Don't even breathe. You can feel what I'm holding to your side, can't you?'

The doorbell rang again.

Cecil said, in a conversational tone, 'It's probably the postman, or someone who's mistaken the door and should be going down to the agency. They'll go away when they get no response. No one's in. Alexander, keep an eye on the hall. We don't want anyone coming up from the office to open the front door, do we? That's it. No one move till I've thought through what we're going to do. Molly, keep very, very still. Yes, this is a sharp little knife, which I took from the kitchen this morning, and it's pricking your skin.'

Bea felt a puff of wind as the French window on to the balcony closed. No one else seemed to have noticed it. There was an empty chair where Piers had been sitting.

The doorbell rang again.

Piers' smartphone is still here on the table, so he couldn't reach that to call for help. He'll go down the stairs to the garden . . . into my office . . . he'll pick up the phone there and ring the police for help. How soon can they get here?

Still no one moved or spoke . . . except Simon, who cleared his throat to say, 'Cecil, no! Please!'

Cecil said, 'Keep out of this. I know what I'm doing.'

Teddy looked at Alexander for a lead and didn't get it.

Bea looked at Karina, who was shaking her head and smiling. 'Oh, Cecil!' she said, 'aren't you going a little too far? That little slut won't make any trouble. She knows which side her bread is buttered.'

Another, even longer ring on the doorbell.

Bea said, 'Cecil, calm down. You know perfectly well that you're not going to spill blood in my living room, in front of all these witnesses.'

'Certainly not,' said Cecil. 'As soon as whoever's at the door goes away, we're all going to leave. And that includes Molly. The Rolls-Royce is circling the block at this very moment. When it stops outside, we'll all pile in and make our way home in time for lunch. We'll drop Molly off somewhere on the way. And there will be absolutely nothing to link us to you in future. No proof. None.'

His intention to kill Molly was clear to Bea, but not everyone was reading him as well as she was.

'Of course,' said Karina, smiling. 'It's getting on for lunchtime. All this excitement has made me feel quite hungry. Simon, what have you planned for lunch today?'

Simon didn't reply. He was washing his hands, over and over, and shifting from one foot to the other. He was dithering. Of course.

Cecil's insane. He can't possibly think he can kill Molly and get away with it, can he? But that's exactly what I see in his eye.

No, he can't. There are too many witnesses! He must see that.

What's happening at the front door? If Piers has got in downstairs now, he should be in the main office . . . all he has to do is dial nine nine nine. And then he has to make his way through the big office and up the outer stairs to the street . . .

Molly whimpered. A bright red stain appeared on her top.

Simon actually decided to act. 'Cecil, let Molly go and I swear I'll not leave you in the lurch. I'll tell the television people I don't want the job. I'll continue to look after Karina exactly as before, and I'll do my best to help her with the media dates that you've set up for her. Molly, I'll do my best to see you get paid for what you've done, but that won't happen if you talk because we might not be able to get the money together to pay you. You understand, don't you?'

Molly opened her mouth but was too frightened to speak. She nodded her head, like a puppet.

Simon tried hard to paper over the cracks. He said, 'And Molly, as for your little friend, what happened to her was all a misunderstanding for which you were partly to blame by leading her on with your stories of a different lifestyle. She got into the wrong car with the wrong person and that's how she died. There's no point in your saying anything else, is there?'

Molly made goldfish movements with her mouth but didn't speak.

Karina laughed. 'Oh, Simon; you silly boy. Of course she won't talk. She knows better than that. There's no proof that anyone has done anything wrong, and there's absolutely no reason to pay her anything now the publisher has got her memory stick. Of course you'll stay with me, Simon. You and Cecil and I are a wonderful partnership and together we're heading back to the stars.'

The doorbell rang once more.

Cecil was annoyed by the noise. 'Alexander, go to the front window. Take care not to be seen but find out who's ringing the bell. Perhaps it's the postman, and you can take the parcel or whatever so that we can leave. We need to get out of here. Teddy, ring Bernie and tell him to bring the Rolls to the front door *now* so that we can all walk out of here, nice and easy.'

Alexander was ready to obey, but said, 'What about the Abbot woman?'

Cecil said, 'She's coming with us.'

Bea shivered. She didn't fancy that at all. She could only too easily imagine Cecil's knife piercing her ribs.

Who was it ringing the bell? Where was Piers?

Alexander was halfway to the window when they all heard the front-door key turn in the lock and Piers saying, 'Straight through. Door on the left!'

'What?' That was Alexander.

'Who?' Teddy, fingers working his phone.

Bea said, '*Now!*'

She scooped up her file of papers and threw it at Cecil . . .

The file exploded, sending papers everywhere . . .

Molly twisted out of Cecil's grasp and staggered across the room to tumble on to the floor by the fireplace.

Cecil whirled on Bea, sharp knife gleaming . . .

Only to be floored by a dark-haired man who appeared from the balcony to sweep Cecil's legs from under him.

The knife arced through the air and fell with a tinkle on the hearth, missing Molly by a hairsbreadth.

Karina screamed.

Hari? Was it Hari? Yes! Hari turned Cecil over as if he were no more than a joint of lamb to be carved and sat on him. *Flump!*

Hari said, 'Sorry to have been so long. Been up all night with my pop star, who was threatening suicide. It's a funny old world, isn't it?'

Karina screamed. 'Cecil! No! Help him, someone!'

Alexander overturned a chair in his haste to get away from the window. 'It's two women out there. I think they're cops! I'm off!'

Teddy froze. 'What . . .?'

Two large women in very solid clothing appeared in the doorway, blocking Alexander's attempt to flee. 'Police. What's all this . . .?'

Piers ushered the police into the room. 'I know you came to enquire about the broken window, but there's a lot more than that going on here. Since you came originally about the window, let me tell you that these two boys were responsible for that.'

'Right!' The newcomers swivelled to give Alexander and Teddy the once over.

Molly, panting, tried to get to her feet and collapsed. 'Help me!'

She reached out to Simon, who picked her up, placed her in a chair and hovered. He kept sending apologetic glances to Karina, but he didn't rush to her side, either.

One of the policewomen said to Molly, 'Is that fresh blood on you? And what's that on the floor? A knife? Have you been assaulted? Who's that sitting on the man on the floor? We need backup.' She accessed her phone to call for an ambulance and reinforcements, while her colleague got out her notebook and said, 'Who's the householder?'

Bea felt rather weak at the knees but made a start on the explanations. 'My husband – that's the man who let you in – and I are the householders. The man who's sitting on the man lying on the floor is a friend called Hari, a security consultant and a friend of mine. He made a citizen's arrest because the man on the floor was about to use his knife on the redhead over there and I think he cut her rather badly and she needs medical attention.'

Piers picked up the story. 'When the knife was produced, I slipped down the back way and through the basement only to meet Hari arriving. I explained there was a man with a knife who was behaving very strangely. I went on up to let you in, while Hari came up the outside stairs and dealt with the problem. Simple.'

He sent an approving nod to Hari, who was holding Cecil down on the floor without difficulty. 'What happened to the pop star?'

'I summoned a psychologist to help him deal with the trauma he'd suffered. I suppose his manager will set the expense off against tax. Good for publicity, though.'

Cecil tried to buck Hari off, and failed. Hari gave a little bounce on Cecil to remind him who was top dog now.

'What pop star?' said the smaller, slighter policewoman, mouth agape.

Karina was gasping, hand to her heart. 'Help me! Help me! My heart's racing!'

Simon made as if to move towards her, only to be yanked back to Molly's side.

One of the police took a long look at Karina. 'Take it easy, lady. You can relax now we're here!'

Piers picked up his smartphone and checked that it was still live. 'I left this here to record what's been going on. Whoever is dealing with the murder of the girl Jolene will be interested to hear this.'

'Oh, oh! I'm going to faint!' Karina knew how to hold her audience.

Molly went one better. She bent over, gasping. 'The baby . . . Oh, the baby! No, no! Please! Don't let me miscarry!' The red patch on her dress was spreading, or was it?

Simon pressed his hand over her side to staunch the bleeding. 'Where's that ambulance! Quick!'

Karina echoed her words. 'Yes, I need an ambulance!'

The smaller of the policewomen said, 'Everyone, calm down! The ambulance is on its way. Lady, if you put your head down between your knees, you won't faint.'

Cecil was going red in the face, wriggling, trying to dislodge Hari and failing.

Karina looked around for support but no one seemed prepared to give it to her. There were tears filling her eyes. In a voice choking with distress, she said, 'Boys!'

The boys flinched but didn't fly to her side. They were trying to work out how this development affected them.

Simon held Molly together, stemming the flow of blood from her side. Her dress was ruined but not much had dripped on to the carpet.

Cecil was otherwise occupied.

Alexander made up his mind. He edged towards the door. 'I've got to go. Got to be places, do things.'

The police weren't entirely sure that Hari was on the side of the angels, since in principle they didn't approve of citizens taking the law into their own hands, but Alexander was definitely out of order. They knew what to do about people trying to leave the scene of a crime. 'Nobody leaves. We wait for backup.'

Teddy shrank in his seat, holding up his phone. 'Bernie's outside in the car. He wants to know what to do. He says traffic's building up behind him.'

Karina got to her feet. 'Then we'll be off. We're done here. You, whoever you are! Let my husband get up. Simon, Teddy, Alexander; we'll be off!'

'No way!' said the larger of the two police.

Karina drew herself up. 'I don't think you realize who you're dealing with!'

The larger woman, in a kindly but not-to-be-ignored voice, said, 'Sit yourself down, Granny. We don't know what's been going on here, but nobody leaves till we tell them they can go.'

Bea suddenly felt tired. The questions were going to go on for hours. She sank down into the nearest chair, saying, 'Someone had better ask Bernie to park the car and join the party. Otherwise he might well motor off into the blue with the Rolls-Royce.'

Reinforcements for the police arrived, as did not just one ambulance, but two – one for Molly and one for Karina.

Bernie parked the car and joined the party. The whole boiling lot were then transferred to the station to sit in separate rooms until called in for questioning.

Piers' happy thought to record what had happened that morning turned out to be the only thing that prevented Hari from being accused of assaulting Cecil. It also helped the police to work out exactly who had done what and to whom.

Cecil said 'no comment' to everything. But with the evidence piling up against him, he was charged with murder and kept in custody pending his trial.

The knife he'd used on Jolene was never found, but the front passenger seat of the car – which Bernie had not torched but lodged in a friend's garage with the intention of selling it – showed traces of Jolene's occupation. And there was evidence of her blood in the boot.

Karina was discharged from hospital that evening and interviewed at the station. She disclaimed, in tears, any knowledge of anything untoward and, with the evidence of Piers' phone recording, was sent home in a taxi to a silent, empty house.

Bernie, when his jacket and its contents were produced, realized his only chance of avoiding a prison sentence was to drop the boys in it. So he did, avoiding a custodial sentence by a whisper.

Alexander and Teddy confessed to burglary and criminal damage, declared they were anxious to make good the damage they'd done and got away without a custodial sentence as well.

Both boys claimed they knew nothing about Molly. Not a thing. Never had had her. Never would have. Nothing to do with them. And their mother? They distanced themselves from her, too, moving out to stay with friends, waiting to see if her career took an upturn with the publication of her memoirs.

Molly was released from hospital the next day, once it was clear she was not going to miscarry. She gave a statement to the police making out that Simon was her white knight for saving her life.

Simon cooperated with the police, who were more than half inclined to charge him as an accessory to murder. They kept him at the station for as long as they could but as he maintained his innocence through long hours of questioning, he was eventually let go.

When Molly was released from hospital, she turned up on Bea's doorstep only to be refused admission.

Molly turned on the waterworks. 'You can't be so cruel as to turn me away after all I've been through. And the police are still holding Simon!'

Bea handed over Molly's tote bag. 'I suggest you make a beeline for Belgravia. Simon will turn up there if he can convince them of his innocence. Besides which, Karina needs someone to look after her. It's a big house and she's got it for at least three months more.'

Molly recoiled. 'She's loathsome! I hate her!'

'And she hates you. You should get on well together, especially if she agrees to share Simon with you. If he gets his television work and you sell the sketch Piers made of you, then you'll be well away. If Karina's memoirs take off, I expect you can get more work or a job in publishing and, if you see that she turns up at all her publicized dates, you'll have enough income between the three of you to move into a smaller place together.'

Molly flushed. 'Over my dead body!'

'You deserve one another.'

Bea shut the door in Molly's face.

It was poetic justice that those three should end up living together.

Bea's ward Bernice came home the next weekend with a scruffy, silent university student in tow. He was, apparently, brilliant at everything except knowing how to behave in normal, everyday life. But disentangling his problems made for another story.